THE MACBETH PROPHECY

THE MACBETH PROPHECY

Anthea Fraser

SEVERN
SH
HOUSE

This first world edition published in Great Britain 1995 by
SEVERN HOUSE PUBLISHERS LTD of
9–15 High Street, Sutton, Surrey SM1 1DF.
First published in the USA 1995 by
SEVERN HOUSE PUBLISHERS INC of
425 Park Avenue, New York, NY 10022.

British Library Cataloguing in Publication Data
Fraser, Anthea
  Macbeth Prophecy
  I. Title
  823.914 [F]

  ISBN 0-7278-4772-4

Typeset by Hewer Text Composition Services, Edinburgh.
Printed and bound in Great Britain by
Hartnolls Ltd, Bodmin, Cornwall.

"What are Macbeth Prophecies? They are forecasts of the future which, deliberately or unconsciously, well meant or malignant, *cause* to happen what they foretell."

Paul Tabori, *Crime and the Occult*
(David & Charles)

Part One

One

Jason Quinn was on television this evening, complacent as ever about the limitations of his narrow world, as abrasively incredulous of anyone who dared question them. I longed to confront him with all that has happened since Philip and I came to Crowthorpe, but of course he wouldn't believe it. There are times when I don't myself but it still goes on, though whether the motivating power is collective human consciousness or something which emanates from those cold, grey stones on the hillside, I'm no longer able to judge.

Seeing his patronizing face took me back to that other programme which alerted us to the full significance of Janetta Lee's prediction, and still farther back – almost seven years – to the selves we had been when we first came to Crowthorpe; jaunty, overconfident, supremely pleased with ourselves and each other.

Part of our high spirits had simply been the result of being together. Identical twins have a unique relationship. Philip is and always has been simply an extension of myself. Even our mother soon gave up her attempts to distinguish us, distributing rewards and punishments equally since she had no way of knowing which of us had earned them. It was a small price to pay for having a doppelgänger.

Over the previous few years however, we'd been unavoidably separated. I had completed my university course and moved first to a college of education and then to a primary school in Swindon, while Philip remained behind pursuing his seemingly endless medical studies. At the time of that holiday he had been qualified for just over a year and we were on the lookout for a move that would bring us together again. Quite simply, we were incomplete apart.

Though perforce a jack-of-all-trades at the primary school, my subject was history and it was in the pages of a history book that I first saw the name of Crowthorpe. It appeared in a chapter recording the notorious witch trials of the seventeenth century, and the entry read: *The Bray twins of Crowthorpe in the county of Cumberland, on trial at Lancaster assizes, confessed to "extreme abominations"*.

The association of twins and crows fleetingly caught my interest, since Philip and I had had a phobia about the birds all our lives. Then, barely a week later, I came across another reference in a different context. Twin brothers from Crowthorpe had been shot as deserters during the Napoleonic Wars. It struck me as incredible that a small Lakeland village had twice in the last three hundred years produced twins famous – or infamous – enough to reach the history books.

Was it only coincidence? Is there, indeed, any such thing? Whether or not, I was sufficiently intrigued to look up the village in my atlas and discover that just beyond it lay an ancient stone circle. That, for me, clinched the matter. One of my main interests was Celtic culture and I had written a paper on it for my thesis. That evening I phoned my brother and proposed that we went there for our Easter holiday.

"*Crowthorpe?*" he'd repeated incredulously. "You can't be serious!"

"But it's in the Lakes, Philip. We were thinking of going up there at Easter. And the place seems to breed twins! One pair in the seventeenth century were convicted of witchcraft and another shot as deserters during the Napoleonic Wars. Don't you think that's a coincidence?"

"The coincidence," Philip said slowly, "is that you happened to read about them."

However his interest was aroused, as I'd known it would be, and the discovery of the proximity of the famous Gemelly Circle settled the matter. Whether purely by chance, or as the result of a nudge from fate, we wrote off for accommodation and the evening before the holiday, met by arrangement at our parents' house in Gloucester.

Philip was anxious to see the leaflets I'd brought with me, but after a cursory glance he nodded and turned away. "Yes, just as I thought," he said. I made no comment. Often it was enough that one of us should read something for both of us to acquire the knowledge. It was an aspect of our closeness which we accepted but never discussed, instinctively shying away from any admission of telepathy. Ironic, now, to remember that former caution.

Our mother, however, with no such convenient methods of divination, wanted all the details of our proposed holiday. "Where exactly is this place you're

5

going?" she demanded as we sat with pre-dinner drinks.

"The northern Lake District," I replied somewhat obliquely, and added, with the forlorn hope of stemming further questions, "a few miles north-east of Keswick."

"But what's it called?"

Briefly my eyes met Philip's, watchful, still not entirely at ease. "Crowthorpe," I said reluctantly. "It's at the northern end of Lake Crowswater." And before I was aware of it, an involuntary shudder trickled down my back.

"*Crowthorpe?*" Mother repeated sharply, no doubt reminded of embarrassing scenes with two hysterical children.

Philip came to my aid. "We're big boys now," he said dryly.

She looked from one of us to the other. "The physician has healed himself? I'm glad to hear it, specially if you've cured Matthew at the same time. But is this some kind of test? There must have been plenty of places up there, without deliberately seeking out a double helping of crows!"

"There's a stone circle we're interested in," I said, almost steadily.

"Well, I can't say it would inspire me to drive all those miles! What you see in those dismal lumps of stone I can't imagine. Why don't you go somewhere where there's a bit of life and you'd meet some nice girls?"

Philip said with amusement, "We don't exactly lead a cloistered existence, Mother!"

"I'm well aware of that, but it's never anything

6

serious, is it? I used to be proud of my handsome sons but I'm beginning to think good looks are a mixed blessing. It's too easy for you, that's the trouble; you just sit back and the girls come running. It's high time you settled down."

"You want to be a grandmother, don't you, love?" my father teased her, winking at us.

"And a wife's one thing you won't be able to share!" she continued, ignoring him. "Don't think I didn't know how you carried on at university, with those poor girls never knowing which of you they were with! Highly unethical, I call it."

"But so convenient!" murmured Philip unrepentantly.

By the next morning we were in a fever of impatience to be on our way and made straight for the motorway, eating up mile after mile of unvarying road until, at last, the Midlands fell behind us, the hills came nearer and the land opened out on either side. We turned off at Penrith and the excitement which had hold of me was no longer pleasant, drying my mouth but making my hands damp and clammy. I sat gripping the road map and hoping Philip wouldn't notice my growing agitation. Perhaps, like myself, he was belatedly doubting the wisdom of staying in a village called Crowthorpe. "We're big boys now," he'd said. But phobias don't end with adolescence.

I forced myself to look out of the window at the stretching fells and the crags looming against the innocent blue of the sky. Some of the higher ones were still capped with snow, reminders of the long cold winter just behind us. A few miles short of Keswick, the road we were watching for opened up on our right. "Barrowick 5, Crowthorpe 11" read the signpost. And now that our journey was almost complete, I was aware of holding back, of wishing the miles that separated us from our destination were lengthening rather than shortening.

In no time it seemed we were through Barrowick, with its parks and gift shops, and the road was running alongside Lake Crowswater – one mile wide and six long, according to the guide book – hugging the western shores closely. On the far side of the water the hills came down almost to the lake and it was obvious that any paths there might be over there would be suitable only for walkers.

I was so intent on the beauty of the scenery that I didn't notice the bird until Philip swore suddenly and the car skidded to a halt. Jerking round, I turned to ice as a huge crow rose almost from beneath our wheels, filling the entire windscreen with its dark menace. Either it moved abnormally slowly or sheer terror made it seem so. Philip and I continued to sit with sweat coursing down our bodies while the creature blundered over to a signpost beside the road, where it sat glaring at us balefully and uttering its hoarse, staccato cry. Finally, just as my nerves reached snapping point, it took off with a clatter of heavy wings, rising in laborious flight towards the hillside directly ahead of us. When I was able to look at him, Philip's face was white and shining, a mirror, I knew, of my own, and I wondered whether the increasing malaise I'd felt over the last hour had foreshadowed this encounter. He nodded to the post where the bird had briefly perched. "Crowthorpe," I read.

"It's gone ahead to announce our arrival."

I forced an uncertain laugh. "Hardly the welcome

we might have hoped for! Perhaps this wasn't such a good idea after all."

"Now he tells me!" Philip said tonelessly. "Got a cigarette?"

I looked at him in surprise. Neither of us had smoked for years. "Sorry. Look—" I moved awkwardly. "Would you like to turn back? We don't *have* to stay here. We could spend the night in Barrowick and then go on to Grasmere or Ambleside."

"Because we were frightened by a bird?" Philip turned his head to look at me. "Matthew, I'm a doctor of medicine, heaven help me. Superstition has no place in my philosophy."

I could still feel the sickeningly irregular beating of my heart. I think I was almost annoyed with him for not taking the chance I offered and reversing the car at once. But perhaps there was no turning back, even then, and Philip had simply recognized the fact before I had. Whatever his reasons, he switched on the ignition and the car moved slowly forward. We had reached the head of the lake and on our right lay the imposing entrance to the Lakeside Hotel.

"Well?" Philip said unevenly. "You're the navigator."

I had the street map ready. "We take the left-hand fork up Fell Lane. Honeypot Lane should be the third turning on the right."

We were still too shaken to make conversation, but the prettiness of the village helped to steady us as Philip drove slowly up the twisting cobbled street. Down near the main road the houses had been imposing, three-storeyed buildings set in large gardens, but as we climbed, these gave way to small cottages which

9

either opened directly on to the footpath or boasted miniature patches of brightly coloured flowers. It was the beginning of the tourist season and everything was fresh and sparkling for our arrival.

We ticked off the turnings as we came to them: Ash Street, Broad Walk, Honeypot Lane. Philip turned into it and stopped outside the bay-windowed, comfortable-looking house which was number twenty-two.

Mrs Earnshaw, our landlady for the next ten days, was small and stout and bustling, but her welcoming smile faltered as she opened the door to see both of us standing there. "Twins, is it?" she exclaimed. "You never said!" Then, recovering herself, "But of course, you wouldn't, would you? Come inside, gentlemen. You're our only guests for Easter, so you must make yourselves at home."

We followed her up the narrow stairs and into the room reserved for us. It was square and neat, furnished with the bare essentials. We had expected nothing more.

"I don't do evening meals, as you know, but there's plenty of choice in the village. There are several pubs where you can get a hot dinner and a café or two on Lake Road or the High Street. Or if you feel like treating yourselves your first evening, all the hotels are open to non-residents."

"How do we get to the Gemelly Circle?" Philip enquired, moving over to the window.

"You can walk there from the top of the village, sir. Just continue round Upper Fell Lane and you'll come to the footpath leading up the hill. There's one of them Ancient Monument signs showing the way."

She moved to the door. "I'll leave a front door key for you on the hall table."

As the door closed behind her Philip turned from the window and I looked across at him. "You're not sorry we came here, are you?"

He moved impatiently. "Why should I be? It seems adequate."

He knew I was referring to the village rather than the boarding house but I was not going to press him. I glanced at my watch. "It's five-thirty. Let's unpack and go straight out, so we can get our bearings before the light goes."

Ten minutes later, collecting the door key left for us, we let ourselves out of the house and by mutual consent, turned up Fell Lane. There were not many people about, but I was uncomfortably aware that we appeared to have a marked effect on those we did meet. Several stopped abruptly and stood staring at us and one, a girl of about thirteen, simply turned and fled. Being identical, we were used to mild curiosity, but it certainly appeared that the residents of Crowthorpe were overreacting. Uneasily I remembered Mrs Earnshaw's unguarded greeting.

However, the attractiveness of the village soon pushed any qualms from our minds. Everywhere there were unexpected turnings, odd little flights of steps, archways crossing the road which, since there were windows in them, were presumably dwelling-houses in their own right. The hotchpotch of architectural styles, whereby a modern bungalow in soft Lakeland stone merged perfectly with its neighbour some hundred years older, added considerably to its charm. We walked slowly, enjoying the prospect of exploring at

11

our leisure all the intriguing alleyways which led off the road we followed, and it was almost with surprise that we came to the National Trust sign pointing up a narrow track between two houses. "Gemelly Circle", it read. "Ancient Monument".

I said casually, "I don't think it's worth going to look at it this evening. It's starting to get dark and we shouldn't be able to see much." And there might be crows up there. I don't know if it was Philip or I who added the silent rider, but we both acknowledged it.

"Right. I'm hungry anyway. Shall we try a pub, or aim high as Mrs Earnshaw suggested? How many hotels are there in the neighbourhood?"

"Three; most of the accommodation is in boarding houses."

"Well, we passed the Lakeside Hotel, and I think I caught sight of another on Fell Lane, just before we turned off. Let's retrace our steps and see if we can find it."

Philip's memory proved correct. Opposite the end of Ash Lane a painted sign and open gate proclaimed the entrance to Greystones Hotel and, belatedly wondering whether ties would be *de rigeur* in the dining room, we walked up the long drive to the handsome house at the end of it. An attractive red-haired woman was seated behind the reception desk, and I went across to her.

"Excuse me, we haven't booked a table but could you fit us in for dinner?"

"I'm sure we can." She looked up from her papers with a smile, but it faded abruptly as her eyes passed from me to Philip just behind me. One hand went to her throat and for a moment there was total silence. Then she said in a strained voice, "If you'd like to wait in the bar, I'll have a menu sent in to you. There'll be a table free in fifteen minutes."

She wasn't looking at us any more. Philip raised his eyebrows and shrugged expressively.

"Thank you." We turned to the bar. There were quite a lot of people there, mainly residents, I guessed, since they were laughing and joking with the barman. There was a momentary silence as we entered, but this time it had a more normal quality, such as we'd been used to all our lives, and almost at once everyone started talking again.

"Great being a freak, isn't it?" Philip said under his breath. A waiter came in, handed us each a menu and took our drinks order.

"We'd better not make this a regular port of call," I murmured. "It's an excellent menu but look at the prices!"

Our drinks arrived and we settled back to enjoy them and take stock of our surroundings. The whole place had the ambience of a country house. There were small personal touches which appealed to us: a dish of *crudités* and assorted home-made dips had been placed on the table with our drinks, and a folded card gave the history of the house, with its terms discreetly printed on the back.

We chose our meal slowly, savouring the dishes in advance, and it was some time before I realized that no-one had come back to take our order. It seemed that the hotel was not as well run as I'd thought; and the quarter-hour wait we'd accepted was almost up.

As I turned to remark on this to Philip, the waiter

13

returned. "Your table's ready, gentlemen, if you'd like to come through."

"But we haven't given our order yet," Philip protested.

The waiter looked surprised. "Surely, sir – your first course is waiting for you."

"And what," I asked a little sarcastically, "has been allotted to us?"

He glanced down at the pad in his hand. "One *paté de maison*, one vichyssoise, to be followed by Steak Diane and roast duckling. Is that correct, sir?"

Philip and I exchanged startled glances. "Quite correct, but how—?"

"I understood you'd given Mrs Barlow your order, sir. It was she who took it through to the kitchen."

"Mrs Barlow?"

"The proprietor's wife. I believe you spoke to her as you came in."

In silence Philip and I followed him across the hall to the dining-room. As he pulled out our chairs I saw that the dishes we'd chosen were indeed waiting for us. Even the bottle of wine we'd selected stood ready for our approval.

"What do you make of that?" I asked in a low voice, picking up my spoon.

"Very mystifying. Perhaps they bug the tables to save the staff legwork! No-one could possibly have overheard us with all that noise going on."

Unwillingly I remembered the expression on Mrs Barlow's face when she registered our presence. It had been a mixture of shock and excitement. *Why* did everyone react to us so strongly here?

The meal was delicious and we relaxed, allowing

the pleasant atmosphere to soothe away suspicions which were surely ludicrous. The sweet trolley was brought for our inspection, and after it coffee and *petits fours*.

"Is Mrs Barlow still about?" Philip asked the waiter as he topped up our coffee cups.

"I'm afraid she's gone off-duty, sir. Can I help you?"

He shook his head. "It's not important." But we both knew that it might be.

The night was clear and cold when we emerged from the warmth of the hotel and walked briskly the few hundred yards back to our lodgings. Our arrival in Crowthorpe had not been without incident, I reflected, and I fell asleep to the confused memory of beating black wings and the frightened look in Mrs Barlow's eyes.

Two

We woke the next morning to the pealing of church bells.

"Easter bloody Sunday!" said Philip, pulling the pillow over his head. "They don't intend the faithless to lie in, do they?"

"I suppose you don't want to go?"

"To church?" Philip raised himself on one elbow to stare at me.

"I only wondered," I said awkwardly.

"Do you?" he challenged.

I hesitated. Neither of us was in the habit of church-going, yet that particular morning I felt a primitive urge to put myself and my future in the care of someone greater than myself. To claim sanctuary, protection —

I said defensively, "Easter *is* one of the major festivals."

"The raising from the dead," Philip returned flippantly. "It's always happening nowadays. Last month a patient of mine 'died' twice on the operating table but they managed to revive him each time, and the last I saw of him he was sitting up in bed tucking into fish and chips!"

"Point taken." I swung my feet to the floor. "We will not go to church; instead, we'll visit the heathen shrine of the stones. Is that more to your liking?"

16

"Decidedly! But first, if I'm not mistaken, there's a delicious smell of frying bacon stealing under the door."

By the time we set off once more along Upper Fell Lane, the sun had gathered some warmth and was spilling prodigally over the daffodils which rioted in the small cottage gardens. In one or two of them, old men pottered, straightening to look curiously at Philip and me as we passed. We reached the sign pointing to the Circle and began to climb the steep slope which brought us out on to the open hillside. There we paused for a moment to look back, surprised at the height already gained. Below us Crowthorpe lay sprawled down the hill and at its foot the stretching waters of the lake glowed a dazzling blue in the sunshine. We were almost completely enfolded by hills and not a soul was in sight, though the distant bleating of sheep told us that we shared the hilltop with at least some fellow creatures.

A few minutes' walking brought us within sight of our goal. On the deserted hill the ancient stones stood in their faery ring, a group of them huddled together at one side. I had the curious sensation that I'd seen them before, but the memory must have come from photographs in the guide book. Philip grabbed my arm.

"Look over there!"

I followed the direction of his eyes and gave a low whistle. The hill was not deserted after all and the stones already had one visitor that Easter morning. Leaning against one, her back to us, was the slight figure of a woman with red hair.

"Perhaps now we'll solve the mystery of last night's

dinner," I commented. We must have made some sound as we approached, for while we were still a few yards away the woman glanced round. Then she straightened slowly and turned to face us.

"Good morning," Philip greeted her. "Isn't it a lovely day?"

"Indeed it is." She was watching us with a stillness that made me uncomfortable. Her eyes, large and grey, moved slowly between us.

"We did enjoy our meal last night," I began purposefully.

She looked at me blankly. "Oh?"

"But there's one thing which puzzled us. How did you know the dishes we'd chosen?"

Her face cleared. "Ah! You dined at the Greystones last night? Then it was my sister you saw, not I."

The implication behind her words was unmistakable and we stared at her speechlessly.

"You're not unique, you know!" she added with a touch of amusement. "We're identical, too." She held out her hand. "Eve Braithwaite, the vicar's wife."

I said the first thing that came into my head. "So there are still twins at Crowthorpe."

Her interest quickened. "You know about the Crow-thorpe twins?"

"Some of them," I replied guardedly.

"Not many years go by without at least one pair, and always identical, which as you know are much the rarer kind. I never cease to marvel that such a tiny place can attract so many."

"Then they're not all born here?"

"Of course not. You weren't, were you?"

"But we're only on holiday."

18

She looked at me oddly. "Are you?"

I moistened my lips. "How many pairs are here at the moment?"

"Only ourselves and the squire's daughters. There was a third, but they – moved away."

"The squire? That sounds positively feudal!"

She smiled. "He isn't really, of course, merely a solicitor and, incidentally, one of my husband's church wardens. But he lives at Crowthorpe Grange, which makes him Squire as far as the village is concerned – and he has twin daughters, nine years old."

Philip said – and I think only I caught the edge in his voice – "Is there any reason for this – abundance of twins?"

"Ah!" Eve Braithwaite smiled again and patted the stone beside her. "You can't have heard the local legend."

During the last few minutes I had become increasingly aware of the presence of the stones; almost as though they were a silent group of bystanders listening to our conversation.

"In Celtic times, this region was the centre of a twin god cult. There was longstanding rivalry between the Bear Twins and the Crow goddess, Macha, who lived under the lake, but as long as the Twins were in harmony, their joint power was too strong for her to overthrow. So one day she craftily sent up a beautiful girl, and as she'd intended both the Twins fell in love with her. Finally the girl agreed to marry one of them, but on their wedding day, the other brother put a powerful drug in the bridegroom's cup and came here to the temple in his place. By the time the betrayed Twin woke and rushed up here, the ceremony was over. Beside himself with fury, he turned on his brother and in that moment, with their power divided, the Crow goddess struck and turned them all to stone."

She pointed to the half dozen megaliths set apart from the rest. "That group is known as the Wedding Stones, the small one being the Bride Stone, the Priest in front of her, and so on. And ever since, the spirits of the Twins have been imprisoned there and the Crow goddess has held sway."

The Crow goddess, black-cloaked and sharp-beaked—

High in the clear air above us a curlew spilled its liquid song. I could feel the blood drumming in my ears. Eve Braithwaite's amused, assessing eyes went from my face to Philip's.

"But one day," she went on, in the tone of a mother telling a story to her children, "so the legend goes, a sufficient number of twins will be gathered here to generate the power to release them. And you can scoff as much as you like, but it's a fact that Crowthorpe has always been known for its twins."

"A very pretty tale for Easter morning," Philip said unevenly. "But I'm surprised you're not at church with your husband, listening to more conventional myths."

It was appallingly rude, but Eve Braithwaite answered calmly, "I was at the eight o'clock service, Dr Selby."

Philip's discomfiture at her knowledge of his name made her laugh. "I heard Mrs Earnshaw was expecting you this weekend, though admittedly I didn't know – and I'm willing to bet she didn't either – that you were twins. I'm surprised Anita didn't mention meeting you, though. Perhaps she tried to phone last night when we were out. What did she do that puzzled you so much?"

Briefly we recounted what had happened and she nodded. "Telepathy. She uses it more and more, though she usually manages to be discreet. I imagine she assumed Louis had gone for your order, and knowing what it would be, didn't wait for confirmation but passed it along the line. Then when he actually was going to collect it, the kitchen staff would have told him it was already in hand." She looked at us steadily. "I'm sure I don't have to tell you anything about telepathy."

I found myself resenting her matter-of-factness. "We've noticed it between ourselves, but not with other people."

"Probably only because you haven't tried it more widely." She pushed herself away from the stone. "Well, I'll leave you to make your obeisance to the twin gods. Church must be out now and Douglas will be wondering where I am."

With a little nod she left us. We stood side by side watching her diminishing figure as she walked over the grass and gradually dropped below the level of our vision. She didn't turn round.

To break the lenthening silence between us, I said, "Odd, that Mother should have complained only the other evening of our tricking girls by pretending to be each other. These blokes were playing the same game thousands of years ago."

He didn't answer me directly. "Doesn't it strike you as ominous," he said musingly, "that we should always have had such a fear of crows?"

* * *

21

Lunchtime came and went without our noticing and we stayed on the hillside till the lengthening shadows warned us that it was late afternoon. We had needed that time alone together, to try to come to terms with something which neither of us had yet formulated.

According to the guide book, the Gemelly Circle was an estimated three to four thousand years old. It was eighty feet in diameter and composed of some forty stones of varying shapes and sizes, and Philip and I moved constantly among them, running our hands over the rough-hewn surfaces, exploring cracks and crevices.

This affinity with standing stones was something we had discovered during research for my paper on ancient circles. Prolonged contact with them always brought a sensation of peace, but never before had I felt such a deeply personal bond as now encompassed Philip and myself. There was something here I didn't understand.

Time and again we returned to the Wedding Group which Eve Braithwaite had pointed out, trying to decide which characters they represented in the legendary marriage service. By half closing my eyes, it was possible to mould the small Bride Stone into the shape of a girl kneeling in her wedding dress, with the Priest in front of her as Eve had said. Poor, petrified little bride. However, there was no groom by her side, just two stones standing confrontationally face to face – doubtless the Bear Twins at each other's throats.

I shuddered involuntarily. It was only a legend, but legends had their roots in race memory and there was often a grain of truth in them.

I started as Philip laid a hand on my shoulder. "Come

on, Matthew. If we don't make a move we'll turn to stone ourselves! Let's walk over in that direction and see if there's another path leading back to the village."

I said thoughtfully, "However she might have discovered our surname, Mrs Braithwaite knew you were a doctor."

"Yes, that hadn't escaped me. Perhaps I smell of disinfectant!"

Over the next rise we could discern the sheep whose bleating had reached us earlier. In the distance lay a small crescent-shaped belt of trees. We made our way towards it but, reaching one end of the windbreak, stopped in some embarrassment. Concealed behind the trees was a small gypsy encampment comprising three shabby caravans and a few lean-to tents. Some scrawny horses cropped at the grass and over a fire a woman, heavily pregnant, balanced a cooking pot. The smell rising from it identified the contents as rabbit stew. Beside her, two olive-skinned, dark-eyed babies played in the dirt.

No-one had noticed us and we were about to withdraw tactfully when a raucous noise shattered the quiet and a large crow – surely the bird which had presaged our arrival – started flapping its great wings without attempting to rise from the shaft of the caravan where it perched. The woman at the fire turned and stared across the intervening space, sullen and resentful of our intrusion, and the children stopped their play to gaze at us open-mouthed.

I said inadequately, "I'm so sorry – we didn't know anyone was here." But the harsh rasping of the crow's alarm call drowned my words. We turned and made our way hastily back round the screen of trees. I was shaking violently and wondered if I were going to vomit.

"One of the goddess's messengers!" said Philip, with a totally disastrous attempt at lightness. "I told you it had gone to announce our arrival." He looked at me closely. "Are you going to throw up?"

"Such a medical turn of phrase! I hope not. About crows," I added carefully, after a moment. "It's never struck me before, but ours is a very selective phobia, isn't it? Plenty of people are terrified of birds in general, but with us it's only crows."

"No-one understands phobias," Philip answered, kicking the turf at his feet. "If we cared to be psychoanalyzed there's no doubt a rational explanation."

"I'd rather not know," I said.

As we'd supposed, a fairly well-worn track led down from the trees, presumably used by the gypsies. It brought us out on to a stretch of Upper Fell Lane near our lodgings.

"What now? Having missed lunch, I'm beginning to feel hungry and there won't be any food at number twenty-two. Shall we take the car into Barrowick and find somewhere to eat there?"

But a letter awaited us on the hall table which altered our plans. Avoiding Mrs Earnshaw's curious eyes, I waited until we reached the privacy of our room before opening it.

The note began baldly: "My sister and I would be delighted if you'd join us for supper this evening – seven-thirty at the Vicarage." It was signed "Eve Braithwaite".

"Well, well," Philip said softly. "That could be interesting. Can you stand another dose of Celtic lore?"

"You think that will be served with supper?"

"Sure to be. And perhaps Mrs Barlow is looking for another chance to practise her telepathy. Brother, this will be a vicarage party like no other!"

We forebore from asking directions to the vicarage. Mrs Earnshaw's curiosity was patent as we came down the stairs and we had no intention of gratifying it. Once in the streets we could if need be enquire the way to the church; the vicarage was sure to be close by.

We turned left at the gate, along the stretch of Honeypot Lane we had not yet explored. It didn't in fact stretch very far, ending in a T junction on Ash Street, which curved round behind it from further down Fell Lane. And almost opposite the end of the road stood the squat outline of a church.

"That didn't take long!" I commented, but Philip shook his head, indicating the noticeboard by the gate. "Our Lady of the Sorrows," I read aloud. "You could be right. There's unlikely to be a wife in that setup! Those would be the bells that woke us this morning, though."

Another winding road led off beside the church and we followed it until we found ourselves at the top of the High Street. "There's Crowthorpe Grange," I pointed out. "I wonder if the squire and his lady are in residence this evening."

"Not to mention their twin daughters," Philip said darkly. "No wonder the locals looked at us askance. They probably feel they have their share of twins already. Matthew, why do you suppose we've been invited to supper? Doesn't it strike you as odd, after so very brief an acquaintance? Especially when there was no mention of husbands being present."

"You think they have designs on us?" I suggested facetiously.

He was pursuing his own line of thought. "I've a feeling they – expect something of us, and since I should hate to disappoint them, I'm counting on you to back me up, even if you don't see what I'm driving at."

We had followed the bend in the road and another church was now in sight lower down the hill, with the vicarage just beyond. As we turned into the gateway, Mrs Braithwaite opened the front door.

"I'm so glad you've come. Douglas is preaching in Barrowick this evening and the boys are having tea with friends. It seemed a good opportunity to get to know each other." She was speaking rather quickly, and the undercurrent Philip had suspected reached me clearly. "Do come through."

She led us into a pleasant square room at the back of the house. The curtains had not yet been drawn and there was a superb view down the sloping garden and the fields beyond to a stream in the valley, presumably making its way to the lake.

"You've met Anita, of course."

Mrs Barlow turned from the fireplace and held out her hand. Seen together, there were marginal points of difference between the two women, but these lay more in their manner than any disparity of appearance. I fancied that the vicar's wife had the stronger personality.

Anita said jerkily, "I'm afraid I disconcerted you last night. I'm so sorry."

26

"It was most impressive," Philip assured her. "Do you read the tea leaves too?"

She gave a light, breathless laugh. "No, I leave that to Janetta Lee!"

"Janetta—?"

"Can I offer you some sherry?" Eve interrupted. "I'm sorry we've nothing stronger."

"Sherry will be fine. Incidentally, we'd better introduce ourselves properly. I'm Philip and this is Matthew." He glanced at Eve. "Or did you already know?"

"No, I—"

"You addressed me as 'doctor' this morning."

She stood looking at him, the sherry bottle in her hand. "Why did you come to Crowthorpe?"

"We told you – for a holiday."

"No other reason?"

"Should there be?"

"When twins come to Crowthorpe, they usually stay."

Feeling it was time I made a contribution, I said lightly, "We were very impressed with your Circle. I suppose it's quite a tourist attraction."

"In the season, yes." Eve turned away and at last began to pour the sherry. I saw that her hands were shaking. "There are several round about – Castlerigg, Long Meg."

I sat down on the sofa next to Anita. "Tell me how you managed to read our minds so accurately last night."

"I hope you don't think I was prying. It's very difficult when one automatically eavesdrops on people's thoughts. I don't mean to – it's just as if they're speaking too loudly and one can't help overhearing.

Sometimes I find myself answering, and as you'll appreciate, that can cause problems."

Eve handed me a glass of sherry. "I was telling them this morning they could do it themselves if they tried. Think what an asset it would be in their professions! Matthew could see the block which was preventing a child from learning his tables—" She broke off. "You are a schoolmaster, aren't you? And Philip would know how his patients were without having to ask!"

I could feel Philip's excitement flicker across the screen of my own consciousness. "Then by all means let us see what we can do." Gently he turned Eve to face him. "Concentrate on something, and I'll tell you what it is. Better still, send the message to me and *Matthew* will repeat it!"

I looked up, startled, but Philip's eyes were already boring into Eve's and almost at once I heard myself saying: "'Thou dost put into our minds good desires—'"

Eve spun to look down at me. "That's fantastic! It was part of this morning's collect. I knew you could do it!" She paused, her eyes consideringly on my face. "You're not too happy about it though, are you, Matthew? Before, it's always been just between you and Philip; a closed shop. I know how you feel but it has to spread. That's the whole point."

I took a gulp of sherry, feeling the brief pressure of Philip's hand on my shoulder. My brain seemed to be racing in an entirely new dimension and no longer felt as though it belonged to me. Was this what the two women had been expecting from our visit? *Do you read the tea leaves?* Philip had asked sarcastically. And, "Who's Janetta Lee?" I asked aloud.

"One of the gypsies at the camp on the hill."

"The pregnant one?"

"No, that's Nell. Poor thing, she has a baby a year when Luke's not in jail. How do you know about her?"

"We came down the hill past the camp. They wouldn't have noticed us if it hadn't been for a crow which set up a tremendous racket."

The women exchanged glances. "That would be Granny Lee's tame one. She goes round with it on her shoulder. Mind you, I use the word 'tame' loosely. It's an evil-tempered old thing."

"How many families are up there?"

"Well, they're all interrelated. There's Luke and Nell Smith and the two babies; he's a blacksmith by trade but seems to spend most of his time in prison for molesting barmaids! Between you and me, though, I think they ask for it. He's a handsome brute – lord knows what he ever saw in Nell. Then there's Buck and Nan. They're distant cousins of the Smiths. You may see their son Benjie wandering round, a boy of about eight. He's slightly retarded, poor lamb."

Eve paused, glanced across at us and then away. "The story goes that he wandered over to the Circle one night and fell asleep between the stones. When they found him the next morning his – his brain was addled. Of course it probably isn't true, but he was certainly normal enough until he was two or three, so *something* must have happened. Most likely he climbed on one of the stones and fell and cracked his head."

She paused again, following some thought of her own. Then she shrugged it aside and finished briskly, "And the third caravan belongs to old Granny Lee,

Nell's mother. She lives with her son Jem and his wife, who've been married only a month or two."

"And it's this young one who reads the tea leaves?" I persisted.

Anita smiled. "You're not going to let me forget that, are you? I don't know about tea leaves, but she can use Granny's crystal. They always have a tent at the Bank Holiday Fair. Go along tomorrow if you dare, and let her tell your fortune!"

"There's a fair tomorrow?"

"Certainly, down in the meadow by the lake. It's quite a gala occasion, people come from miles around."

Eve stood up. "If you've finished your drinks, I'll take the meal through. You must be ravenous."

We were still seated round the table when Douglas Braithwaite returned with his two sons. He was a pleasant-looking man in his early forties, but although he greeted us politely there was a slight reserve in his manner. However, any hint of awkwardness was covered by the boys.

"Mummy, they're putting up the stalls for the fair!" young William broke in excitedly. "Can we go down first thing in the morning?"

"There's a Ferris wheel, too," Edward added. "You can see almost to Barrowick from the top!"

For the sake of politeness we stayed a few minutes longer, joining in the general conversation. Then Philip caught my eye and we rose to go. Douglas Braithwaite walked with us to the gate.

"You know the quickest way home? Cut through Broad Walk there, and along Ash Street to the end of Honeypot Lane. You'll soon find all the backcracks."

I opened my mouth to say we'd only be here for another week, and closed it again. Somehow I didn't think we'd be able to leave Crowthorpe quite as easily as that.

Three

Easter Monday dawned with a late frost on the grass but by mid-morning the sun had melted it and was shining out of a cloudless sky. The wind was south-easterly and carried the sounds of the fair up the hill to our open bedroom window – odd snatches of tinny music and the blaring loudspeaker.

"What shall we do?" I asked Philip as we stood staring down into the quiet street. "I don't want to spend the whole day at the fair, do you?"

"Heaven forbid! We'll just look in for an hour or so this evening. We'd better go out somewhere, though, I have a suspicion Mrs Earnshaw is hovering with the Hoover. We could take the car and explore a little further afield. We've not been out of the village yet."

Crowthorpe was surprisingly congested. Crowds were pouring down Fell Lane and there was a queue of cars coming from the Barrowick direction into which we had to filter to reach the road to Caldbeck. As we crawled along Lake Road we had ample opportunity to look at the brightly coloured booths and marquees set up in the meadow by the lake. Down here the noise and excitement was intense and as we reached the corner and turned north, we met another stream of cars coming into the village.

"At least now the queues are in the other direction," Philip commented. "If you ask me, we're well out of it."

Caldbeck was peaceful by comparison and we joined the trickle of visitors making their way to the church and John Peel's grave. From there we drove back to Keswick by another route, taking time to search for and find Castlerigg stone circle in the hills beyond. I wondered if it too had some dark legend attached to it, but any atmosphere was dissipated by a crowd of Japanese tourists busily photographing the site.

On the way home we stopped in Barrowick for our evening meal, and by the time we approached Crowthorpe it was almost dark and the lights and music reached out to us across the lake. We were lucky enough to find a parking space in the market place off Lake Road, and joined the crowds still flocking along to the fair.

"No wonder it's become traditional," I remarked. "It must be quite a moneyspinner." Fairy lights strewn in the trees lighted the path from the main road to the uneven grass of the meadow and as we stepped off the concrete we were caught up in the general excitement, part of the holiday crowd. From somewhere overhead a loudspeaker was blaring out the latest pop tunes, interrupted at regular intervals by the even shriller screams of the passengers in the roller-coaster which had been set up in the lee of the hill.

Despite our recent meal we stopped to buy a bag of freshly cooked popcorn, eating it as we walked along and burning our fingers.

"Pity we haven't a couple of girls with us," Philip said with his mouth full. "I'd welcome a spot of dalliance by the darkening waters!"

"There are plenty about. Take your pick!" We were causing our usual stir and a couple of giggling girls stood nearby watching us.

"There really are two of you, aren't there?" one of them asked, catching my eye. "I thought at first I was seeing double!"

I bowed. "Madam, we are twain."

"It's uncanny, really – like Tweedledum and Tweedledee."

"That," said Philip, wiping his greasy hands on his handkerchief, "does positively nothing for our image!"

"Sorry – they were short and fat, weren't they? How does it go – something about a crow . . ."

Her friend obliged her: "'Just then flew down a monstrous crow, as black as a tar barrel, which frightened both the heroes so, they quite forgot their quarrel.'" She laughed. "It's good, that. 'A monstrous crow' – and here we are in Crowthorpe!"

I said thickly, "If you'll excuse us—" and amid their murmurs of disappointment, I steered Philip into the densest part of the crowd. "Come on," I added with a touch of desperation, "I'll take you on at the coconut shy."

"Well done!" said a voice behind us as I managed to dislodge one of the giant coconuts, and I turned to see Douglas Braithwaite with one of his sons.

"Now you'll be lumbered with that for the rest of the evening!" he added with a laugh as the showman handed it over to me. "So, Messrs. Selby, what do you

34

think of our little village? At least it has the distinction of being the only one hereabouts which has positively no connection with the Lakeland poets! Neither Wordsworth, Coleridge nor Ruskin ever slept here!"

William tugged at his father's hand. "Dad, you promised me a go on the Dodgems!"

"Here." I pushed the coconut into his arms. "You take this. I wouldn't know what to do with it."

They were swallowed up into the crowd and Philip and I allowed ourselves to be pushed along by the general flow. Our conversation with the girls still hung on the air between us and the fortune-teller's tent caught me by surprise. I'd forgotten about Janetta Lee.

"Learn What is Written for You in the Star's!" invited the large, uneven letters.

Philip grinned, reading my mind as usual. "Go in and correct her grammar at least!"

I lifted the tent flap and peered inside. It was very dim, but a revolving red light from the merry-go-round lit it every few seconds with a lurid glow. A singsong voice came out of the shadows.

"Come in, pretty sir. Want your fortune told? Then cross me palm wi' fifty pence."

I let the flap fall behind me and took the empty chair opposite the girl. She looked extremely young, not more than eighteen, with lustrous dark eyes and long jet-black hair. I caught myself wondering if she'd be prepared to accompany me down to the lake. Then I heard her gasp, and knew with resignation that Philip had come in behind me.

"Might as well make it two for the price of one!" he said cheerfully. "Since we were born at the same time, it follows we must have the same fate. Right?"

35

She had flinched back in her chair and her eyes were now plainly frightened. "Please, young sirs, I made a mistake. I've got another appointment – the gentleman will be here directly. I can't—"

Philip bent forward and with deliberation placed a pound coin in front of her. "Don't worry, I was only teasing. You shall have your pound of flesh – or your pound sterling, at any rate."

She looked at him blankly. "Sir, I—"

I pushed the crystal ball towards her. "Come on, now, you've got our money. You must keep your side of the bargain."

Her eyes fell unwillingly to the crystal and the cheap jewellery jangled on her wrists as her hands came up to cup it. When she spoke again, her voice was different from the light tones with which she'd greeted me, a low throbbing whisper which added import to the words.

"You must stay in this place."

Philip made a sudden movement and I leant forward the better to catch what she was saying.

"Great power awaits you," she continued haltingly. "Over body and soul, life and death. It is your destiny to bring about—"

"Janetta! Howd thi tongue, lass!"

Philip and I turned swiftly and the girl slumped forward, her forehead resting on the crystal ball. Just inside the tent stood a small elderly woman in a black and red shawl. She was staring as though hypnotized at Philip and myself, both of us now on our feet.

"You will please go, gentlemen," she ordered, her voice shaking. "The girl sees nowt. She was deceiving you."

"She was doing very well," I protested, since the girl was clearly incapable of defending herself.

"Please go!" The woman swooped forward, snatched up the pound coin still lying on the table and pushed it into my hand.

"But look, surely she deserves—"

"She don't want your money." She glanced briefly down at the motionless figure. "I must see to her."

We had no option but to leave. I followed Philip out of the tent and by unspoken consent we shouldered our way past the throngs to the practically deserted lakeside.

"I wonder what upset the old woman," I said at last. "Fortune-telling's always a con but they don't usually admit it."

"Perhaps this time it was the truth." Philip stared out across the water. "What did you make of it, all that power-not-given-to-many?"

"A load of rubbish!" But it had intrigued me, too. The classroom in Swindon held out no such promise.

Philip bent, selected a pebble and hurled it into the darkness of the lake, waiting for the distant splash as it fell. "Shall we accept the challenge – take over the village? You can see to their minds and I'll look after their bodies! Far more scope here, I imagine, than in that grotty surgery in High Wycombe!"

A joking reply was called for but I was unable to supply it. There was an undisciplined excitement about him which disturbed me, especially since I could feel the undertow of it myself.

"Well, well, if it isn't you two again!" The girls we'd seen earlier had loomed up out of the shadows.

"Did you follow us?" Philip demanded ringingly.

"You flatter yourselves!"

"Did you?"

"No, we – well, we just caught sight of you some way ahead, and—"

"Have you heard what happens to girls who follow men?"

She stared at him, trying to see his expression in the twilight, and giggled uncertainly.

"They might," said Philip deliberately, "get more than they bargain for. Such as this!" And putting his arm round her, he pulled her against him and kissed her thoroughly.

"And this!" I added, following suit with the other girl. And at the feel of her soft yielding body I knew this was exactly what we needed to dispel the strangeness. Thoughts that had nothing to do with the supernatural surged into my head and I welcomed them wholeheartedly, letting mental excitement give way to physical. Pulling the willing girl behind some bushes, it was swiftly gratified. And it was about this unlooked-for but easy conquest that Philip and I joked as we prepared for bed that night. We made no further reference to the fortune-teller.

But we were not to be allowed to forget the gypsies.

A couple of mornings later as we walked above the village, a tall dark man came hurtling out of a clearing just in front of us, cannoning straight into me and knocking me off balance. He caught at my arm to prevent my falling.

"Beg pardon I'm sure, sir, but I'm that bothered to get to doctor, I—"

"Something's wrong?" Philip interrupted. "I'm a doctor."

The man registered him for the first time, and as his eyes went from Philip's face to mine, his hand shot out towards us, the forefinger and pinky extended in the age-old gesture to ward off evil. "No – no, sir, I—"

"Look man, I can be there quicker than anyone else. What's happened?"

"It's Nell, sir. Her pains have started but it's not like the other times. It's bad and the women can't do nothing with her."

"Then lead the way," Philip instructed tersely, "and hurry!"

We were nearer the gypsy camp than I'd realized and as we ran a shrill scream rang out over the trees. We rounded the screen, the caravans came into sight, and I fell back, letting the others race on ahead. I had no wish to be involved in Philip's obstetrics. He and Luke Smith had disappeared into one of the caravans and a moment later the girl from the fairground came down the steps, hesitated for a moment then walked slowly towards me.

"I hope you didn't get into trouble the other evening," I said.

She gave me a strained smile and shook her head. Another scream made us flinch.

"What's going on in there?"

"Oh sir, poor Nell's awful bad!" Her huge eyes filled with tears. "The Granny wouldn't let me stay. Said as I'm too young to be present at child-bed, but I'm a married woman, sir, and my time will come. Does it always hurt so bad?"

"I shouldn't think so," I said reassuringly from my

position of male immunity. "Don't worry, Philip'll sort things out. He's a very good doctor." My mind had swung back to those moments in the tent, and unable to resist this unexpected chance to question her, I said compulsively, "What did you mean, about my brother and I achieving power?"

She gave a little shiver and looked up at me. "Did I say that? I don't remember."

Her eyes met mine unwaveringly and to my frustration I saw that she was speaking the truth. There was nothing to be gained by further questioning.

Luke Smith had now also emerged from the caravan, evicted, no doubt, by Philip. He didn't approach us, nor we him. He squatted down by the shafts and began to roll a cigarette. The shrieking from inside was by this time almost continuous and I could feel the sweat breaking out along my hair line. Presumably there was no means of anaesthetizing the poor woman. The toddlers we had seen before began to whimper and Janetta bent to soothe them.

"There now, don't cry. Mammy'll soon have a new brother or sister for you."

They could only have been one and two years old themselves and obviously understood neither the commotion nor the explanation. I took out my handkerchief and embarked on a long-forgotten trick of twisting it into the shapes of various animals. The babies were enthralled, and Janetta too.

Time crawled by and I had begun to wonder whether the screams or the inexplicable silences were the harder to bear, when at last came a short, sharp shriek, followed almost at once by the cry of the newborn. I stood up, unknotting the handkerchief, but my relief was short-lived. Another cry reached us, and immediately a flood of screeching invective broke out, jerking Luke Smith to his feet and sending him hurrying back up the steps. Janetta and I, appalled, stood staring towards the caravan. The abuse continued unabated and at full volume for some minutes until Philip, pale and dishevelled, appeared in the doorway and came slowly towards us.

There was a strange expression on his face which I couldn't interpret. As he reached us a sudden fear grasped me. "She's not – she didn't die, did she?"

Janetta gave a little gasp and fled towards the caravan. Philip shook his head. "No, no. All's well. Very well, considering. It was a particularly nasty breech birth and there was nothing I could give her except some cheap alcohol. It had to serve as disinfectant too. God, the place was crawling! If she doesn't get puerperal fever it will be a miracle, but come to think of it that's where she's had her other confinements."

"Then what on earth was—"

"The tirade, brother dear, was because I delivered Nell of twins. Identical twin boys," he added heavily as I stared at him. "And the sweet, white-haired old lady accused me of – well, malpractice isn't quite the word. Witchcraft would be nearer the mark." He drew a deep breath. "She insisted that until I arrived there had been only one baby in the uterus and by my charms I'd split the foetus in two for my own wicked purposes! Tell me, Matthew, are we or are we not living in the late twentieth century?"

"But she couldn't have believed it, surely?"

"She's not enamoured of twins, that's for sure. And to have some turn up in her own family –

that was too much. Look out, here comes the proud father."

Luke was shambling towards us rather shamefacedly. "I'm much obliged to you, Doctor. You musn't mind the Granny, she's set in her ideas. But – well, we can look after Nell ourselves now. There's no call for you to come back, like."

"She ought really to go to hospital."

He looked alarmed. "There's not summat you haven't told us?"

"No, no, but she needs rest after that ordeal, and the strictest hygiene. That really is essential, both for her and the babies."

"Aye, well Nan'll see to it. She knows what to do."

"And you want me to stay away, is that it?"

He hung his head. "There's no call to drag you up again."

"I presume it was your own doctor you were setting out to fetch? As a courtesy I'll have to let him know."

"Ain't no need. We don't trouble him for the babbies, only when someone's ill and herbs ain't working."

Philip sighed. "Very well, but if she shows signs of fever—"

"If need be we'll get Dr Sampson, aye."

And with that, Philip had to be content.

Thoughtfully we made our way down to the village.

"Despite what he says I'm going to contact the surgery," Philip remarked. "I don't want anything on my conscience."

"So Crowthorpe has another pair of twins."

"Yes." He gave a short laugh. "You should have seen them. Lying there squawking away, with their black hair and scrawny little bodies, they looked just like a pair of crows themselves!"

We stopped at a public call box and Philip found the doctor's number in a tattered directory which hung on a string. I waited outside, reluctant to hear the medical details of Nell's confinement.

"Sounds a nice old boy," Philip announced as he rejoined me. "We're invited round for drinks before dinner – nineteen, Caldbeck Rise. Know where that is?"

"It'll be on the street plan. We're doing well, aren't we? Supper at the vicarage, drinks at the surgery!"

"At least I feel better now I've off-loaded poor Nell. It won't be any hardship dispensing with a return call up there."

Dr Sampson and his wife were a pleasant couple in their sixties. To our relief, his only comment on seeing us was, "Twins, is it?" We'd become more than a little self-conscious of the relationship since coming to Crowthorpe.

"Not thinking of settling up here, are you Selby?" the doctor enquired suddenly when they'd finished their discussion. "You're just the sort of chap I'm looking for. Finding it too much for me now, all on my own. Decided I'd better take on a junior partner before I'm too old to shape him to my ways."

"He works far too hard," put in his wife anxiously. "I've been telling him for some time he should take things more easily, but it was only this last winter, when he had bronchitis, that I persuaded him to approach the FPC."

Philip looked across at me, his eyes shining. "I suppose there aren't any staff vacancies in the village school?"

The doctor seemed surprised at the change of subject. "I believe there will be," he replied, "in September. I was talking to Bob Sedgewick the other week. Why do you ask?"

For a long moment Philip and I looked at each other. Then he said slowly, "In that case, Doctor, I might well be able to help you. I've a feeling there'll be yet another pair of Crowthorpe twins before long."

"You mean that? You were already thinking of settling here? My dear chap, that's splendid news! Of course, the correct procedure will have to be followed, but as Dora said I've already been in touch with the FPC and they admit this area is under-doctored. Subject to the usual references and so on, there shouldn't be any problem.

"And your brother's a schoolmaster?" He turned to me. "I imagine Bob will be more than interested. He's not had much response to his advertisement, he was telling me. He's on holiday at the moment, but if you were to write to him I'm sure he'd send you all the details."

He leant back in his chair and regarded us benevolently. "It's beginning to look as if these positions were tailor-made for the pair of you!"

Which was exactly how it had struck me, and I was less than sanguine about it. It was all too neat, too convenient, the way the wheels had turned. I said as much to Philip when we had left the

44

Sampsons and were walking down the hill for our evening meal.

"But why fight it?" he replied. "We've always wanted to get together again, and this gives us the chance. I was fed-up in High Wycombe; you were in Swindon. And don't forget we've been promised unlimited powers here!"

"That's surely not what decided you?"

"No, what clinched it was when I realised, back in that filthy, stuffy little caravan, that there were two babies waiting to be born. It seemed an omen, somehow – fate, that a twin should be instrumental in delivering twins. What's more, if I hadn't been there I doubt if either they or their mother would have survived. Old Sampson certainly couldn't have got there in time. He told me he was at one of the outlying farms all afternoon – he'd just got back when I phoned."

"I suppose Luke was grateful enough for your ministrations, but he wouldn't have accepted you if there'd been any choice. I didn't care for that sign he made when he first saw us."

"No, it was a bit off-putting. Odd how superstitious people still are. I remember reading that ancient civilisations considered twins to be very powerful. Some venerated them, and others left them out to die. I wonder which way the Romanies were inclined."

"Do you realize that a week ago there were only two pairs of twins living here, and now the number's about to be doubled?"

"Perhaps that's why it feels so right for us. Eve said there have been twins in Crowthorpe for centuries. If

45

you remember, that's why it caught your attention in the first place."

We'd reached Lake Road and turned into a pub in the market place that we'd noticed earlier. It was called, fairly predictably, the Crow's Nest, but neither of us referred to that. There was quite a nautical air about it – fishing nets draped on the wall and an elderly-looking salmon mounted in a glass case. In the tiny dining-room behind the bar we did full justice to a home-made steak pie and when we'd finished, took our beers through to the public bar. We were curious to inspect the people who would soon be our neighbours, though how many in the small crowded room were Easter visitors it was not easy to assess. No-one came to talk to us, but they nodded across in a friendly enough fashion and we were satisfied.

A light drizzle was falling as we started to walk home and the air was quite chill. Spring wasn't in any particular hurry that year and it was still only mid-April. I was glad to reach the dry warmth of the boarding house and we went straight upstairs, pursued by the sound of the Earnshaws' television. Philip had moved to draw the curtains when he stopped suddenly, his hand still gripping the cheap material.

"What is it?" I joined him quickly, thinking he'd seen something in the street below, but it was empty. He let his hand drop and turned to face me.

"What did Eve say about that gypsy child, the retarded one?"

"That he'd spent a night in the Circle and it – I think the phrase was 'addled his brain'. Why?"

"Come on!" Philip moved suddenly, catching up his jacket again and pulling open the bedroom door.

"We're going up there. I want to check on those babies."

"Now? But good God, Philip—"

He was already clattering down the stairs and as I hurried after him, I heard him knock on the living-room door. "Sorry to trouble you, but have you such a thing as a torch? I must have dropped my cigarette lighter outside somewhere and I should hate to lose it." Philip, the non-smoker.

A torch was produced amid exclamations of concern and minutes later we were hurrying along Upper Fell Lane. Automatically I turned up the path we'd come down that afternoon but Philip tugged at my sleeve and hurried me past the opening.

"We're going to the Circle first."

"Philip, are you mad? You said you wanted to see the babies!"

"Bear with me, Matthew. I'll explain later."

The rain was heavier now and we didn't speak as we made our way over the uneven grass of the hillside. Philip kept the torch trained on the ground immediately ahead but even so I stumbled and wrenched my ankle. It was slightly lighter up here, the huge arc of sky a paler purple than the land below, and the last quarter of the moon only just behind the clouds.

The stones loomed, blotches of darkness against the sky, and despite myself I felt a clutch of apprehension. Who knew what mysterious rites had been enacted up here in the primeval past? Surely such a wealth of worship, sacrifice and bloodshed must have left some trace behind?

Philip stopped and, head down, I bumped into him. "Now what?" I said irritably, to mask my nervousness.

"Now," he answered grimly, "we're going to search this place inch by inch."

"Are you ready yet to tell me why?" There was an edge to my voice, and he turned, his hand contritely on my arm.

"Sorry, I thought you were with me. You nearly always are. I want to satisfy myself that the babies aren't here."

"Here? How could—"

"Let's just look, shall we?"

It was impossible in the semi-darkness to see far ahead and I envisaged that our search would be a lengthy one. We embarked on it methodically, flashing the beam of the torch round the base of each stone before moving onto the next one, and had inspected about a dozen when Philip suddenly lifted his head.

"My God," he said softly, "I was right!" He set off into the centre of the Circle and the faint sound which had alerted him reached me too – a tremendous cry. I think my eyes picked out the paleness of the bundles a second before the torch found them, and I stood by Philip in the cold wet darkness, staring down for the first time at the Smith twins. Philip knelt quickly beside them, feeling the temperature of their skins.

"They haven't been here long, but these shawls are drenched. Get your jacket off, Matthew. Here, take this one."

Gingerly I accepted the shapeless bundle, disentangled its soaking wrapper and, following his example, enfolded it in the bulky tweed of my jacket. In less than ten minutes we were hammering on the door of the Smiths' caravan.

It took a while for Luke to open it, his eyes gummed

with sleep, but at the sight of what we carried he came instantly awake and fear crossed his face. Behind him a child, disturbed by our knocking, began to cry and a woman's voice called, "What is it, Luke? Not the coppers?"

"Not this time, Nell." Philip brushed past Luke and strode over to the untidy bed where she lay. "They may well be here in the morning, though. Can you tell me how your newborn babies came to be out in the rain in the stone circle?"

She gave a cry, reaching to lift the child Philip had laid on the bed. Silently I relinquished my own charge and reclaimed my jacket.

"Oh dear Lord!" she whispered, clasping both babies to her. "Why? Why?"

"That's what I'm waiting to hear." Philip turned to Luke.

"The Granny took them," he mumbled. "She said as Nell needed her night's sleep and she'd bring them back in the morning. Honest, sir, we didn't know nothing."

"Can I trust you to look after them, or shall I take them to someone who will?"

Nell was crying softly. "I'll not let them out of sight."

"Just one thing more." I'd never seen Philip so stern and authoritative. "Tell Granny Lee that if anything happens to these babies – if they so much as get a cold in the head – the authorities will be informed about tonight. Do you understand?"

Luke nodded, sullen but frightened, and Nell caught at Philip's hand. "Bless you for fetching them back, sir."

"Whatever made you think they might be up there?" I asked curiously, as we went down the hill. "And what was the point, anyway? If Granny was trying to kill them it would have been better to leave them unwrapped."

"To answer your first question, it was association of ideas. We knew that for some reason the old woman hates twins. She'd broadcast her fears sufficiently widely for both Luke and Janetta to react when they first saw us. I suppose I was thinking of that, and about primitive people either venerating twins or disposing of them, and I suddenly remembered – Benjie, was it? – who seemed to have lost his faculties after a night in the Circle. Regarding your other question, I don't think Granny was trying to kill them, but she probably reasoned it would be as well to – disarm them, as it were, before they had a chance to develop any power. If they grew up simple, the danger would be averted."

"She put those kids out there with the express purpose of turning them into idiots?"

"That's what it looks like."

"But Philip, that's – diabolical!"

"I agree."

"And you're not going to report it?"

"There's no need. They'll be quite safe now."

"Only thanks to you!"

"We found them, that's all that matters, and she won't dare try anything else."

By the time we let ourselves into number twenty-two we were both shivering. The living-room door opened at once.

"Goodness, you are wet! Let me have those jackets

and I'll dry them for you in the kitchen. Did you find the lighter?"

We looked at Mrs Earnshaw blankly for a moment, then Philip said, "Oh – yes. Yes, thank you, we did."

"Well, that was a stroke of luck! You were so long I was beginning to get worried, but since you found it I suppose it was worth the trouble."

Philip smiled at her and handed back the torch. "Yes, Mrs Earnshaw, it was certainly worth the trouble," he said.

Four

The few remaining days of our holiday were spent trying to find accommodation for our return in July which, of course, would be at the height of the holiday season. Having been in lodgings for years, we'd decided to look for a flat but Barrowick estate agents held out little hope of our finding one. We were on the point of leaving yet another office when the man we'd been speaking to suddenly said, "Hang on a minute!" and spoke into the telephone. A moment later a girl brought in a file and laid it on his desk.

"This came in only this morning and we haven't had time to type the particulars but it could just be what you're looking for: a self-contained flat at the top of a house in Ash Street. How would that appeal?"

I was already on my feet. "When can we see it?"

"Well, it's not officially on the market yet. Apparently the owner's brother-in-law and family will be there for another month. I don't know if they're thinking of letting it long-term, mind. You'd have to sort that out for yourselves. Would you like me to phone and try to make an appointment to view?"

Which was how we found Rowan House. It was a tall, three-storey building in traditional Applethwaite stone and it stood in large gardens at the corner of

Ash Street and Fell Lane. The Staveleys welcomed us cautiously.

"We weren't really expecting anyone so soon; we only phoned the agents this morning. Still, since you're leaving in a day or two, my sister-in-law says you're welcome to go up and have a look. It's self-contained as you can see. We had a staircase built outside, so they'd be completely independent."

The flat, as we knew at once, was ideal. The original attic windows had been enlarged to frame magnificent views down towards the lake and the whole effect was light and airy. There were two bedrooms, a fairly large sitting-room, and bathroom and kitchen. Since the other Staveleys were emigrating to Canada they were proposing to leave their furniture which, as Philip and I had none of our own, was a further asset.

Back downstairs, we talked terms with Mr and Mrs Staveley. They had intended to let the flat for the holiday season and then find permanent tenants in the winter, but since barely six weeks would elapse between the present family's departure and our own arrival, they were prepared to hold it for us. Once again, things had gone our way.

It was only later that it struck me as strange that, with nothing settled regarding our careers, Philip and I had been confident enough of our return to pay a deposit on the flat. Perhaps, though we were unaware of either its significance or its potency, Janetta's "Macbeth prophecy" had already taken hold of us. Subconsciously, we were not prepared to relinquish the promises made.

I remember very little of the last term in Swindon,

but one incident sticks in my mind since it was less than comfortable. On the day I received a letter from Mr Sedgewick inviting me for an interview, I could contain my exhuberance no longer, and broke into the general conversation in the staff-room with my news.

"Isn't it the most incredible luck?" I continued jubilantly. "My brother and I will be together again, and in such lovely surroundings! It's a most attractive place, all narrow, twisting little streets and courtyards, with the lake at the bottom of the hill and the Gemelly Stone Circle at the top. And you know my passion for ancient monuments. I can potter around to my heart's content, while—"

"Just slow down a minute, Matthew," John Dobson interrupted at last. "Are we to gather from all this gobbledegook that you intend to leave us?"

"Most certainly I do – at the end of this very term!"

"It might be kinder to be less enthusiastic at the prospect!"

"Sorry, but to be brutally frank, I can hardly wait! Philip's already applied for a post there, and I'm off for my own interview next week."

"In other words, being brutally frank in my turn, you haven't actually landed the job yet?"

"Oh, I'll get it all right!"

"I hope you won't be disillusioned. Does the old man know of his impending bereavement?"

"Of course. I handed in my notice on the first day of term."

"Without a definite job to go to? Haven't you heard of all the unemployed teachers walking the Embankment—"

Whatever he had been going on to say was lost for ever. Without warning, Sue Anderson, whom I'd taken out on one or two occasions, startled us all by bursting into tears and rushing out of the room.

Margaret Pearson surveyed me coldly. "Callous devil, aren't you? That poor kid's been carrying a torch for you for years. When you asked her out, she was over the moon. And now here you are, shouting to all and sundry that you can't wait to shake the dust of the place off your feet."

"I didn't know any of that," I defended myself. "There was never anything serious."

"Not to you, perhaps. It was serious enough for her. The trouble is you're too damned good-looking for your own good. You've never had to worry about girls, have you? They just come flocking."

"Oh now look," I protested, embarrassed as much by her back-handed compliment as by her accusations.

"Can you honestly tell me there's ever been a girl you fancied who didn't come running when you snapped your fingers?"

"Well, I—"

"No, you can't!"

"Hold on, Maggie, it's not Matthew's fault if the girls all go for him. Wish I had his problem!"

The bell sounded for the end of break, releasing me from my discomfiture, but when later that afternoon I bumped into Sue, red-eyed and subdued, in the staff cloak-room, my conscience belatedly asserted itself. She gave me a watery smile and would have passed me, but I caught hold of her arm.

"Sue, I'm sorry about this morning. I—"

"You've nothing to be sorry about, Matthew. It's I who should apologize, for making such a fool of myself. It was – just the shock, that's all."

"I didn't realize you—"

"Of course you didn't. I never intended that you should."

"Perhaps we could have a drink together?" I asked tentatively.

"Perhaps, but not this evening." Her control was beginning to slip again. "Goodbye, Matthew," she finished in a rush, and, escaping from my fingers, hurried out of the door.

At least I'd tried. Putting the matter thankfully aside, I went home to phone Philip. And here another setback awaited me, and one which caused considerably more regret. When I told him of my coming interview, he replied: "The best of luck. Let me know how you get on, but I'm sure it'll be OK."

"Let you know?" I frowned, not understanding.

"You weren't expecting me to go with you? Matthew, we're run off our feet here. A measles epidemic is in full swing, and between you and me I'm not very popular at the moment anyway. My resignation didn't go down too well."

I tried to swallow my disappointment. "Have you heard from Dr Sampson?"

"Nothing definite. He's taken up my references and my papers are with the Cumbria FPC. It all seems to be going smoothly."

Remembering Sue, I said suddenly, "Have you broken the news to that district nurse you were running round with?"

"I have. There were a few tantrums but we survived."

I suppressed a smile. If I really was "too good-looking for my own good", then so, too, was Philip.

"I presume you had similar problems?" he asked astutely.

"A few."

He laughed. "Couple of heart-breakers, aren't we? Sorry, Matthew, I must dash. I'm on early duty at the surgery this evening. Phone me when you get back from Crowthorpe."

His words were still with me as I started to prepare the following day's lessons, and I allowed myself a moment of self-congratulation. As usual, we'd managed to extricate ourselves from our romantic entanglements without too much trouble. Dismissing the two girls with no further qualms, I had picked up my pen when I suddenly remembered our mother's words. *A wife is something you won't be able to share.*

For the first time, uneasily, I wondered what would happen if Philip and I really fell in love, and which of us would succumb first. I was aware of an immediate wave of resentment towards Philip's hypothetical wife, whoever she might be, and the unpleasant sensation lingered with me for the rest of the evening.

The long journey north was tiring with no one to share the driving, but I arrived in ample time for my interview and was taken aback to find several other men waiting in a small room next to the headmaster's study.

I'd been so sure of success that I hadn't even considered other applicants. One of them was ushered into the study as I arrived, and the others gave me a quick, furtive inspection as I sat down. From being so confident, I was suddenly panic-stricken that my application would be passed over and by the time my name was called, was more nervous than I would have believed possible.

There were three men waiting for me. Robert Sedgewick stood up behind his desk with a welcoming smile and held out his hand. "Come in, Mr Selby. I'm sorry to keep you waiting. May I introduce Mr Pemberton and Mr Williams, who represent the school managers. Now, take a seat and we'll just go through your papers."

The interview progressed in a fairly standard manner, but my agitation had increased to the stage where I was having difficulty keeping my mind on my answers. God, what would happen if I didn't get the position? I *had* to come to Crowthorpe, and this would probably be my only chance!

"Mr Selby?"

"I – beg your pardon?"

"I was wondering if there were any questions you'd like to ask. I imagine this school is considerably smaller than where you are at the moment. Do you feel you'd be happy in such a different atmosphere, country instead of town, and so on?"

"I'm sure I should, sir. My brother and I were up here for a holiday and liked the area very much. He's – hoping for an appointment here too."

There was a pause and I surmised they were waiting for some questions. I had none; I desperately wanted the job, that was all, but I forced myself to ask, "How many children are there?"

"A hundred and twenty at the moment. We have four classes from age five to eleven, so a slight overlap is necessary – about a year and a half usually. I teach myself, of course, and there are four other members of staff."

"And where do the children go from here?"

"The nearest secondary school is in Barrowick. A school bus leaves every morning from the depot in the market place and brings them back at the end of the afternoon."

I saw one of the managers glance at his watch and, feeling time run out, said rapidly, "I hope very much my application will be successful, sir. I'm sure I should be very happy here and would enjoy the challenge of a smaller school."

"Thank you, Mr Selby. We'll let you know as soon as we have reached a decision."

I was out in Broad Walk again and it was not yet four o'clock. I sat for some minutes in the car with the window wound right down. It was a cloudy day and rain was not far away. If only Philip were here!

Eventually I switched on the engine and drove slowly out on to Fell Lane. At the corner of Ash Street, Rowan House stood large and dignified behind its garden wall and I remembered the euphoria that had gripped Philip and myself when we had signed the lease. What had made us so certain of our return? Surely not a few words whispered by a gypsy girl?

But in swift contradiction to the disclaimer, confidence flooded back and I almost laughed aloud. Of course I should get the job: Janetta Lee had implied as much! It was naive, utterly illogical, but my doubts vanished instantly and there was an idiotic smile on my face as I drove back to Barrowick in search of somewhere to sleep.

After some difficulty I managed to find a small room in an hotel on the outskirts, and on impulse booked it for two nights rather than the one I'd intended. Then, desirous of company, I phoned Anita Barlow. Even if she didn't, as I hoped, invite me straight round, I had the excuse of booking a table for dinner the following evening. In the event, the result was a compromise.

"Matthew! How long are you here for? Is Philip with you?"

"He couldn't get away, unfortunately. I came up for my interview and decided to stay over Saturday night as well."

"That's fine, because we're having a few friends for drinks tomorrow. It will be a chance for you to meet them, and you must stay to dinner afterwards."

For the moment, though, I was reduced to my own company and decided to look round Barrowick, mingling with the crowds in the cobbled streets, admiring the old clock-tower and stone archways.

Eventually I found an alley leading to the lakeside and strolled down it to the water's edge. Here, even on this grey evening, the motor launches had been busy and the last one was just returning to the jetty thronged with holidaymakers. Around the edge of the water, ducks and swans strutted and stretched, accepting titbits thrown to them by the crowds. Lake Crowswater, beneath which the Crow goddess had her home.

I was suddenly cold, and, turning away from the darkening water, made my way back to the hotel.

* * *

The following morning I awoke to heavy rain and resigned myself to a few hours in the dim dark lounge with the newspaper. About lunchtime, however, the weather cleared with the rapidity I was coming to associate with the Lakeland climate, and after I had eaten I drove back to Crowthorpe. I intended to spend the afternoon acquainting myself more thoroughly with the village which, if the gods of chance played fair, would soon be our home.

I parked in the market place and walked down to the jetty, a smaller less commercialized counterpart of that at the other end of the lake. Behind me, the Pavilion Café spilled its clientele on to its broad terrace and to the right the grounds of the Lakeside Hotel stretched down to the water. I could see one or two private jetties with small boats moored alongside.

Turning my back on such opulence, I walked instead alongside the stream, following it under the bridge of the main road and along the valley which stretched to the north. Some distance to the left, Crowthorpe climbed its hillside and I guessed this would be the view we'd glimpsed from the vicarage windows.

The grass was wet with the morning's rain but the racing clouds were high and fluffy and the breeze which sped them on their way ruffled my hair. I stopped suddenly, looking down at the gurgling water beside me, at the lush green fields and beyond them the slowly rolling hills. A wild surge of happiness exploded inside me. This without doubt was where I belonged, and the thought of having to return to Swindon for two more months was almost unbearable.

I continued my leisurely stroll along the path until I came to a fork in it. One branch led up the long slope towards the village, and after a moment's hesitation I took it. It was quite a stiff climb which eventually brought me out towards the top of the High Street just short of Crowthorpe Grange. I was well satisfied with my afternoon's exploration and regretted only that I had not been able to share the enjoyment of it with Philip.

When I arrived at the Greystones that evening, Anita greeted me warmly. "What a shame Philip couldn't be with you! Never mind, come in and meet some of the local community." She tucked her hand into my arm and led me through to her private sitting-room.

"Here's our prospective new schoolmaster, everyone. Isn't he gorgeous? Douglas, of course, you've already met, and Dr and Mrs Sampson. This is my husband George, and here are Geoff and Felicity Marshall who, as I told you, are also lucky enough to have twins in the family! And this is David Buckley from the Lakeside Hotel, his wife Sally, and Tom and Vera Chadwick, from the Meadowlands."

The sea of smiling faces was a little confusing, but of all the names tossed into the air, the ones which had really registered were, of course, the Marshalls, and as soon as I could I edged myself back to where Felicity was standing.

"Are your daughters absolutely identical, Mrs Marshall?" I asked with interest.

"We can tell them apart, if that's what you mean. I suppose it's easier with girls – you can do their hair differently and so on. We've always made an effort to treat them as individuals rather than as a collective noun. I think that's important, don't you?"

She looked up at me smilingly – a fair, pretty woman, Felicity Marshall.

"I'm not sure," I answered. "Speaking personally, my brother and I were never interested in separate identities. We preferred to be thought of as one entity."

Her eyes flickered uncertainly and at my side Eve came to her rescue. "Take no notice of him, Felicity. He and Philip are uncannily alike, more clones than twins! Perhaps they *are* clones!" She looked at me laughingly, with raised eyebrows.

I smiled and turned back to Mrs Marshall. She didn't really look old enough to have nine-year-old girls. "And your daughters are quite happy to be – dissociated?"

"That's a forceful word," she protested. "I only mean we give them the opportunity to grow up as sisters rather than twins."

"How do you feel about it?" I challenged Eve. "Do you think of Anita as your sister first, or as your twin?"

"Well, we're close, of course, but probably not as close as you and Philip. We've often had fights, and so on. I rather imagine you haven't?"

"No." It came as a shock to me that two such integral halves could ever be at odds with each other.

"Do Claire and Nicola fight?" Eve asked Felicity.

"Like cat and dog, at times!"

"Perhaps by your treatment of them you've forced them apart," I said.

"Oh come now—"

"I'm sorry," I said quickly. "I didn't mean to sound critical. Obviously my brother and I are the odd ones out. I hadn't realized all identical twins didn't feel as we do." Suddenly Philip's absence was an aching void. This talk of friction between other twins served only to emphasize how in tune we were, and how much we needed each other.

Anita touched my arm. "Philip's on the phone, Matthew. You can take it in the call box in the hall."

With conflicting emotions I hurried from the room and into the wooden kiosk. I snatched up the receiver and said rapidly, "Oh God, Philip, I wish you were here!"

"That's why I'm phoning. How did the interview go?"

I forced my mind back to the previous afternoon, my earlier doubts and fears forgotten. "Famously. I don't think there'll be any problems but of course it has to go through the official channels." I paused, realizing I hadn't told him I should be at the Greystones. Still, perhaps that hadn't been hard to deduce. I added, "I timed it well, too. The Barlows have some friends in and I've just met the 'squire's' wife. I think I was probably rather rude to her."

"No doubt she'll survive. I have next Thursday off, by the way. All right if I come over?"

"Of course. I'll wangle a free day, too. It's ages since we saw each other."

He laughed. "Don't start playing hooky just because you're leaving – bad for discipline! I'd better go, someone's waiting to use the phone. See you Thursday."

"Thanks for phoning."

"I needed to talk to you."

The phone clicked in my ear. I drew a deep breath,

rubbed my hands on my handkerchief and went back to face the crowd.

When we sat down to dinner an hour or so later, it was only the Barlows, Braithwaites and myself. George Barlow was a tall, worried-looking man with horn-rimmed spectacles and a shy smile. He treated his wife with the gentle, rather touching affection I'd noticed before between childless couples.

Not unnaturally, the conversation turned again to the subject of twins.

"You certainly gave Felicity pause for thought!" Eve teased me. "I don't think she found your views very comfortable."

"I only said it was pointless to deny the fact that twins *are* twins."

"In a way, though, I see what she means. Mothers of twins, especially identical ones, tend to dress them exactly alike, talk about them in one breath and so on. I suppose it could cause a child some crisis of identity."

"On the other hand, our mother tried from the start to make us different, if only for ease of identification, and failed hopelessly."

"So there will shortly be four pairs in Crowthorpe," remarked Douglas. "It's remarkable how self-perpetuating the thing is. Twins hear of the story and willingly come along to bolster it."

"What brought you here?" I asked Anita.

"It was 'who' rather than 'what', since we were only babies, but it was certainly because of the legend. Our father was a professor who married late in life. He was steeped in Celtic mythology and had known about Crowthorpe for years. When his wife presented him with twin daughters he was just about to retire, and made a point of settling here. So although we weren't actually born in Crowthorpe, we've been here virtually all our lives."

"I hadn't realized," George put in, "how comparatively rare identical twins are. There was a talk about them on the radio the other day. Apparently twins occur once in every eighty or so births but identical ones only every four thousand. Scientists are appealing for volunteers to take part in a series of tests on immunity to disease, hereditary weaknesses and so on."

"Perhaps they should come to Crowthorpe!" Anita said laughingly.

"It would be fertile ground. At this rate, you'll soon outnumber the rest of us!"

"So they're doing tests, are they?" Eve mused.

"Yes, on quite a wide field: diabetes, psychology, and the old bone of contention, heredity versus environment."

"I wonder what form the psychological tests would take," I said, and felt both women glance at me – anxiously, I thought. Perhaps their husbands didn't approve of the parlour games we'd indulged in at the vicarage.

George for his part had looked across at Douglas. "Oh, the usual, I imagine. Behaviour under stress, personality characteristics and so on."

"Telepathy?" I prompted.

"Quite possibly."

Anita said, "Eve and I once had the same dream. I started to tell her about it the next morning, and she finished it off for me."

"I've read," I said, "of twins dying at the same time as each other. One of them has an accident and the other, miles away, dies at the same instant of no apparent cause. I've always taken it for granted the same thing would happen to Philip and me. We couldn't survive without each other."

There was a brief, uncomfortable pause. Douglas Braithwaite cleared his throat. "Without wanting to sound pompous, I'm not too sure I approve of that philosophy. Each life is sacred; a completely separate being, however close one might feel to another. The fact that two people are born at the same time most certainly does not infer they must also die together."

"Nevertheless, it does happen."

"Very seldom, I think you'd find, and for quite valid reasons. Good gracious, man, even at the rate of one in four thousand, there are vast numbers of identical twins throughout the world. Imagine their reaction, if someone suggested they should die simultaneously! It's reminiscent of throwing a wife on her husband's funeral pyre!"

I put my hands up in mock self-defence. "Far be it from me to frighten anyone! I only said it has been known, and whatever you say I'm quite sure it will happen to us. I hope it does."

"You won't insist on it, will you Anita?" Eve queried humorously, and in the general laughter the conversation edged on to more comfortable topics.

I recounted it to Philip the following week when he came over to see me, but the discussion took a turn I hadn't expected.

"You know, I'd like to have another go at that mind-reading stunt," he said slowly. "I know you weren't too keen, but just consider the possibilities!"

I frowned into my glass. "I've a feeling we could easily get out of our depth."

"If we don't experiment, we'll never know what our depth is. Suppose it really is possible to read a patient's symptoms telepathically. It would be an enormous advantage; people are so bad at expressing themselves." He looked at me shrewdly. "Eve was right, wasn't she, about your being slightly jealous over that demonstration we did? Surely you know there's no reason to be?"

We changed the subject then, but that he hadn't forgotten it was made only too apparent a few days later. When Philip and I phoned each other, it was always in the evenings at each other's lodgings. Yet suddenly, in the middle of one afternoon, I felt an urgent need to contact him. I tried to play it down – for one thing it was in the middle of a class – but the necessity became too strong for me. I set the children some work and hurried to the nearest phone. There was no reason whatever to expect Philip to be at home at that hour of the day, but he answered the phone on the first ring.

"Bless you, Matthew!" he said exultantly, before I'd even spoken. "Look at your watch, will you? I can't stop now but there's a letter in the post which will explain." I was left standing with the dead phone in my hand, feeling flat and oddly frustrated. As instructed I looked at my watch. It was four minutes past three.

The promised letter arrived the next morning. It had been scrawled hurriedly, but as Philip had said, provided an explanation, albeit a disturbing one:

I've been thinking how often we use telepathy unconsciously, as when I phoned you in Crowthorpe, and I've thought up a little test to see if we can do it to order. This afternoon, at precisely three o'clock, I shall be signalling you to phone. If you don't – well, we'll have to work at it a bit harder. But if you do – and somehow I think you will – then Crowthorpe had better watch out!

I was in a thoughtful mood for the rest of that day.

A week or so later I received notification that my application to Crowthorpe Primary School had been successful, and when in jubilation I phoned Philip to report the good news, he had just received similar information from Dr Sampson. At last the stars were in their courses and our return to Crowthorpe doubly assured.

The last few weeks of term passed as always in a welter of exams and sports days. I did not keep my promise of contacting Sue again. Inevitably we came across each other during the course of the school day, but her unhappy face reminded me of the embarrassment she'd caused me in the staff-room and I told myself it was better to leave well alone rather than open old wounds. A pity: she'd been an agreeable and acquiescent companion before her unexpected outburst.

All in all, I was relieved when the final day of term arrived. The school duly presented me with a leather brief-case and, amid expressions of goodwill from my colleagues, I was at last free to put Swindon behind me and begin my new life with Philip at Crowthorpe.

Five

That summer was one of the happiest times I can remember. Philip had arranged to leave High Wycombe on the same day that school finished and, side-stepping our parents' invitation, we set off immediately for Cumbria. His appointment was due to take effect from the end of August, which gave us a month in which to relax and settle into our new surroundings.

I remember, those first weeks, spending a lot of time standing at the picture window in the sitting-room staring out from our vantage point at the magnificient panorama before me. Immediately below was the garden, with gnarled old trees, outcrops of rockery and masses of every coloured rose imaginable. Over at the far end of it stood a little bungalow that I hadn't noticed on our first brief visit. It was built of stone like most of the houses in the village and a low picket fence surrounded it to ensure its privacy; a garden within a garden. I wondered idly who lived there.

Beyond the high wall stretched the gardens of other houses further down Fell Lane, and beyond them again the main road. On the far side of it I could just see the roof of the Lakeside Hotel and to the left the jetty from where boats plied continually across the lake. It was an outlook which never failed to fascinate me.

"Back at the lookout post?" Philip enquired laughingly, coming in one day to find me in my usual position.

"I still can't believe our good luck."

He joined me at the window. "Will we ever get blasé about being able to see mountains, lakes and woods without moving from our own sitting-room?"

"I doubt it," I said.

There was a table under one of the windows and we formed the habit of eating our evening meal there, watching the ever-changing parade of holiday-makers strolling down Lake Road or making their way to the Pavilion for the nightly dancing. And over coffee we'd watch the lights come on all down the hill and feel the still, dark closeness of the surrounding hills.

Once or twice we hired a boat and drifted lazily in the water for hours at a time, putting in at various little bays and rocky beaches on the eastern shore, where the mountain came down to meet the lake. I showed Philip the path I'd discovered alongside Minnowbeck, the stream that flowed along the valley, and by chance we discovered the site of the village's third hotel, whose owners I'd met at the Greystones. And finally, the week before Philip was due to join Dr Sampson, he said one morning, "I want to go up to the camp and check on the twins."

I had been awaiting this decision ever since we arrived but felt it to be his rather than mine. He had twice saved the twins' short lives and regarded them, I knew, as his protégés.

Nell Smith was draping tattered nappies on the nearby bushes when we arrived. She was a small, pale woman with straggling nondescript hair and she

71

wore down-trodden bedroom slippers and a greasy apron. Over by the caravan stood a battered old pram without wheels and from its depths I could see a small fist waving. Nell saw us, hesitated, then, wiping her hands on her apron, came towards us warily.

"Good morning, Nell. We've come to enquire after the twins."

"They're well enough." Her eyes were not inviting and there was an unpleasant odour about her, a general unwashed smell which pricked at the nostrils.

"May we have a look at them?"

She jerked her head in the direction of the pram and we walked over. The babies had filled out amazingly in the intervening four months. Black eyes regarded us with interest from either end of the pram. Nell had followed us across, like a bitch, I thought uncharitably, which waits for praise when someone admires its pups.

"They're fine babies," Philip said warmly. "What are their names?"

"Davy and Kim."

"Can you tell them apart?"

"Never tried. There's two mouths to feed, that's all there is to it."

Philip gave a short laugh. "And Granny? She hasn't interfered with them at all?"

Nell shook her head, glancing nervously over her shoulder.

A young boy came wandering towards us, sucking his thumb. His shambling gait and vacant eyes proclaimed him to be Benjie, who had once spent a night within the Gemelly Circle. Before he could reach us, his mother Nan swooped on him and bore him away.

"We've come to live in Crowthorpe," Philip told Nell. "I'd like to come up from time to time to see the twins."

"There's no need," she said resentfully. "They'll not come to no harm."

"I'd just like to keep in touch," Philip returned smoothly.

A young man came down the steps of the adjacent caravan. He was small and slight, his whole appearance marred by a truly horrific squint. He hesitated when he saw us, gave us a surly nod, and set off in the direction of the village. We took our leave of Nell and followed him at our leisure, assuming that since he was not old enough to be Nan's husband, he must be Janetta's – and Granny Lee's son.

This was confirmed by Eve when she called round that evening to bring us some shortbread she'd made. "Yes, that would be Jem all right. Poor lad, he has his work cut out with Janetta! People say she only married him because he couldn't properly see what she was up to!"

"Has Granny still got her crow?" Philip asked casually.

"As far as I know, but I haven't seen her for a while. She's the most restless of the bunch, probably because she was on the road for the best part of her life. Every now and then she takes her caravan, leaving Jem and Janetta to shack up as best they can, and sets off by herself for weeks at a time."

I for one did not regret Granny Lee's departure. It would have suited me very well if she never returned.

So the summer slid slowly away, the bright red berries appeared on the rowan trees, and Philip and

I took up our respective employment. I found my new colleagues pleasant and friendly, and although I was pleasant and friendly in return, I didn't encourage any close friendships. I had no need of them, now Philip was with me, and having learned my lesson from Sue Anderson, I resolved not to form any ties with either of the female staff. In a village this size, as I knew from Eve, gossip was rife and would not be as easy to ignore as it had been in Swindon.

However, friendships in which Philip shared were welcome, and we continued to see Eve and Anita fairly regularly. There was a closeness between the four of us which had some deep mainspring we hadn't yet plumbed, and we felt the need of each other's company. How their husbands felt on the subject, Philip and I never bothered to discover. Occasionally they would join us for coffee or drinks when we met at their homes, but although both men were included in return invitations, they never accompanied their wives to our flat. Nor was either of them present at the Greystones one October evening when Philip again broached the subject of telepathy.

"I've been thinking over what you said in the spring, Eve, about the need to extend rather than just use it between ourselves."

Eve's eyes dropped. "Did I say that?"

"I think you're right. If one has a gift, one should develop it, wouldn't you say?"

"I'm not so sure. Douglas didn't even approve when Anita and I used to do it. He regards it as an intrusion on another's privacy. If he knew we'd tried it with you—"

"Then don't tell him!"

She stared at him wide-eyed and Anita gave an

74

excited laugh. There was a look in her eyes which reminded me of the first time we'd seen her.

"In any case," Philip was continuing, "I wasn't just referring to the four of us. We know we can all read each other's minds. I want to reach out farther still and see what happens."

"Oh God!" Eve said softly.

"It was you who started it," I reminded her.

"I can't imagine why. I suppose it was the shock of suddenly seeing you both – and at the Circle, too. I should have left well alone." She gave a little shudder.

Anita said ringingly, "Well, I think you're right, Philip! It *is* time we extended our field. How do you propose to go about it?"

"If we start right away, we'll have to choose whoever's available. Is George around?"

"You're not going to try him, surely? He's much too down to earth to respond to such things!"

"But is he in the hotel?"

"Yes, he'll probably look in later. He's finishing off some figures for the accountant."

"Let's see if I can bring him earlier than he intends."

We sat in silence for some minutes. I had gauged Philip's intentions and didn't see how they could possibly be fulfilled. But shortly afterwards George Barlow came into the room. As Philip signalled everyone to silence, he sat down on the floor in the centre of the carpet and to his wife's amazement proceeded to remove his shoes and socks. He then stood up, circled an armchair three times in complete silence, solemnly replaced his footwear and left the room.

As the door closed behind him, Anita said stiffly, "You didn't have to make him look ridiculous."

"No harm was done. He won't remember anything."

"Then it's more like hypnotism," Eve pointed out. "From a distance, too. Rather frightening."

"Whatever you like to call it, it's simply mind control." Philip sounded slightly aggrieved that his feat hadn't been more wholeheartedly applauded. "The human brain is vastly underrated, as you know. If we can see some way of developing further, it could be of enormous benefit."

"Or harm," Eve put in unexpectedly.

The subject dropped by mutual consent, but it was at our next meeting that the Marshall twins arrived.

We were at the vicarage and when the doorbell rang, Eve went to answer it. We could hear her quite clearly. "Hello girls. What can I do for you?"

A child's voice said hesitantly, "We've come to see Mr Selby."

Anita and Philip turned to me and I shook my head in mystification.

"You'd better come in, then."

It was obvious who they were: two pretty little girls, fair-haired like their mother, one with a long ponytail, one with plaits. My heart had started to beat with slow, heavy thuds. "You wanted to see me?"

The one with the ponytail answered pertly, "It was you who wanted to see us."

I was aware of a constriction in my chest. Some twenty minutes earlier, the idea had crossed my mind that it would be interesting to meet this other pair of twins. They went to a private school in Barrowick, so

I hadn't come across them in the course of work as I'd hoped. But it had been only a passing thought and I'd done nothing about it – consciously.

Philip said softly, "How did you know my brother wanted to see you?"

The child with plaits – Claire, as we later discovered, answered with a little frown, "He called us."

"'Called'?" Anita repeated. "In what way? You mean he phoned?"

"No, just – called." Claire looked about to cry and Eve said quickly, "It's lovely to see you, anyway. Come and sit down and I'll bring you some milk and biscuits. Does Mummy know you're here?"

They shook their heads, settling on the floor like puppies.

"Then I'd better ring and tell her you're safe."

Ten minutes later Geoff Marshall called to collect his daughters. "I really do apologize for the intrusion. I can't imagine what possessed them."

Possessed them? I felt a chill on the back of my neck.

Eve said smoothly, "Don't worry, it was nothing. Just some misunderstanding, I gather."

"You know, I feel quite odd in here with the rest of you," Geoff said with a laugh. "Three sets of twins – and me. It's an uncanny sensation."

I said, "I don't think you've met my brother, Philip."

"Oh, sorry!" Eve exclaimed. "I'd forgotten he wasn't at the drinks party."

Philip stood up and shook his hand.

Geoff looked from him to me. "I must admit I

couldn't have said which of you I'd met! There's no point of difference at all, is there?"

"I told Felicity they were clones!" Eve said with a smile.

When he had gone, herding the little girls in front of him, everyone turned to me. I spread my hands helplessly. "I thought I'd like to meet them. I promise you that's all."

"It was enough," said Eve. "If you now only have to think something in passing for it to happen, this is getting beyond a joke. I think we'd better put the wraps on it for a while. We don't want the entire village turning up at our coffee evenings!"

To be truthful, the arrival of the Marshalls had shaken me considerably. Being able to influence someone as a result of deep concentration, an effort of will, was exhilarating. But as Eve had said, that a casual thought, no sooner formed than forgotten, should have had such instant ratification was something else entirely.

When we set out for home that evening, Philip put a hand on my shoulder. "Don't worry about it. We'll need it eventually but the time is not yet. It developed more quickly than we expected, that's all."

"But suppose I can't control it?" I heard my voice shake. "Hell, I can't help what I think. It's like the old fairy story of being granted three wishes and not taking time to choose carefully."

"Except that you're not rationed to three. Nobody's counting, as far as I can see. Perhaps this is what Janetta meant when she spoke of the power we should have. I don't suppose the Marshalls had any intention of calling at the vicarage until they received your 'message', which means you didn't just *read* their thoughts but actually influenced them. A kind of hypnotism, as Eve said – even brainwashing. However—" as he felt me shudder under his hand "—we must take things slowly. We don't want to alarm anyone. Relax, Matthew. I'll help you to suppress it until we know which direction to take. In the meantime, as Eve said, we'd better cool it for a while."

So "cool it" we did, for over two years in fact, though it's hard to believe, looking back, that so much time could have passed. For myself, I was happy enough to leave well alone. The upsurgence of unlooked-for power had worried me, not least because of the ideas it had given Philip. I put it firmly to the back of my mind and developed the habit of breaking any train of thought which threatened to become too concentrated, and having satisfied myself everything was under control again, I was able to relax and enjoy my new life to the full.

The routine of village life sucked us into its comfortable predictability, the seasons came and went, and we were content. It was only after our third Christmas in Cumbria that I began to feel uneasy again.

Several times that spring I experienced a sudden and inexplicable draining of energy, so devastating that I could only slump to a chair and wait for it to pass. It usually occurred during school hours, and more than once my sudden stumbling lunge towards my desk caused suppressed titters. I was completely at a loss to account for these attacks and too frightened to mention them. Only when I began to hear the first whispers of Philip's growing reputation did an inkling of their cause begin to filter into my mind.

These unsolicited testimonials, overhead in shop or pub, were broken off at my entrance with embarrassed grins and murmurs, but they began to add up in my brain and it finally became clear that my extreme lassitude and Philip's successes were not unconnected. He was beginning to flex his psychic muscles again and since we apparently shared our power source, these experiments took their toll of me as well.

"You might have warned me!" I burst out furiously one evening up in the flat. "How do you think I've felt, imagining for weeks that I'm suffering from some incurable disease?"

"I'm sorry, Matthew, really. I'd no idea it would affect you so much, and you never said anything. I'll try to spread it a bit. There's no reason why we should take the full impact."

I paused in the act of getting a can of beer from the fridge. "I'm not sure that I follow you."

"I don't see why Eve and Anita shouldn't contribute their share. Come to that—" he was avoiding my eyes "— the Marshalls as well. The more there are in the 'pool', the less hard it will be on individuals."

"Philip—" The coldness from the can had moved up my arm and across my shoulder-blades. "What exactly are you planning to do?"

He smiled, and the light in his eyes did nothing to reassure me. "Create Utopia, Matthew, that's all. An ideal state!"

I moistened my lips. "How long have you been thinking along these lines? Why didn't you discuss it with me?" What I meant was, why hadn't I known what he was thinking?

He said gently, "It was for your own sake. You panicked when you realized how much power was on tap, so when I began working things out, I felt it wise to – block you off for a while."

"You put up a barrier to stop me reading your mind?"

"Not a barrier, only a screen. It can come down now, if you're ready to join me."

Slowly I poured the beer into a tankard.

"Matthew? You're not angry, are you? I wasn't trying to shut you out, only mark time till you could accept it."

"Accept what?" My voice was still stiff.

He perched on the edge of the kitchen table. "Remember what Janetta said?"

I moved impatiently. "For God's sake! Only fools believe in crystal balls!"

"The crystal had nothing to do with it. She could sense something in us, something which was bound to find expression, which couldn't be stopped. 'Power over body and soul, life and death'."

"So you're planning a Brave New World?"

"A corner of it, perhaps. I want to see if it's possible, by the power of thought, to influence things for the better. Why don't you try it? Pick out one of your pupils – someone, perhaps, who isn't particularly bright – and try to instil knowledge into him telepathically. You might well find yourself with a class of Einsteins!"

I had a sudden picture of the dark lake that Easter nearly three years before, and Philip saying, "I'll take care of their bodies and you look after their minds!" And I'd thought he was joking.

"The Smith twins are psychic."

"What?" Abruptly I came back to the present.

"Davy and Kim. I can contact them any time."

"Philip, they're *babies*!"

"Even babies have minds. As a matter of fact they're very self-sufficient for their age. They've had to be, poor little blighters. The rest of the crowd up there are frightened of them. They get food and shelter and precious little else."

Philip had been paying regular visits to the Smiths. Sometimes he invited me to go with him, but I preferred to spend my Sunday afternoons relaxing with the papers. Now I furiously resented this further evidence of our separation.

"They're intelligent boys," he went on. "They talk pretty fluently and they're not three yet. I've great hopes of them."

Jealous of his interest in the Smiths, I switched back to his original point. "You mentioned involving Eve and Anita."

Although the four of us still met regularly, telepathy had not been mentioned since the evening of the Marshalls' visit, and our meetings now took the innocuous form of bridge evenings. I suspected this also satisfied their husbands as a plausible reason for our meeting at all.

"Yes, we've soft-pedalled long enough," Philip answered firmly. "I don't think Anita will take much persuading, but Eve has Douglas to contend with. And it's also time we began to take the Marshall girls in hand. There's a lot of untapped potential there."

It was getting dark, but neither of us made a move to switch on the light. Our conversation was more suited to the shadows.

"Eve and Anita perhaps," I said finally, "but I don't like meddling with children's minds. We should leave the Smiths and Marshalls alone."

"Absolute nonsense! There has to be some reason for this concentration of twins. Four pairs in a village this size – a veritable power-house! It's not as if we're going to hurt them; in some cases they won't even know they're being used. I just want to open the channels and see what happens. And *if* we can overcome disease, just here, on our own small patch – and *if* we can produce extra-bright children in our local school, well, there's no knowing where it could lead! To a Nobel Prize at the very least!"

"Given the choice, people might prefer illness and thick kids to a mental take-over."

But my objections were only token, because Philip had progressed so far without me. Already I could feel a stirring of excitement as I mentally took stock of my class with a view to selecting the first guinea pig.

A week or two later, Jason Quinn came into our lives.

"Would you mind if we didn't start playing straight away?" Anita asked when she and Eve arrived for our bridge evening. "There's a programme I'd like to see on television and you might find it interesting too. Have you seen any of the Jason Quinn interviews?"

Philip lifted the card table to one side. "No, but the name sounds familiar."

Eve said, "He wrote that play there was such a fuss

83

about a few years ago – *The Temple Builders*, wasn't it? Now he's started these interviews on TV, making a point of choosing people whose views he disagrees with, and there seems to be no shortage of them! Poor souls, he gives them no quarter at all!"

"I'm surprised they agree to appear. Who's his victim tonight?"

"A medium." Anita's voice shook slightly. "That's why I thought you'd be interested."

Philip said softly, "And we're to presume he doesn't agree with mediums either?"

"There's not much doubt about that. He has absolutely no patience with the supernatural."

"Then it should be an interesting half-hour."

Certainly it was no disappointment. Dr Arnold Fosdock was, we could see at once, a lost cause. A small thin man, balding and with rimless spectacles, he fidgeted nervously with his tie and took several sips of water from the glass in front of him while Jason Quinn, smooth and unhurried, began the interview with a series of deceptively innocuous questions. It was a classic case of the lion amusing itself till it was ready to pounce and destroy. Nor was the metaphor of a lion misplaced, considering the mane of brown-gold hair and lazy, assessing eyes.

There was something about the man which instilled in me a strong dislike while at the same time commanding my attention. He was so casually immaculate, so totally at his ease, that I was conscious of an increasingly powerful desire to ruffle him out of his complacency. So engrossed was I in my analysis that by the time I began to listen to the exchange, Quinn was already moving in for the kill.

"And you actually believe that this – ectoplasm – flows from your body to clothe the 'spirit'?" His voice was politely incredulous.

"Of course I do. Yes." And, as Quinn didn't speak, "Yes, I do."

"But if as you say you're in a trance at the time, presumably you're not able to see it?"

"Not personally, but everyone else does."

"You see, Doctor, that's precisely my point. These phenomena always seem to be experienced at one remove, which I find strains my credulity to the limit."

"But it's actually been photographed!" Fosdock began to rummage frantically through the papers in front of him.

Jason Quinn raised a hand. "I believe I've seen some of those photographs." His tone made clear his opinion of their authenticity. "I might add that in the cause of research I've attended séances myself, but regrettably nothing whatever materialized at them."

"I'm not surprised!" muttered the doctor.

Quinn smiled. "Naturally I don't doubt your sincerity; I merely suggest that it's misplaced."

So it went on, deceptively gentle, entirely merciless, until the poor doctor had contradicted himself several times and in struggling to retrieve lost ground, became hopelessly stuck in the quagmire prepared for him. It was a relief to all of us when the programme came to an end. Philip leant forward and switched off the set.

"What a bastard!" he commented. "Anyone's drink need freshening?"

But I was unable to dismiss Jason Quinn so lightly from my mind, and as is often the way, having

85

once been brought to our notice, his name kept cropping up repeatedly over the next few weeks. His programme had become a cult, and secure in their own living-rooms, the viewing public relished each ensuing destruction as voraciously as had the crowds in Roman arenas or the *tricoteuses* at the guillotine.

One Sunday in April a leading newspaper featured his profile, and leaving Philip to pay his customary visit to the gypsies, I settled down with some interest to read it.

. . . Physically, Quinn is an imposing figure, over six feet and with the well-known thatch which reviewers have not been slow to dub 'Jason's Golden Fleece'. At Cambridge, where he read classics, he was in constant demand for debates, always appearing against rather than for the motion, and frequent invitations to speak at College dinners soon earned him a reputation as a brilliant raconteur. It was at Cambridge that he met his first wife, writer Penelope Russell, though they didn't marry till some years later. For a while after coming down he worked with a firm of stockbrokers but found his true vocation with the outstanding success of his brilliantly satirical play *The Temple Builders* in the early eighties. Two more plays followed, and although they didn't attract such wide critical acclaim, one of them, *Lord Moses*, was adapted for television and it was this that first fired his interest in the medium. Shortly afterwards he was invited to take part in the quiz programme *Next Question*, where his caustic wit and wide general knowledge were an immediate success.

His new series, *Jason Quinn Interviews* which he hosts himself, has already attracted high viewing figures and though his cavalier treatment of guests seems to be making him a man the viewers love to hate, he must nevertheless be admired for his sincere dislike of chicanery, into which category he uncompromisingly groups most of the fringe sciences. "The supernatural," he once said, "has nothing to recommend it. It's dangerous to the gullible and unacceptable to everyone else."

. . . He was divorced from his first wife last December and shortly afterwards married the actress Tania Partridge . . .

There was quite a lot more and I carefully tore out the page for future reference. I had the obscure conviction that it would come in useful.

Whether due to Jason Quinn's scepticism or Philip's willpower, it was only a week or so later that Anita said tentatively one evening, "Do you think perhaps we should try some more telepathy? As you said, it seems wrong not to make use of it."

Philip and I avoided each other's eyes, but a wave of triumph surged between us. This time, we knew, there would be no back-tracking. Our real work in Crowthorpe was about to begin.

Six

During the months that followed, the four of us conscientiously exercised the psychic powers we shared, and were excited to find how steadily these increased. Yet as the time passed, I was puzzled by the frequency with which the Gemelly Circle injected itself into my thoughts. I began to accompany Philip up the hill on Sundays, and to wait by the stones while he went on to the camp. He didn't altogether approve of this practice and I had the impression that he resented my preoccupation with them.

"What do you find to do up here, all by yourself?" he demanded. "Not planning another paper, are you?"

"No, I'm just recharging myself. There's some kind of force here; don't you feel it? I first noticed it years ago, when we came up searching for the babies that night. It's as though the stones have soaked up centuries of powerful emotions which can be drawn on as required."

He frowned. "Required for what?"

I shrugged. "The psychic experiments, perhaps."

He said oddly, "I thought those were our own idea."

"How do you mean?"

"I don't know. Sometimes I have a feeling that

perhaps we're not quite as much in control as we think we are. Would you say it's possible that we're being used?"

I stared at him, coldness moving over me.

"All of us, I mean. You and I, Eve and Anita, the Marshalls, the little Smiths. Perhaps the power we're generating is of use to someone else – or something. The something that has been striving all these centuries to bring twins to Crowthorpe. You must have asked yourself why."

I glanced apprehensively at the stones which surrounded us. "The legend, you mean?" I forced a laugh. "You're suggesting we're being primed to overthrow the Crow goddess?"

But Philip didn't return my smile. He simply shrugged without replying and began to walk towards the crescent of trees.

Then one Sunday we had an experience which completely devastated us. We had been preparing supper and came out of the kitchen to find a strange light flooding into the hall from the open sitting-room door.

Philip said, "What the hell—?" and went ahead of me, pushing the door wider. Then he stopped so abruptly that, hard on his heels, I went straight into him. He reached out and gripped me tightly as I edged round him to locate the source of the light. Over in the far corner, the television set was bathed in a lurid glow and superimposed on the screen was a picture of the Gemelly Circle. As we stared unbelievingly, the image began to pulsate and fade, to be replaced by a man's face filling the whole screen. It was a strong face, elderly and lined, and the staring eyes had the mad look of a prophet. It took a moment to realize that they were staring inwards and the man was in fact blind. Then that picture also faded, the glow left the screen, and the television set merged back into the shadows of the room.

For long minutes Philip and I stood immobile. Then he let go of my arm and said tonelessly, "The set isn't even plugged in."

I reached out convulsively for the light switch and in the sudden brightness we gazed at each other's white faces.

"See what I mean?" Philip said.

"But what was it all about? Who was that man?"

"God knows, but I have a feeling *we* will shortly. His powers seem to be greater than ours, and it's all connected with those stones. I've been trying to ignore that possibility, but this clinches it."

"It couldn't just be Eve or Anita, experimenting, could it?"

He shook his head. "There's someone else," he said positively, "and when he arrives, whoever he is, we'll have at least double the power we have now."

It was June, and the holiday trade was beginning to build up again. In the warm evenings Philip and I occasionally walked along Lake Road to watch the boats and listen to the strains of the disco drifting from the Pavilion. One evening we met Steve Ellis, one of my colleagues from school.

"Come and have a pint at the Crow's Nest," he suggested. "It's been taken over by a new landlord and I want to make sure the beer hasn't changed!"

We hadn't been to the Crow's Nest since the night we

rescued the Smith twins, but I remembered the faded nets and the stuffed salmon, still staring glassily out of its case. I was looking at it when a sudden shock jerked me round and I found myself staring across the room at the face which had filled our television screen. Yet something was different: there was undoubtedly sight in those eyes, and inexplicable recognition.

Unaware of the rigidity which gripped Philip and me, Steve was making his way over to place his order, and woodenly we followed him. The man behind the bar, ignoring Steve, spoke directly to us.

"Evening Mr Selby; Doctor. It takes one to know one, doesn't it?"

I found my voice. "I – beg your pardon?"

"Twins, sir. Takes one to know one."

"You're a twin?"

"I am that. My brother Fred lives with us. Isn't married, you see." He held out his hand. "Name's Tom Hardacre, and that's the wife, Mabel."

A pleasant, round-cheeked woman further down the counter nodded and smiled before placing two brimming glasses on the bar top.

"And – your brother—"

"Blind. Not that it bothers him. Uses my eyes, does Fred." He tapped his forehead. "Telepathically, see."

"Bitter, Matthew?" Steve's voice came from a long way off. I nodded.

"Like to see you sometime, would Fred. And the ladies too."

Other customers were claiming the landlord's attention and Steve pulled my sleeve. "Wake up, lad! Take your glass – I can't carry all of them!"

91

Obediently I moved against a wall, glad of its support at my back.

"Did that chap say he was a twin? Good God, not *more*! You seem to attract each other like magnets!"

When he arrives we'll have at least double the power, Philip had said. And there had proved to be not one man but two.

From that first encounter it was tacitly understood that the Hardacres should attend our meetings with Eve and Anita. Also the Marshall girls, now aged twelve, began to arrive uninvited and sit silently in a corner. Gradually we were all growing closer together, and our power grew correspondingly. We evolved a format, beginning each meeting with basic tests of willpower, on others as well as ourselves, and progressing to increasingly more difficult feats of thought control. The evenings ended with a session at which we all reported progress since the last meeting.

"The headmaster sent for me this morning," I told them one evening after the start of the new school year. "He wanted to congratulate me on the high standard in my class. Waxed quite poetic about the values of discipline and enthusiasm!"

"Well done, Matthew. Who's next?" We took turns in chairing the meetings and on this occasion it was Eve.

"Me, please." It was Nicola Marshall who spoke. She was abnormally pale and holding tightly to her sister's hand. "But I hope you'll say it wasn't me after all." She turned to Philip. "It's about Mark Saunders."

He looked up quickly. "You know what happened?"

Her mouth quivered. "He was fooling around," she said unsteadily. "Kept bumping into me – that sort of thing. He's been doing it for weeks. We get the same bus back from school."

She paused and I tried to remember Mark Saunders. He must have been about fourteen then; I'd taught him for one term before he went to secondary school in Barrowick.

"Yes?" Eve prompted gently.

"Yesterday I was by myself – Claire stayed behind for her music lesson – and when we got off the bus, he followed me up the hill. I pretended not to notice, but when there was no one else about, he pushed me into a corner and gripped hold of my arms. He was hurting me and he wouldn't let go and – and I lost my temper. I glared at him, thinking – I don't know – just that if he wouldn't stop when I asked him to, I'd have to make him. And" – her voice wavered – "he suddenly cried out and fell back and I ran home. But later, I heard people talking."

Philip was staring at her fixedly, and after a moment's silence I said urgently, "Well, what happened? Philip!"

He turned towards me but his eyes hadn't refocussed and for a sick moment he had a look of blind Fred. "I can only repeat what Dr Sampson told me," he said unevenly. "The boy was found in a state of deep shock and rushed to hospital. There was no outward sign of injury, but X-rays showed that his brain was crushed, as though it had been repeatedly battered with a heavy instrument. The case has the whole place by the ears, it's so utterly incomprehensible. Or it was." He added heavily, "Only one thing's sure. Even if he lives, he'll never be right again."

Nicola put her hands over her face and began to sob dryly. It was the only sound in the still room.

Claire said tearfully, "She didn't mean to hurt him!"

"I know," Eve said gently. "It's a lesson to us all, though. We've all got this power and we must be constantly on our guard as to how we use it."

"I think," I said suddenly, "we should go up to the stones." I felt Fred Hardacre's sightless eyes on my face. I went on, feeling my way, aware of his prompting. "We can use them as a safety valve, pour the excess power into them when it reaches danger level. I thought it was they who supplied the power, but perhaps it works both ways. At least it's worth a try."

We went in procession through the village and on to the hill – Philip and I in the lead, Anita and Eve, Claire and Nicola, Tom and Fred. It was no surprise when we arrived to find the Smith twins already playing there. We each chose a stone and stood closely against it, shutting our eyes and letting the energy flow in whatever way should prove necessary. And when the simple ceremony was over, Nicola's tears had dried and we all felt safe again. It was the first of many such expeditions.

The months passed. From time to time I took out the profile on Jason Quinn, reading and rereading it until I felt I knew the man intimately, though why I should have felt this compulsion to understand him, I had no idea. Nor, for some reason, did I ever discuss him with Philip.

Christmas came and went, and no-one spoke of

Mark Saunders, condemned to spend his life in a mental home. I think it was about this time that the nightmares started. Philip and I, each in our own bedroom, would wake at the same instant, drenched in sweat and convinced the house was full of crows. We didn't realize we were sharing these dreams until we met one night in the kitchen, both searching for something to help us sleep again.

"Do you ever see Granny's crow when you visit the Smiths?" I asked him, shivering in my bathrobe.

"Occasionally, but it never comes near me. I've schooled myself to ignore it."

"So the repressed fear expells itself in dreams?"

"Possibly. If so, I'm sorry to inflict them on you as well."

I'm not sure whether the knowledge that we both experienced the dreams lessened or added to their importance. Nothing was clear any more. At school I was now able, by glancing at any boy or girl I chose, to instil instant knowledge in the subject I was teaching. How fleeting such knowledge was I couldn't assess, and I doubled my efforts when exams came round.

Occasionally, too, we all inadvertently "summoned" each other, so that we'd arrive on one another's doorsteps uncertain why we were there. Our closeness had not gone unnoticed in the village. We must have made an odd group by any standards, and certainly Geoff and Felicity Marshall did everything they could to keep their daughters away from us. Finally the girls informed us tearfully that they were to be sent away to boarding school.

"They can't split us up, don't worry!" Anita assured

them agitatedly. "We can still contact each other any time we choose."

I looked at her with some misgiving. She'd become noticeably distrait lately; her eyes had a wild glint and there was a general unfocussed air about her. She had of course always been the least stable of the group.

But Philip and I were apparently exempt from any doubts Crowthorpe might have had about its twins. Now widely regarded as a brilliant diagnostician, his opinion was increasingly sought by eminent men in their own fields of medicine, while I basked in my reputation as an outstandingly successful teacher. Which was how things stood that September, when Madeleine came to Crowthorpe and nothing was ever the same again.

We'd had little contact with our landlady over the four years we'd been at Rowan House and the only member of the family we saw with any frequency was her precocious daughter Deidre, whom we were continually having to avoid. But that summer the outside of the house was to be painted while Philip and I were away, and it was arranged that we should leave the key with Mrs Staveley so she could open and close windows as the decorators required.

By this time it took a physical effort for Philip and myself to leave Crowthorpe, as though our roots had literally gone down into its soil. However, our father had suffered a heart attack earlier in the year and we had no choice but to go home. It was a dreary wet summer, and the house in Gloucester seemed dark after our airy rooms at the top of Rowan House. Nor were relations easy with our parents. We had grown apart over the years; they considered us, rightly no doubt, to be selfish and inconsiderate, while for our part their refusal to be impressed by our achievements caused us no little irritation. Tempers grew short as the weeks passed, and it was with a sense of liberation that we finally set off once more for Cumbria.

"I'll collect the key while you put the car away," I told Philip, jumping out and humping my case from the back seat; and I jauntily rang three sharp notes on the doorbell. But the girl who answered it was someone I'd never seen before. I don't know what it was about her that so completely captivated me. She wasn't pretty in the conventional sense, but she had a stillness, a dignity, that I'd never encountered before, and I was at a loss to know how to deal with it.

"You must be from upstairs," she said when I didn't speak. "My aunt said you'd be calling for your key. Will you come in for a moment while I find it?"

Numbly I followed her through the hallway into the large kitchen. The obnoxious Deidre, sitting with a glass of milk at the table, simpered up at me. "Hello, Selby." She'd taken to addressing us both thus, since she couldn't tell which was Dr and which Mr. "Did you have a nice holiday?" I nodded absently, my entire attention focussed on the other girl as she retrieved the key from a drawer and handed it to me.

"Are you the schoolmaster?" she enquired. "I'm starting there myself next week. My name's Madeleine Peachey."

"Welcome to Crowthorpe. You say Mrs Staveley's your aunt?"

"Yes, she's kindly invited me to stay here during term-time."

97

"That's certainly good news!" With any other girl – any girl at all – the mildly flirtatious remark would have produced an answering smile, but Madeleine merely nodded and moved to the front door to show me out. We reached it at the same time as Philip, and I saw her eyes widen.

"My goodness, you are alike, aren't you?"

"My brother Philip," I introduced briefly. "Mrs Staveley's niece, Madeleine Peachey."

Philip put down the case he was carrying, but if he'd hoped for any conversation he was to be as disappointed as I.

"Good afternoon," Madeleine said, including us both, and firmly shut the door.

Philip glanced at me, pursed his mouth and picked up the case again. In silence we went up the newly painted staircase to our own flat. I think that by the time we reached it, I was in love with Madeleine.

Instinctively I concealed the depth of my feelings from Philip. Though girls we had had in plenty, neither of us had even remotely considered ourselves in love before. We'd always been completely self-sufficient, and now things had changed I didn't know how to tell him. For although I wanted Madeleine with an intensity that alarmed me, Philip had to be my first consideration.

In this necessarily cautious approach I was helped by Madeleine herself. At first she seemed mildly surprised by my attentions, but it was natural enough that we should fall into the habit of walking to and from school together and gradually some of her reserve melted, though her attitude towards me could best be described as one of guarded friendliness.

All I could do was school myself to patience and

in the meantime forestall Philip's awareness of my feelings by means of the mental block he had once used against me.

Meanwhile, the exercises in psychic control continued. The Hardacre brothers were of immense help, and under their tuition our powers strengthened considerably. Apparently Fred had been blinded during the war and the trauma reverberated on Tom, who also temporarily lost his sight. When Tom's vision returned, they discovered that Fred was able to "see" with his brother's eyes and this had intensified the deep psychic bond which had always been between them.

Nicola and Claire, now away at boarding school, wrote frequently to Eve, who circulated their letters, and occasionally, in an uncanny way which I could never get used to, we were aware of their "presence" with us at our meetings.

One day that autumn I persuaded Madeleine to come up after school for a cup of tea.

"You and Philip are very close, aren't you?" she said, as we sat at the kitchen table. "I think Aunt Alice is a little frightened of you!"

Alarm bells rang in my head. We were constantly on the alert for any hint of suspicion against us, but I only said lightly, "I can't imagine why!"

"Because you're twins, I think, and so friendly with all the other twins. She says you've both changed since you came here."

Silently I cursed Alice Staveley and her prattling. I couldn't have Madeleine of all people becoming wary of us. I was having enough trouble getting through to her as it was.

"I know it sounds silly," she continued, "but I think

she expects trouble of some kind. She says there often is when there are twins in the village, and there've never been so many as there are now. Did you know some were burned as witches? And during the Civil War when Crowthorpe was strongly Royalist, the current twins supported Cromwell, which caused fighting actually in the village."

"Your aunt doesn't blame us for that, I hope?"

She smiled very slightly. "I shouldn't think so."

I said unwisely, "Is that why you're always so careful to keep me at a distance?"

She looked up, startled, and her face flushed. "No, Matthew, that isn't the reason."

Philip's key sounded in the door and I had never in my life been less pleased to see him. His eyes went from Madeleine's pink cheeks to me. "Sorry to interrupt the tête-à-tête. Have you left me any tea?"

"Of course," I said smoothly, "bring another cup and saucer."

"You're getting very pally with the little school-teacher, aren't you?" he remarked when she'd gone.

"Why not? She's a nice girl."

"Not your type, I'd have thought."

"Meaning she's not yours?"

"I dare say she could grow on you. She's different, anyway."

"She's unique!" I said, and feeling his quick glance, regretted the indiscretion.

One November Sunday, when the hills above the lake were blanketed with mist, Madeleine accompanied Philip and me on our walk to the Circle. It was dank and cold, the ferns withered, the grass wet with heavy dew. Philip took his leave of us and strode away as usual towards the camp. Madeleine stood looking after him.

"Why does he want to see those children?"

"He feels responsible for them, having delivered them."

"But it's more than that, isn't it?"

I didn't reply and she shivered suddenly.

"Cold?" I drew her towards me, and suddenly knew I could hold back no longer. She stood quite still while I kissed her, her lips cool and soft under mine. It wasn't the ecstatic surrender I was used to, but I had not expected that from Madeleine. Above the pounding of my heart, I said as lightly as I could, "Well, at least you didn't slap my face!"

"Did you expect me to?"

"It was on the cards. You haven't exactly been encouraging. Madeleine, that day at the flat I asked you why you kept me at arm's length. You didn't have a chance to reply."

She stirred and moved out of my arms. "At first I thought you were just fooling about and I was determined not to be added to your scalp belt."

She hesitated and I prompted gently, "And later?"

"Later, it occurred to me that although we were together quite a lot, you seemed to be holding back too, and I wondered why. It didn't seem in character."

So that was all it had been! I drew a sigh of relief. "It was because of Philip," I said.

She looked at me blankly. "Philip?"

"I couldn't think how to tell him I'm in love with you."

Her eyes flew to my face. "Oh Matthew, don't say that – please!"

"Whether I say it or not doesn't alter the fact. I've loved you since the first day I saw you. I'm sorry if I confused you, darling, it was only because I was so terrified of putting a foot wrong. I've never felt like this in my life, and I didn't know what—" I broke off because unbelievably her eyes had filled with tears.

"Oh Matthew," she whispered, "I'm so sorry."

"*Sorry?*" Alarm sharpened my voice. "What is there to be sorry about?"

"Well, I – you see, I don't love you."

I stood staring at her, panic rising inside me and she went on rapidly, "I was sure I'd fall for you, that's why I held back really. I couldn't believe you were serious, and I was afraid of being hurt. It was the strangest feeling, waiting to fall in love. But to my surprise it didn't happen and didn't happen, and I couldn't understand why not. I told myself it would all come right when you kissed me. But it didn't." She looked up at me helplessly. "I'm sorry," she said again.

Part of me – a very small part – wanted to laugh aloud. There was an ironic justice here, that at last I should be paid back for the havoc Philip and I, knowingly and uncaringly, had been causing for the last twelve years. And though I'd had a dozen reasons to account for Madeleine's reserve – some of which she had herself given me – that she didn't love me had never once entered my head.

"Matthew?" She raised a hand and tentatively touched my face. "Don't look like that. Please."

"Perhaps you just need more time." It was the only hope I had.

"Perhaps."

"There isn't anyone else?" At least that might have salved my pride.

"No-one. And I am very fond of you."

I pulled her against me, more roughly this time, and started to kiss her, forcing her lips apart and trying with increasing desperation to instil some of my own passion into her. She made no attempt to push me away, but nor did she respond. Despairingly I let her go. My eyes went hungrily over her face with its wide, caramel-coloured eyes and polished skin.

"I'm not going to give up, you know," I said abruptly. "God help me, I'll *make* you love me."

Her eyes held mine. "I hope you can. I think I must be out of my mind not to."

"I'm certainly out of mine."

She reached up and kissed me gently, and on a wave of despair I turned away and rested my forehead against the nearest stone. Immediately, a sense of calm flowed comfortingly into me. Since meeting Madeleine, I hadn't been giving the stones enough of my time. Unresentful, they had waited until in my hurt I turned to them, and then had consoled me. Perhaps in time they'd give me Madeleine.

Seven

During the Christmas holidays Madeleine returned to her home in Lancaster and grimly I tried to hide the sense of loss that afflicted me. Once or twice I felt Philip's eyes consideringly on my face, but he made no comment. Then, with the blustery new year, she was back and life became bearable again. From time to time she came up and had supper with us and those evenings were especially happy ones for me. With both Philip and Madeleine beside me, I was complete.

It was on one of these occasions that Philip, looking in the paper to see what was on television, remarked, "I see Jason Quinn's a guest on this new current affairs programme. They'll be discussing his latest play."

"Surely you don't want to watch that!" Madeleine exclaimed. "Personally, I can't stand the man – far too opinionated and full of himself."

"If you don't mind," I said, "I'd rather like to see him. With luck, the interviewer might give him a taste of his own medicine!"

"Not a chance!" she retorted. "They'll kow-tow to him as they always do, and make him more conceited than ever!"

But I had not forgotten the curious reaction Jason Quinn had aroused in me, and despite Madeleine's protest, I switched the programme on, interested to find out if he still affected me so strongly.

A brief synopsis of his play, *Clouded Crystal*, revealed that the plot centred on the exposure of a charlatan fortune-teller.

"Typical!" said Philip under his breath.

"I should have thought, Mr Quinn," continued the interviewer smoothly, "that with your well-known views on the supernatural you would regard all fortune-tellers as charlatans?"

"In a sense yes, I suppose that's true. However, quite a large number sincerely believe they have this power. I consider them deluded rather than actual fakes."

"But you don't yourself believe the future can be foreseen?"

"Of course not. Does anyone, seriously?"

"Perhaps you'd like to answer that, Professor."

The camera switched to the guest at the other end of the table.

"I should explain to our audience that Professor Hudson from the University of Denver, Colorado, is a leading psychologist. His latest book deals with an exhaustive study of brain-waves in connection with telepathy, clairvoyance and so on. Now, Professor, since clairvoyance is presumably synonymous with future gazing, what is your reply to Mr Quinn?"

The Professor cleared his throat. "Firstly, if you'll pardon me, that last assumption is not necessarily correct. Clairvoyance *can* be linked with precognition but it can also be contemporary – a momentary flash of something which is happening at the same time some distance away. I must assure Mr Quinn however, that there is sufficient evidence on all these subjects for them to be taken very seriously indeed. With regard to so-called fortune-telling, for instance, I wonder if you've ever come across the phenomena known as 'Macbeth prophecies'? In such cases, a forecast is made which actually *causes* what it predicts to take place."

Across the room Philip moved suddenly. I didn't look at him but I knew of course precisely what he was thinking. All at once this mildly entertaining programme had assumed enormous significance.

"In effect," the professor was continuing, "they're not so much prophecies as conscious or even unconscious suggestions – a primitive but very effective method of brainwashing. The person allegedly foreseeing the future plays on the known weaknesses of his subject – egotism, for example, or greed – to instil an idea in the form of a prophecy. I guess that's where the Macbeth reference comes in: if Macbeth hadn't been told he'd become Glamis, Cawdor and King, his ambitions might never have crystallized in that direction. But once the idea was implanted, everything he did was directed towards fulfilling the prophecies. You could say the witches' prediction was responsible for the whole tragedy."

Jason Quinn moved impatiently. "But you're not suggesting this is a common occurrence, surely?"

"It might well be, Mr Quinn, and it's certainly not confined to a fortune-teller's booth. Going back in history we have many examples of its effectiveness when used by false prophets, dictators, witch-hunters—"

The camera flicked back to the interviewer in time to catch him glancing at his watch. "Gentlemen, this is fascinating but I'm afraid we're running out of time. One last comment from you, Mr Quinn?"

"Merely that I'm interested in the professor's thesis but regrettably unconvinced. I'm unable to accept predestination in any form. If—"

"Sorry, Mr Quinn, I'll have to cut you off there. Thank you very much, gentlemen."

The camera switched to another part of the studio and I turned off the set.

Into the silence Madeleine said, "You might know the professor was wasting his breath. Jason Quinn would never accept anything that didn't comply with his own rigid formula."

"And do you?" Philip asked quietly. "Do you accept what the professor was saying?"

"If he's done so much work on it he must know what he's talking about, as anyone but Jason Quinn would admit. I can't say I like the idea, but I suppose we're all guilty to some degree of manipulation by flattery. This is just going one step further. I'd be interested to read his book. Anything to do with the mind is fascinating, isn't it, telepathy and so on? I read that identical twins have it to a greater degree than other people, because their brain-waves are similar. When there's a change of brain rhythm in one twin, a matching change occurs in the other. Weird really, as though genetically they were the same person." She looked up with a smile. "I don't know why I'm telling you this – you must know it already."

"We have our moments," Philip said dryly.

Moments of susceptibility too, I reflected with misgiving, for we should not have made our home in Crowthorpe had Janetta Lee not promised us such power here, nor striven so actively to achieve it. We were ourselves snared by a Macbeth prophecy.

*　　*　　*

107

During that cold wet spring Madeleine, Philip and I drew a little closer but she still gave no sign that she might love me. I had to be content with held hands and brief, snatched kisses, and it was not enough. Sometimes I thought she seemed equally fond of Philip, and for the first time in my life found myself resenting him.

"Did you know Philip's twins have started school?" she said one day after the start of the new term. "Their elder sister's in my class – Cora Smith. She's a nice little thing but she insists on following me round all the time and she never stops talking! I suppose she doesn't get much attention at home."

"It's something that they come to school at all. Isn't there an elder boy as well?"

"Bobbie, yes. He's with me too; there's barely a year between them. They're strange children. They seem younger than the rest in some ways but incredibly mature in others, probably because they've had to fend for themselves."

On the Sunday of half-term I found myself alone. Madeleine was spending the week in Lancaster and Philip had been called out to a difficult confinement. More from force of habit than any other reason I walked up to the Gemelly Circle in reflective mood. How quickly the years had passed since we'd first met Eve here and she'd told us about the Crowthorpe twins. She had known even then that we would stay. Once twins came to Crowthorpe they were unlikely ever to leave.

At the back of my mind a long-forgotten memory stirred. Hadn't she said, though, that first day, that one pair of twins *had* moved away? I felt suddenly that it was imperative I should learn about them. Leaning back against a stone, I closed my eyes and willed Eve to come to me, and twenty minutes later she appeared over the brow of the hill.

"I hope this is important," she greeted me. "Douglas was expecting me to mow the grass and he wasn't best pleased when I announced I had to come out."

"I think it's important, yes. Didn't you tell us once that a pair of twins had moved away from here?"

"That's right, the Carters – Miss Sarah and Miss Jane. They're in a mental home near Carnforth, poor loves; the same one as Mark Saunders."

I felt a sense of shock. "How long have they been unbalanced?"

"All their lives, but they were pretty harmless. They lived here with their mother for many years. She didn't die till she was over ninety, and she wouldn't allow them to be sent away. Once she'd gone there was no-one to care for them, so they had to go."

"They must be quite elderly, then?"

"In their sixties, certainly. Anita and I used to visit them fairly regularly at first. They were twins after all, and there weren't any others then except the Marshalls, who were only toddlers. But since you and Philip came I'm afraid we've not bothered. I haven't even thought about them for years. You make me feel guilty."

"How ill are they? What form does it take?"

"Basically they're just simple. They can't talk properly – only a succession of grunts – and occasionally, through frustration I suppose, they have odd spells of violence. That was really why none of us could cope when their mother died. She was always able to calm them down." She paused, looking round her. "They were very fond of the stones. They used to move round patting them and making those odd sounds. It gave you quite a funny feeling, as though they were actually – communicating with them." She looked at me closely. "Why this sudden interest in the Carters?"

"I think Philip and I should meet them."

"If you want to, of course. We can salve our own consciences at the same time. But why?"

I said, "You didn't by any chance try to reach them telepathically?"

She stared at me, her eyes widening. "My God! Do you think—?"

"Did you?"

"No, of course not. We never bothered much with that in those days. There were just odd flashes between Anita and me. Certainly it never occurred to us that—"

"It might be worth a try."

"Matthew—" She hesitated. "I don't want to risk hurting them in any way. I mean, if they got over-excited or anything—"

"But couldn't it be the most tremendous relief to them, if after all these years behind a barrier, they could suddenly communicate?"

"I suppose it could, but that's not the main reason you're interested, is it? Nothing so altruistic!"

I smiled a little. "How well you know me, Eve. It just occurred to me that here might lie another as yet untapped source of power."

Her answering smile faded. "Don't you think we've enough already? So much, in fact, that we regularly have to – to empty it into the stones."

"The point is that we've no way of knowing how

110

much we'll need. We mustn't overlook any opportunity of increasing it."

"But what will we need it *for*?"

"I don't know. Sometimes when I'm up here I get an inkling, but it always fades before I can grasp it properly. I just know we must go on amassing it so that we're not caught unprepared when the time comes."

She shivered. "I wish you wouldn't talk like that. It frightens me."

"It frightens me too, but it has to be faced. How soon can you arrange a visit?"

"Relatives go more or less any time, but I think other visitors are restricted to weekends. The patients get disturbed if there's too much coming and going."

"Then shall we make it next Saturday? We can all drive down together."

The week that followed seemed to crawl past. It was incredible that my subconscious should have allowed me to overlook the Carter twins for so long, and I was impatient now to rectify the omission. Consequently I was absent-minded even with Madeleine, and finally, sitting on the grass of the playing field one lunch hour, she tugged at my sleeve.

"Matthew, will you please listen to me!"

"Sorry, darling. What did you say?"

"I was telling you about Cora. I mentioned before how she keeps chattering all the time."

"So?"

"I never really bothered to listen but when I did I had a shock. It was about the twins, Davy and Kim."

She had my attention at last. "Yes?"

"They seem to get up to some very nasty tricks,

particularly for such young children. They ought to be stopped, though I'm not sure how."

"What do they do, Maddy?"

"For one thing they catch small animals – with their bare hands, I gather – and cut their throats in some grotesque kind of ceremony and smear the blood over the stones in the Circle."

I stared at her, my own blood suddenly thundering in my ears. "Cora told you that?"

"In passing, yes. She didn't seem to attach much importance to it. And apparently there's a most peculiar atmosphere between the twins and the old woman up there. Is she their grandmother? The twins told Cora that she'd tried to kill them once, but you know how children exaggerate. They were probably only trying to make an impression."

In the recesses of my mind I saw again the small damp bundles wrapped in my jacket and Philip's. "Probably," I agreed out of a dry mouth.

"It doesn't seem a very healthy environment for children to grow up in," Madeleine went on. "I hate to think of those poor little animals, quite apart from the effect it must be having on the twins themselves. Since Philip seems to have so much influence with them, I was wondering if you'd ask him to speak to them."

"I'll see what I can do," I said.

As I'd anticipated, Philip was greatly excited to learn of the doings of his protégés. "So that's what they get up to, the little devils!" he exclaimed, with an unmistakable note of pride in his voice. "I wonder what the significance is. Blood for the stones to replace the old-time sacrifices? I'll ask them about it but they won't tell me anything they don't want to and they're very adept at raising the mental block in a flash to prevent any probing."

"I suppose you never said anything about our rescuing them that night?"

"Of course not. Why?"

"I was just wondering how they knew."

Philip smiled irritatingly and did not reply.

Saturday came at last and after an early lunch Anita, Eve, Philip and I set off for Carnforth. It was a glorious summer day and the surrounding countryside lay rich in its new greenery. Our route took us through some of Lakeland's loveliest scenery, alongside the blue waters of Thirlmere, through Grasmere and Ambleside, whose narrow streets were already blocked with tourists, past Windermere and so down to the outskirts of Carnforth and the grey stone building we were seeking.

"The Miss Carters are in their room," the nurse at the desk told us. "We weren't expecting any visitors for them and they prefer to be alone. Would you like them to be sent for?"

"We'll go up, if that's all right," Anita said quickly. We were all anxious to have no onlookers at this meeting.

"Of course. It's room nineteen, on the first floor. There's a nurse on duty up there."

In silence we went up the wide, linoleumed staircase. There was a murmur of voices from the common room below and a sudden, high inane laugh. For the first time I wondered how I'd react to this latest pair of twins. Philip was used to illness and the other two knew what to expect. I alone was likely to be out of my depth.

"The Miss Carters," Eve said to the enquiring eyebrows of the duty nurse.

"Room nineteen. If you need me, just press the bell by the door."

We knocked, paused – although hardly expecting an answer – and went in. The two women were seated side by side on one of the beds. They wore neat grey skirts and cardigans and their hands were resting in their laps. They had short grey hair and pale blue, inward-looking eyes, which showed no emotion whatever as the four of us entered the room.

Eve and Anita went forward, talking quietly, apologizing for their absence as though time had meaning for the women sitting there. Then suddenly the pale eyes lifted and seemed to register Philip and myself for the first time. A flicker of interest crossed the smooth, unlined faces.

Without opening my mouth, I said inwardly, 'Good afternoon. I hope you're well.'

Both women stiffened, their faces turning towards me like flowers to the sun, a look of wild, unbelieving hope flooding over them which was painful to see. The answer came hesitantly, 'Who are you?'

Anita replied, also silently. 'I'm sorry. May I introduce Matthew and Philip Selby? They live in Crowthorpe too.'

Excitement snaked across the room, stinging my mind with its whiplash.

'Matthew? Matthew?'

Eve glanced at us with a startled frown. 'Yes, Matthew and Philip.'

'Not – Philip.'

Philip said, 'Sorry, but that is my name.'

The level of excitement was by this time distressing to us all. The grey-haired women hadn't moved from the bed, but eyes, brains, consciousnesses were examining us minutely, stretching towards us in search of something we couldn't grasp. It occurred to me that if this meeting had taken place downstairs, we would have seemed to any onlooker merely to have been staring at each other.

Their concentration was still centred on Philip. 'You have perhaps another name?'

I halfsmiled, knowing how Philip detested his second name. He said reluctantly, 'I was called Arthur, after my father.'

Their fervour became tangible, swelled, exploded. 'Artio and Matunus! We were not mistaken! Hail, all hail!'

And before we could stop them, the elderly women had slipped off the bed and prostrated themselves on the ground. Instinctively I reached for the buzzer to summon help, but Eve caught my hand.

"No – wait a minute!" She'd spoken aloud and her voice was shaking. "Tell them to get up, for God's sake."

"Please—" I knelt down and touched one of the women's shoulder. "Please don't do that. We can't talk when you're in that position."

Slowly, to our infinite relief, they rose, but they didn't resume their seat on the bed. They stood waiting with bowed heads like supplicants at some papal audience.

Philip said silently, 'We don't understand. Why are our names so important?'

'The Bear Twins have returned to Crowthorpe!'

Philip's fingers bit into my arm, but another question was flowing towards us.

'My lords are making use of the stones?'

'We're – building up power, yes.'

'Excellent. You have two years, perhaps. No longer.'

'What will happen then?' Eve asked anxiously.

'The spirits will be released and the Crow put to flight.'

'We'll need your help' I told them.

'Of course, my lord. As always, we are ready, and there is much to do.'

It was impossible to know which twin was transmitting. Perhaps they used the same source jointly.

'How wonderful,' they added shyly, 'to reach out and be understood.'

When we took our leave of them, they again bowed low and remained in that position till the door had closed behind us.

In the privacy of the car, Philip said jerkily, "They can't really believe we're the bear gods, surely?"

"They are unbalanced," Eve reminded us. "Having tuned in to them, it's hard to remember that, but you must have recognized it, Philip?"

"I don't know what I recognized," he said flatly. "The whole affair shattered me. That instant contact and then the – the act of worship. It was mindbending."

"Had you heard the names of the Bear Twins before?" I asked Anita.

"No, but I know that words beginning a-r-t and m-a-t have bear connotations in Celtic, and that's coincidence enough."

When we got back back to Crowthorpe, Anita invited us to tea at the Greystones. Some of the unease still lingered and, hoping the everyday atmosphere of the hotel would dispel it, I was pleased to accept. To my surprise, though, Philip declined.

"You go, Matthew, but I promised to contact Dr Sampson about some results he was expecting from the path. lab. Don't hurry home; I'll see you later."

So I went to the Greystones with Eve and Anita. George joined us – it was some time since I'd seen him – and we all had drinks on the terrace looking down the sloping gardens to the clear blue lake.

Later Anita brought salad and fruit and we sat talking desultorily, grateful for the blessedly normal presence of the hotel guests further along the terrace. For that short space of time we could pretend we were no different from them.

It was after ten when I returned to the flat and to my surprise Philip was not there. Perhaps the Sampsons had invited him to supper. The flat seemed strange and empty without him. I flung the windows wide and leaned out, watching the lights of the cars along Lake Road and the mooring lights bobbing at the water's edge. And I thought of the old ladies in exile in Carnforth, and of the twin gods Matunus and Artio, whose quarrel over a girl had been their downfall.

At last, I heard Philip's car come round the corner of the house, its door slam and voices laughing. Madeleine's voice. And something cold and hard and frightening closed round me.

I was still standing at the window when Philip's key turned in the lock and a moment later he came whistling into the room behind me.

"Hi! Been back long?"

I turned and he came to a halt. "You've been with Madeleine," I said.

"What if I have? It's all in the family!"

"You told me you were going to the Sampsons."

"So I did. And as I left I met Madeleine coming back from the church fête. She thought I was you!"

"Did you disillusion her?"

He moved uncomfortably. "Look, Matthew, I don't know what you're making such a fuss about. We've always shared everything."

"Did you tell her who you were?" I repeated stonily.

"Eventually."

I moved blindly forward, my hand raised, but he caught hold of it and held it fast.

"Matthew! For God's sake, it's me – Philip! Look, we've done this before, both of us! It's never mattered!"

"It matters this time."

"Yes, I see it does." He let go my arm. "Are you in love with her?"

"Yes."

"Why the hell didn't you tell me? Does she love you?"

"No."

He let his breath out softly, as though my answer was the one he'd hoped for. The leaden weight continued to press down inside me. After a moment he said, "What are you going to do?"

"Keep trying, so you can bloody well stay away from her."

"You have rather thrust us together, you know. Had you forgotten we have the same taste?" His eyes moved over my stiff face. "Relax, Matthew," he said heavily.

118

"It was supposed to be a joke but obviously it misfired. Of course she knew it was me."

It was an effort for me to speak. "Is that the truth?"

"For a moment she did think I was you, but as soon as she caught up with me she said, 'Oh, sorry! It's Philip, isn't it?' So you see after all these years there's one person who can tell us apart. Perhaps that's a good omen for you."

My breathing was still laborious. "But you spent the evening with her."

"It's not a crime, is it? We just had a drink together. I felt in need of some normal company after the afternoon we'd spent. Look, brother mine, don't make a heavy drama out of this. If I've ruffled your feathers I'm sorry, but it's your own fault for not telling me how you felt about her." He held out his hand with a tentative smile and after a moment I took it. "That's better. Now for God's sake let's forget it. OK?"

I nodded and he moved away, loosening his tie. "Lord, it's hot up here. We should draw the curtains when we go out, to keep the sun off. Did you have a pleasant evening?"

"Not as pleasant as yours, I imagine. It was all right."

"Are you going to have a shower?"

"You go first, if you like."

"Right." He left the room and I went on standing there. We'd shaken hands but things still weren't right between us. It was the first time I'd ever had so much as a disagreement with Philip, and the facf that it was about Madeleine made it all the worse. Remembering that little sigh of relief, I wondered bleakly how he would have replied if I'd had the courage to ask if he loved her himself.

Eight

Several months have now passed since that day, but its events have been far-reaching, for the sudden upsurge of power contributed by the Carter twins has tipped the balance from the manageable level to the dangerous. Nor, on subsequent visits, have we been able to establish any coherent links with them and such messages as we receive are garbled; wild imagery and disconnected ramblings. Perhaps, as Eve feared, our first visit had unhinged them further, or perhaps the power they contribute has diminished them in some way. It may even be that, having established the longed-for contact, they are content to let lucidity slip away again; a kind of heathen "Nunc dimittis".

For myself, I no longer seem to have any discrimination in the way I use my influence, satisfying passing whims rather than adhering to the "grand design" with which I'd originally set out. Once, I clamped a boy's mind shut during an important test, because I'd overheard him making a snide remark about me. I didn't even realize what I'd done till I found him in tears afterwards.

Philip is finding the same thing, but with more serious consequences. One afternoon I came back from school to find him with a glass of whisky in his hand.

"Starting a bit early, aren't you lad?" I chided lightly, trying to hide my disquiet.

"I've just killed someone," he said.

I felt for a chair and sat down abruptly, my eyes on his face.

"He was desperately ill but I knew what the trouble was, and how to save him. I deliberately did nothing and he died before my eyes. My God, Matthew, *what's the matter with me*?"

I shook my head. "Remember asking me if I thought we were being used? We both know the answer now."

"But why in this way? What's the point in destroying life?"

"It's a symbol of power, that's all. An arbitrary toss of the dice. Yesterday you might have elected to save him, today you didn't."

He took another gulp of his drink. "Power like that is only justifiable if it's used for good."

"Is it even then? Remember our plans for a Utopia, the healthiest people, the brightest pupils? The trouble is that power works both ways; it affects the one who wields it as well as his subject. We should have thought about that before we stockpiled so much of it."

The television set in the corner crackled into life and Fred Hardacre's face materialized on the screen. "Tonight at the Crow's Nest. Seven-thirty."

Philip and I hadn't moved. After a moment he said flatly, "We've all infected one another, battened on each other to increase our own faculties. It's – grotesque."

"If we went away—"

He gave a short laugh. "Too late, Matthew. It was always too late. We'll have to see it through."

121

The day after this conversation, because I felt there ought to be some record of how it all built up, I started to write this account. I'm almost up to date now and I daren't go on much longer. The controlling power is exerting considerable pressure to make me destroy it and I'm finding it harder and harder to resist. Just a few more pages, and then I'll stop.

In all these months Philip and I have never again discussed Madeleine. I don't think either of us dares to. Our three-way friendship continues but I don't seem any nearer to winning her round. Sometimes I catch Philip looking at her and there's a terrible fear in me.

Granny Lee has been down to the village several times lately. I don't know why, she never speaks to anyone. We found her once standing on the corner of Ash Street, that obscene bird perched on her shoulder, staring up at our windows. I heard from Eve that she'd been hanging round the Greystones too and George had to ask her to move away because she was alarming the guests. Not to mention poor Anita: she hasn't been too well these last months.

Philip has finally stopped his long-standing visits to the camp. The need for them is gone, since the boys come to all our meetings now, but privately I think he was finding it impossible to face Granny's crow. To my shame, I still resent his closeness to the Smiths, particularly since with their glossy black hair and bright eyes they resemble a pair of crows themselves. Which reminds me of an episode a week or two ago, which caused me acute embarrassment:

One Saturday Madeleine and I set out with packs on our backs to walk up the mountain alongside the lake. It was a gorgeous day, clear and bright and with no trace of the mist which occasionally conceals the peaks. The ground was firm and springy and it was exhilarating to feel the tug of muscles as we made our steady progress.

"We'll be coming to the waterfall in a few minutes," she told me. "It's possible to walk round it; there's a rickety little fence screening the drop, but it's safe enough if you've a head for heights."

Crowswater Falls were spectacular. We went in single file up the narrow gorge while the torrent, swollen by the rains of a generally wet summer, hurtled in spumes of spray to the lake far below. Here, amid the overhanging foliage, it was dim and damp, and lush ferns grew along with a few marshy flowers. The roar of the water made conversation impossible. When we came out at the top of the ravine and the path branched upwards again on to the open hillside, we laughed aloud for sheer exuberance.

I felt more relaxed than I had for months. Up here alone with Madeleine it was possible briefly to forget the strains and anxieties which were now so much a part of everyday life. But I was not to be allowed to forget them for long.

We stopped for our picnic in the lee of a barren crag, which afforded some shelter from the stiff easterly breeze. The view before us was breathtaking. We were roughly midway down the lake, and from this height it was possible to see the cluster of houses that was Crowthorpe rising up the slope at one end, while on our left the more concentrated buildings of Barrowick were also visible.

We ate hungrily; chunks of new bread and cheese, crisp apples and slices of pink ham. And when we'd

123

finished I tossed what little remained of our feast in the direction of a small inquisitive bird. At the same moment there was a sudden flapping sound and to my horror a large crow landed on the rock immediately behind us. I started to my feet, knocking over the vacuum flask, and leapt to the other side of the clearing.

"Whatever's the matter?" Madeleine asked in surprise. "It's only after the food!"

But the bird, aware of my discomfiture, started flapping its wings and uttering a high-pitched rasping screech which seared into my brain. I clasped my hands to my ears and the creature suddenly swooped down at me, filling my nostrils with its rank dusty odour, the wind from its wing-beats blasting in my eyes. It was then that I screamed and Madeleine, her face white and uncomprehending, finally succeeded in chasing it away.

Sweating, nauseous, shaken beyond all reason, I sank to the ground and sat with my head in my hands, my breath tearing through my lungs like dry, convulsive sobs. I was too ashamed to face Madeleine, but after a moment she sat beside me and I felt her arms come round my shaking body. Gently she pulled me against her, cradling my head against her breast and murmuring soothing platitudes while the thunderous pounding of my heart gradually abated.

"I'm sorry," I said thickly at last. "That was quite an exhibition, wasn't it?"

"I'd no idea you felt like that about birds. You've always seemed to like them."

"It's only crows."

"Big birds, you mean?"

"Not 'big birds'; not ostriches, flamingos, eagles, pelicans, storks or dodos. Only crows."

Her fingers were still moving gently over my forehead and as the last of the panic receded I caught her hand, pulling her down into my arms. She must have understood that my wild kisses were partly reaction, because she allowed them to go on longer than usual. Even so, I didn't want to accept her limits.

"Maddy, I love you! Don't you care for me at all?"

"You know I do, Matthew."

"It's been two years now. Surely I mean something to you?"

"Of course you do."

"More than Philip?" I hadn't meant to say it.

I felt her surprise but she replied calmly, "I know you better, don't I?"

It was not the answer I wanted, and I said unfairly, "He has this crow phobia too." I didn't intend my disgraceful behaviour to be to Philip's advantage.

"What started it, do you know?"

"It's something we've always had. No doubt there's some Freudian explanation. I'm sorry I made such a fool of myself."

"Don't be silly, you couldn't help it."

"That's no comfort." I rubbed my hands over my face. "I could use a stiff drink but I spilled even the last of the coffee!"

"Do you want to go on, or shall we turn back?"

"We'll go on," I said.

So we continued our climb, but the day was spoiled. I knew my irrational behaviour had disturbed Madeleine and I even blamed her for having been there to witness it. Nor was my discomposure limited to that afternoon. During the week that followed I was constantly on edge and my resulting lack of judgment led to a course of action I instantly regretted.

Glancing at a newspaper during a free period, I came across a review of Jason Quinn's play which had just changed theatres, and its title, *Clouded Crystal*, vividly recalled the American professor and his talk of Macbeth prophecies. Almost without thought, I tore a page from one of the exercise books in the pile at my elbow and wrote in large block letters:

IF YOU STILL DOUBT THE EXISTENCE
OF MACBETH PROPHECIES, COME TO
CROWTHORPE AND SEE ONE FULFILLING
ITSELF!

I found a used envelope in the waste paper basket, scrawled out the address and substituted Quinn's name, care of the theatre where his play was running. I sealed it with sticky tape, then, before I could change my mind, went straight out and posted it in the pillar box at the corner of Broad Walk.

Almost immediately, I wished I could reclaim it. It was a childish thing to have done and I hadn't even had the courage to sign my name. I told myself that Jason Quinn must be used to anonymous letters and would pay no attention to it, and with that bleak comfort I had to be content.

The summer crawls on. I've developed the habit of going for long, solitary walks over the fells. I have this compulsion to keep testing myself, to see if on my next encounter with a crow I could make better account of myself. Then what? Should I run to Madeleine and say like a child, 'Look – this time I wasn't afraid!'?

Philip came in the other day while I was working on this account. It was the first time he's found me with it since I usually write in my room at night.

"What's that?" he asked curiously.

"A record of the things that have happened since we came to Crowthorpe. A kind of diary, really."

"Evidence for the prosecution?"

"Perhaps."

He said uneasily, "You're not putting everything down, are you?"

"Most of it. It's no use unless it's a full account."

He shrugged and turned away. "Well, if you've nothing better to do with your time . . ."

But this afternoon when I came in from school I found him in my room with the papers in his hand. He turned sharply as I entered.

"You've certainly been dotting the i's and crossing the t's. Do you think it's wise?"

With forced calm I took the papers out of his hand. "It won't do us any harm. If anyone ever reads it, we'll be well out of their reach."

He frowned. "You talk in riddles these days."

I made some noncommittal reply and the moment passed. But it was a warning I can't afford to ignore. I was aware the power might compel me to destroy this, but I'd overlooked the possibility of its using Philip. Perhaps if I'd been a few minutes later he might have removed it, taken it away somewhere to burn or tear up at his leisure. Because Philip is as deeply committed in all this as I am, and as much in thrall to whatever it is that governs us.

So this page will be my last entry. Tomorrow I shall parcel it up and take it to the bank with instructions that it be held unopened till Philip's and my death. Thereafter, it is to be handed to Douglas Braithwaite to deal with as he thinks fit.

So, Douglas, if the time ever comes for you to read this, say a prayer for all the Crowthorpe twins. We shall have need of it.

Part Two

Nine

"My God!"

"What now? Death and disaster in the evening paper?" Jason Quinn held out a brimming glass and the other man took it.

"Death, certainly, and in one of the villages where I stayed last month." He took a sip of his drink and lifted the paper again. "'The victim, Patsy Lennard, 19, was a chambermaid at the Lakeside Hotel. Her body was found early this morning near the megalithic monument known as the Gemelly Circle. The eyes had been removed – 'pecked out', according to a witness – and the throat savagely torn as though an implement such as a beak had been used. There are carrion crows in the area, but since they rarely attack people, the police are treating the death as suspicious.'"

"Should do wonders for their tourist trade!" Jason commented, leaning back in a corner of the sofa. "Where is this place?"

"Up in the Lakes – a village called Crowthorpe. In fact, that was where—"

"Crowthorpe?"

"You know it?"

"The name rings a bell. I've a feeling that was the place mentioned in a crank letter I received a few months ago. Unsigned, naturally. I threw it in the waste basket with the rest, and then for some reason retrieved it."

He went across to his bureau and flicked through the pigeon-holes. "Yes, here it is: postmarked last September. I remember now; it intrigued me because it referred back to Macbeth prophecies. Remember that programme I did with a Yankee professor? See what you make of this: 'If you still doubt the existence of Macbeth prophecies, come to Crowthorpe and see one fulfilling itself!'"

"A crank, as you said."

"Written on a torn piece of paper and the envelope has been used before. The address is scratched out but still legible. Crowthorpe Primary School, Broad Walk, Crowthorpe, Cumbria. Not quite as anonymous as our mystery writer intended, perhaps. 'Light thickens, and the crow makes way to the rooky wood.'"

"If you're going to quote from the Scottish play," said a light voice, "I shall leave again at once!"

Jason looked up and Ted Latimer rose to his feet as Tania pushed the door shut behind her and come down the three steps into the sitting-room.

"Sorry I'm late, blame it on the traffic." She pressed a cheek against Ted's and went over to her husband, dropping a kiss on top of his head. "Hi, lover. A large brandy, if you please, and pronto!"

Ted watched her with a jaundiced eye as, tossing her jacket over the back of a chair, she ran her fingers through her blonde, frizzy hair, making it stand out even more.

"God, it was hot at the theatre! I'm not sorry we're coming to the end of the run."

"Nor am I," Jason murmured. "We'll be able to eat at a civilized time again."

The clock on the mantelpiece showed it was past eleven.

"Anything else lined up?" Ted asked dutifully.

"Not till the autumn, thank God. Then we go into rehearsal for the new Pinter." She flopped into a chair and took the glass Jason held out. "What was that sinister quotation in aid of, anyway? You should know it's bad luck to quote *Macbeth*."

"Only backstage, they tell me. There are gruesome goings on up in Cumbria, in a village someone asked me to visit."

"What someone?"

He picked up the sheet of paper. "The letter's unsigned, but at least it's not abusive for once."

"What does it say?"

He read it to her, adding, "My quote was simply association of ideas: Macbeth and crows." He looked at Ted. "And crows are mentioned in the paper, too. The girl's eyes were apparently pecked out."

"Thank *you*!" Tania rose in one fluid movement. "I shall take my glass with me to the bathroom and have a quick shower. Shall we eat outside? It's still very warm and I love seeing all the lights. What has Françoise left for supper? I'm ravenous."

"Cold soup and crab salad. I saw them when I put the wine in the fridge."

"Fine. Give me ten minutes, then we'll eat."

Ted watched her go. "I saw Penelope today," he said abruptly.

Jason smiled. "Sublety was never your strong suit."

"Sorry. I didn't think it showed."

133

"That you don't approve of Tania? I've always known, though whether it's just jealousy on Pen's behalf—"

"She's worth ten of this one. If you weren't such a stubborn so-and-so you'd admit it."

"I never discuss my wives, Ted, past or present. How was Pen?"

"Fine, as usual."

"Did you meet by chance?"

"No." Ted held Jason's eyes steadily. "I might be your agent, but I'm damned if I see why I should break off diplomatic relations with Penelope just because you were misguided enough to leave her. Though from what she was saying I gather you see quite a bit of her yourself."

"I drop in from time to time."

"Can't say I blame you. All right – sorry! Young Emily's not too well, though. A touch of tonsilitis, Penelope thinks. She's kept her home from school all week." He looked across at his friend curiously. "Don't you ever miss your children, Jason?" As he spoke, he wondered if such directness would be resented. Jason Quinn was not one to encourage confidences.

However, Jason merely answered lazily, "I've never been a family man. You know that, Ted."

Perhaps that's why he'd been such easy game when this self-centred little tart set her cap at him. While Penelope – Ted's fingers unconsciously tightened round his glass, remembering how she had turned to him for support. Not for anything else, though, he reflected ruefully, and marvelled, not for the first time, that neither she nor Jason had any inkling of his own feelings for her.

"Right, supper coming up!" Tania had changed into linen trousers and a sleeveless silk top the colour of her eyes. "Make yourselves useful, both of you. Would you set the tray, Ted, while Jason opens the wine? I went on to the balcony after my shower, and the temperature out there is perfect – incredible that it's only mid-May."

"I hope you were decently clad," Jason murmured, with a wink at Ted.

"Starkers actually, darling, but it was dark, so who cares? Not that anyone could have seen me in broad daylight. That's the advantage of a penthouse flat."

And not the only one, thought Ted, looking round the luxurious apartment, though for himself he preferred the homely atmosphere of Penelope's little house in Blackheath.

Strategic lamps lit the roof garden, where pots and containers of all shapes and sizes spilled over with late spring flowers. A young vine had been trained up one of the white trellises and a pink magnolia contributed its oddly pungent scent of raspberry sorbet.

The iced cucumber soup was excellent, the conversation light and amusing, but Ted's mind kept returning to the newspaper report. He could almost visualize that poor girl lying there on the hilltop—

He dropped his spoon with a clatter, feeling the hair on the back of his head begin to rise. Jason and Tania looked at him enquiringly.

"You can't have burnt your tongue, Ted!"

"I'm sorry. I – just remembered something."

"All right, I'll buy it," Jason said good-humouredly. "What did you remember?"

"Well, I was about to say earlier that it was in

135

Crowthorpe that I had that attack of amnesia I told you about."

Tania said, "I've heard quite enough about Crowthorpe, thank you. If you're going to start talking about dead bodies again—"

"No, I'm not. At least, not human bodies." He hurried on before she could speak. "I was on a walking holiday and spending a couple of nights there before going on to Keswick. The first evening, I went up to have a look at that stone circle where – well, that we were talking about earlier. I remember reaching it, and examining a few of the stones, and then – whoosh! From one moment to the next, nothing. Completely blank."

"You mean you passed out?"

"I don't know what the hell happened. If I did, it didn't affect my mobility, because I managed to get myself down the hill and back to my lodgings. I came to as I was closing my bedroom door."

Jason frowned. "You don't remember going back?"

"Not a thing."

"How peculiar. Have you had these attacks before?"

"Never. I don't mind telling you it put the fear of God into me. The next day I went to the nearest hospital and asked for a full check-up. I was terrified it could happen again, when I was in the car or something. They were very thorough; went into all my past history, gave me a full neurological examination, tested my eyes and reflexes, the lot. What's more, they referred me back to my own doctor, suggesting I went to see a neurologist, which in due course I did. But none of them could find anything wrong."

"Did you go back to the Circle?"

"Too right I did, though it took a bit of doing. And

nothing untoward happened at all. I walked round and round the stones without so much as a flicker."

"And you never remembered that blank half-hour or whatever?"

Ted stared down at his cucumber soup. "Not until now."

They waited expectantly.

"It suddenly came back, just a minute ago. I was thinking of the report in the paper, and the stones, and – it was there, every missing detail. I almost wish it wasn't." He smiled faintly. "Sorry, Tania. I'd better stop or I'll spoil your appetite."

"Oh, you'll have to go on now. I shan't eat another mouthful till I know what you saw."

"OK, if you can take it. I hope I can! I remember going round behind one of the stones and seeing a couple of boys a few yards away. Only small, six or seven, I'd say, and gypsies from the look of them. They were bending over something on the ground, but I couldn't see what it was. Then someone called from a distance away and they started to run off without seeing me. I was curious enough to go over and look at what they'd left lying there. It was a dead sheep."

Jason raised an eyebrow. "That's the punch-line? I should think sheep-stealing's fairly common among gypsies."

"No doubt. But you don't usually find the abandoned carcass with its throat slit and all the blood drained out of it."

Tania's hand went to her mouth and a sudden breeze bent the candle flame.

"Go on," Jason said quietly.

"I stood staring down at it, feeling decidedly queasy,

I admit, but still perfectly clear-headed. Then I heard a faint sound. I remember wondering if the boys had come back, and if so what I could say to them. They were there all right, as alike as two peas – twins, I suppose – but I didn't get the chance to say a thing. They stood gazing at me, and so help me I felt a kind of paralysis creeping over my brain. Can you imagine that? I could actually *feel* myself forgetting – the stones, then the dead animal, and finally the kids themselves. And I remember turning like a robot and trotting meekly back to the village, for all the world as though that was what I'd been 'programmed' to do. What's more, I doubt if I'd ever have remembered what happened, if it hadn't been triggered off by that report in the paper."

Jason was looking at him with narrowed eyes. "You're suggesting the episode was deliberately blotted out of your memory?"

"I'm damn sure it was. I tell you I could feel it happening."

Tania said on a high note, "Are you going to finish your soup?"

"Sorry. Yes, of course." He picked up his spoon and sipped the last of the pale green liquid. Somehow it didn't taste quite as good as before.

No-one spoke while Tania removed the plates and put the salad on the table.

"Do you think the two things are connected?" Ted asked then. "The – throat seems to have been attacked in both cases."

Jason pushed the salad bowl towards him. "You never struck me as a likely case for brainwashing, Ted."

"All right, we all know your views on such things. I was inclined to agree with you, till this. And brainwashing is a fact of life. Look at all those prisoners of war—"

"By specialists, under rigorous conditions, yes. But by a couple of small children on a Cumbrian hillside?"

"Perhaps," Tania said shakily, "you're lucky they stopped at brainwashing."

"Oh, come now, darling! You surely don't imagine those little boys had anything to do with the girl's death?"

"As Ted said, there are similarities: location, method of killing. The sheep, that is, not Ted!"

"Thank God!" muttered Ted under his breath.

"It could be," Tania continued, "that your unknown correspondent had a point, and there *is* something strange going on."

"You're sure you do remember all that, Ted? Could your memory perhaps have been 'assisted' by what you read in the paper?"

"Not in the way you imply. I swear, Jason, I remember it all perfectly clearly now. And as I said, I rather wish I didn't."

"I wonder what the Macbeth prophecy was," Jason mused. "The one which is supposedly fulfilling itself. If, of course, it hasn't already done so by now. You know, this village of yours is beginning to interest me." He glanced at his wife. "How do you fancy a holiday, my love, when the play comes off? A touch of clear Cumbrian air would revive you wondrously."

"If you're planning to cut my throat," she answered tightly, "you don't have to take me all that way to do it."

139

Ted shifted uncomfortably. "I'm sorry. I seem to have put a blight on the dinner party."

"Scarcely a dinner party, just a little light refreshment."

"On the little light refreshment, then," he repeated woodenly. "About holidays, though, have you made any plans? You could both do with a break." He thought privately that Jason was looking strained. The grooves from nose to mouth were etched more deeply and the usually piercing eyes looked tired. Tania's last comment had lifted for a second the curtain they meticulously kept over their private life. He'd suspected for some time that things were not going smoothly and had heard her name linked more than once with the leading man in her current play. He hoped the rumours had not reached Jason.

"Tania's anxious to go somewhere bright and noisy," Jason said now, and the tiredness was in his voice as well. "The south of France or the Canaries. For myself, I just want peace and quiet; the chance to relax."

"The trouble with you, my sweet, is that you're such a stick-in-the-mud." Regardless of the food on her plate, Tania flicked open her cigarette case. "Without me to take you in hand, you'd be old before your time."

"Possibly. More wine, Ted?"

The evening moved to an end and it was with relief that Ted took his leave of them.

"What a bore that man is!" Tania exclaimed as the door closed behind him. "A bore and a boor! Fancy bringing up that disgusting story when we were eating."

"You did tell him to go ahead," Jason reminded her mildly.

"Well, naturally. By that time he'd aroused my interest. And it was so uncharacteristic of him, that flight of fancy. Usually he's so abysmally solid and unimaginative."

"Which, to my way of thinking, adds weight to his story."

"Well, you brood over it if you want to. I'm going to bed."

But when he joined her a few minutes later, it seemed she'd also been "brooding". "You weren't serious about going to that god-forsaken place?"

He looked across at her. The light behind her made her hair a fluffy gold halo and the wispy lace nightdress did little to conceal her lovely body. He wondered dispassionately why she so seldom roused him now; she was as beautiful as ever. Perhaps he'd just out-grown her.

"Well?" She turned challengingly to face him, her arms behind her head as she struggled to unfasten the clasp of the chain she was wearing. He went to help her.

"I don't know," he said, replying to her question. "It could be interesting."

"Not to me." She paused. "If you won't go to the south of France, should you mind if I did?"

He slid his hand round in front of her to catch the chain and she caught it and held it against her breast. He said evenly, "Alone?"

"Do you really want me to answer that? Ask no questions and you'll hear no lies. Wasn't that the arrangement?"

"Your arrangement, yes."

She turned to face him, her arms going round his neck. "Have I ever denied you anything?"

141

"Only your undivided attention."

"Which you've never shown any sign of wanting." She surveyed him critically. "Damn it, Jason, you're a very attractive man. You could easily have kept me in line if you'd only taken the trouble." Her fingers moved up into his thick hair and he allowed her to pull his head down to hers, but his mind was elsewhere.

"I'll make a bargain with you," he said minutes later. "You can go abroad if you must, but first we'll spend a week or two in the Lake District."

"Oh no!" She moved angrily away. "You can't expect me to bury myself up there?"

"It's not much to ask, surely?"

"Just because that bloody man spins us a yarn—"

"That's not the only reason. Admittedly I'd forgotten about Crowthorpe, but it interested me from the start. That's why I kept the letter; I thought it might be worth going to have a look at the place. It's a beautiful part of the country and I *am* tired, Tania. I need a rest, and I might even feel tempted to do a little writing up there."

"That'll be riveting for me."

"Two weeks at the most, I promise."

"But we don't know anything about the place, except that there's some ancient monument. Big deal!"

"There's also a Lakeside Hotel. That'll do for a start."

"Come to the Lakeside and spot the next murder victim!"

"That's not in the best of taste."

"Nor is this morbid interest in the scene of the crime."

"That's enough, now," he said quietly. "I'm going,

142

and you're coming with me. As part of the arrangement."

Jason's decision was unchanged in the morning.
Pulling the phone towards him, he dialled directory
enquiries and minutes later a pleasant voice said in his
ear, "Lakeside Hotel, Crowthorpe. Can I help you?"

"Please. I'd like to reserve a suite for the first two
weeks in June."

"I'm sorry, sir, we haven't any suites. I can offer you
a double bedroom with bath, but I must ask you to
confirm the reservation in writing. We're getting very
booked up for June."

"I suppose that will have to do. Is it a good room?"

"Very nice, yes sir. A lovely view across the lake."

"All right, I'll take it. The name's Jason Quinn."

There was a startled pause. "*The* Jason Quinn?" the
voice enquired incredulously.

A brief smile touched his mouth. "I doubt if there
are two of us."

"Thank you very much, sir. If you'll confirm the
reservation I'll see you have the very best room. It's
usually possible to juggle them round a bit."

"Thank you. I'm most grateful."

He turned from the phone as Tania emerged, yawn-
ing, from the bedroom. "Who were you speaking
to?"

"The Lakeside Hotel. We're booked in for the first
fortnight in June."

"Determined devil, aren't you?"

"You could say that. Where's Françoise?"

"She has an English class this morning. I hope she
left some coffee."

"She did. I've already had two cups." He glanced

at her. "You don't really mind, do you? Coming with me?"

"It's a bit late to ask, after all this high-handedness."

"I want you to enjoy it."

"Oh, I'll have a ball, I don't doubt." She moved towards the kitchen. "More coffee?"

"No thanks. I'm going round to see Pen. I heard from Ted that Emily's not well."

"Nothing infectious, I hope."

"Tonsilitis. Will you be in for lunch?"

"No, I'm – lunching with Derek, before the matinée."

He said steadily, "Then I needn't hurry back. Good luck for the performance."

As he started the car he wondered dispiritedly whether he was doing the right thing in rushing off to the Lake District. If Tania spent the time sulking it could be difficult. No doubt it was Derek Paterson who was so anxious to take her to France. He knew quite well they were having an affair. God, why did his marriages go so disastrously wrong? He smiled sourly at himself in the driving mirror. Not like him to indulge in self-pity. He must be in need of a holiday.

"Jason! What a lovely surprise!"

"Hello, Pen." He kissed her cheek. "Not disturbing anything, am I?"

"Of course not. Alexander's out playing cricket and Emily and I are just pottering. She's had a sore throat this week, but I think she's over it now."

"So Ted told me."

"That's right, he was dining with you last night, wasn't he? How's Tania?"

144

"Tired, I think, though she won't admit it. The last weeks of a run often get her down."

He had followed her through to the sitting-room, where his daughter looked up from a book. Small for her twelve years, with brown eyes, high cheekbones and a fringe of dark hair, she was her mother in miniature.

"Hello, Daddy." She came over dutifully for his kiss.

"Hi, poppet. I hear you haven't been well. Sorry about that." To his own ears his voice sounded stilted. He was never at ease in the presence of children, his own or anyone else's. Fleetingly he thought of the gypsy twins who'd had such a profound effect on Ted.

"I've had tonsilitis but I'm better now." She was a quiet, polite child, Emily. The epithet "old-fashioned" came to mind, but out of a sense of loyalty he suppressed it.

"Can you stay for lunch?" Penelope asked.

"I'd be glad to."

"Lovely, then we can take our time and get talked up to date. Alexander's been picked for the First XI, incidentally. That's why he's not here. He'll be sorry to have missed you."

Privately, Jason doubted that. His son, like his daughter, was always constrained in his presence.

"How's the writing going?" he asked, settling comfortably into a chair. "I read a very glowing crit of *Sheridan* in the *Telegraph*."

"Yes, it was most gratifying. I've chosen a female subject for the next one, Philippa of Hainault. I became interested in her years ago, when I was working on *The Black Prince*, and of course those notes will be a help.

145

How about you? Any dates for a world première I can note in my diary?"

"Not as yet, but I'm at the restless stage, always a sign I should get down to writing. The TV business is a distraction but we've only a couple of shows to go in this series. I'm hoping to make a start on a new play during the summer."

Lunch was a simple family meal, unlike the often pretentious fare at home. When it was over, Emily retreated to the den to watch television and he and Penelope settled in the sunshine in the small back garden. The unseasonal heatwave was continuing. After a while he closed his eyes and slept.

He woke to find Penelope watching him, and struggled up in his chair. "Sorry about that! The height of bad manners!"

"Nonsense. It's a compliment that you feel so relaxed."

"I'm not making a nuisance of myself, am I, dropping in unannounced like this? I seem to be doing it more often lately."

"We're always glad to see you, you know that. You're looking tired though, Jason. Can't you get away for a bit?"

"As it happens, we're off to the Lakes for a couple of weeks at the end of the month."

"That should be nice, but watch out for the mad axe-man or whatever it is they've got up there. Did you see the papers?" She shuddered. "Very gruesome."

"As a matter of fact," he admitted, "that's where we're going."

Her eyes widened. "You're not serious, are you?"

"Completely. We're booked in at the Lakeside Hotel, Crowthorpe."

"Isn't that where the girl actually worked? Surely you'll cancel it now?"

He smiled. "You don't understand, Pen. I only arranged it this morning."

She stared at him. "You mean you deliberately—?"

"Yes."

"Jason, why?"

"Because I have a feeling something might be going on up there and I'd like to get to the bottom of it. In fact, I was more or less challenged to do so." And he told her about the anonymous letter.

"Even more reason, I should have thought, for keeping well away. How does Tania feel about it?"

"She's coming under sufferance, on condition she can then go to the south of France with Derek Paterson. Sorry, Pen—" as pain darkened her eyes – "that was a rotten thing to say. Forget it."

"But it's true, I suppose?"

"Oh, it's true. It's surprising you haven't heard; nearly everyone else has. I've only myself to blame. It was I who insisted on our marrying, you know. She'd have been quite happy to go on living together, but honest old-fashioned Jack here—" He broke off and rubbed his hand across his face. "I *must* be tired! Once again, I apologize."

She said softly, "I'm so sorry it hasn't worked out."

"You wouldn't have me back, I suppose?"

She looked at him quickly, saw that although he was smiling he was waiting for her answer, and regretfully shook her head. "There's no guarantee it would work any better than last time. And though I'm still fond of

147

you, I'm not in love with you any more. That's why things are so comfortable between us. Let's keep it that way."

"You're right of course." His contentment in her company had clouded the memory of the unhappiness that had gone before. Their marriage hadn't been a success even before he had met Tania.

He stood up, stretching luxuriously. "I'd better be going. I have a recording session at six. Thanks for lunch, tea and sympathy." He kissed her gently, on the mouth this time, and put his head round the den door on his way out. "Goodbye, Emily. Take care of that throat."

Driving back through the late Saturday shoppers, he was aware of an aching loneliness. They were happy without him, his little family in Blackheath, and though they dutifully welcomed his visits, they didn't want him back. He couldn't blame them, and it seemed his present marriage was going the same way.

He had a brief vision of himself on future Saturdays, visiting ex-wives all over London. Was it possible that he was as bigoted, arrogant and opinionated as his critics maintained, and incapable of any lasting relationship? At forty-one, wealth and fame notwithstanding, it was a sobering thought.

Ten

"Quite a backdrop, isn't it?" Tania had joined him as he stood at the window gazing across the lake to the wood-covered slopes beyond.

"Spectacular." He slipped an arm round her waist. "It seems a comfortable hotel, too. You might even enjoy the next two weeks."

"As long as you don't closet yourself away working on your new play. Will there be a part in it for me?"

"Do you want one?"

"It would be a guarantee of employment!"

He laughed. "I don't think you need worry about that. Shall we stroll down to the lake? There's an hour before we need change for dinner."

"You do realize we'll be recognized?"

"What do you suggest? Permanent dark glasses?"

"I'm used to people looking at me but you hate it."

"I can take it as long as they keep their distance and don't start haranguing me on something I said on the box weeks ago. That happened to me in Oxford Street the other day, did I tell you?"

"Well, you stir up a hornet's nest every time you appear. Better be extra careful here, though," she added, pulling the bedroom door shut behind them.

"They have an unfortunate way of dealing with people they disagree with!"

"Talking of which, I intend to question the chambermaid and see what I can get out of her."

"About the girl who was killed? Why?"

"I'd like to know what she was doing by the stones. She might even have mentioned something she'd seen up there." He pushed her ahead of him through the swing doors.

"Don't tell me you believe that weird story of Ted's?"

"Not as it stands, but there are fascinating possibilities. I'd also like to visit the school on some pretext and see if I can winkle out my correspondent."

"Jason, why are you bothering with all this? Are you on one of your debunking missions?"

"Not necessarily, but I feel the embryo of a new play taking shape. You must admit I've been handed some promising ingredients."

Tania said reflectively, "They haven't found the murderer yet, have they?"

"Not according to the papers. Does it worry you that we might pass him in the street?"

She stopped abruptly and stared at him. "You don't think he's still here?"

"Beloved, I'm not a detective, but if this murder was some kind of ritual, which, judging by the unusual features of it, seems quite likely, I should say the killer is almost definitely someone local."

"Then for God's sake let's keep away from that Circle, in case *we* see something we shouldn't."

She slipped her hand through his arm and they walked slowly through the garden, with its croquet lawn and tennis courts, to the private jetty at the edge of the lake.

"Like to take a boat out?"

"Not just now; I want to leave time for a leisurely bath before dinner. Perhaps tomorrow. I can't get used to having all this time at our disposal after the tight schedules we've been living with."

"Still planning to go to France later?" His eyes were on a boat out on the lake.

"You wouldn't mind, would you?"

"Only if it makes me look a fool. Discretion is essential to this arrangement."

"Lover, if you're in the public eye people will talk about you, whether you give them cause or not."

"So you might as well derive the benefit?"

He felt her tense, prepared to argue her supposed rights, and cursed himself for raising the subject at so inopportune a moment.

"Forget it," he said shortly. "This isn't the time or place for recriminations. Look at that bird down there. Is it a crow? You don't often see them as close as that."

The chambermaid was turning down the bedspreads when they returned to their room. Tania was amused at the awed look she darted at Jason, who promptly set himself to be charming. Leaving him to his interrogation, she caught up her peignoir and went through to the bathroom. His question about France had caught her offguard and she was relieved when he'd dismissed the subject almost at once. Forced into each other's company for the next two weeks, they would have more chance of making a go of things if France and Derek were left out of the conversation.

She stood for a moment surveying her reflection in the mirror over the basin: wide grey eyes, dark-lashed, petulant mouth and a cloud of pale hair. No sign of a wrinkle yet, which was just as well. Skilfully she removed her make-up, caught her hair up in a bandeau and stepped into the bath.

"Your turn," she announced ten minutes later, returning to the bedroom. "How was the first witness?"

"Quite informative and surprisingly ready to talk."

"She probably hopes you'll find her a job in television! What did she say?"

"That Patsy, the dead girl, had some kind of running feud with the gypsies. One of them does odd jobs around the village and it seems she caught him nicking something. Sharon wasn't too clear on the details."

"Sharon?" Tania raised her eyebrows.

"My informant. But the tie-up with the gypsies is interesting, wouldn't you say?"

"You reckon it was them what done her in, Guvnor?"

"Give me a chance! At least they're a common denominator, as is the stone circle. And I'm afraid you'll have to be a brave girl, because that will be our first port of call in the morning."

Anita Barlow looked up as someone came pushing through the swing-doors.

"Matthew! I didn't expect to see you this evening!"

"Why not? I usually drop in on a Saturday."

"But this weekend there's considerable competition. Haven't you heard who's staying at the Lakeside? None other than Mr and Mrs Jason Quinn!"

Matthew stopped abruptly and stared across at her. "You're sure?"

"Of course I'm sure! I was talking to Sally on the phone earlier."

"My God!" he said softly. "What's he doing up here?"

"Having a holiday, I should think, like everyone else."

But Matthew's mind had gone back to the note he had so unwisely sent some nine months previously. Could it have any connection with Jason Quinn's arrival? It hardly seemed likely that he would pay much attention to it, but perhaps Patsy's death had jogged his memory. There were a lot of sensation-seekers among the holiday crowds at the moment.

"Not seeing Madeleine tonight?" Anita asked, as he did not speak.

He pulled his mind back to the present. "She's gone home for the weekend."

"Where's Philip, then?"

"He said something about a game of golf with Dick Willoughby."

Anita made no comment. She and Eve had noticed over the last few months that the Selbys weren't as inseparable as before. Shrewdly she wondered if Madeleine were the reason behind it.

"I think if you don't mind," Matthew was saying, "I will desert you after all. I'd be most interested to see Jason Quinn in person."

"If you speak to him, be careful what you say. He has a mind like a rapier, that one."

Matthew smiled. "Relax, love. My mind's a match for anyone!"

The cocktail lounge was crowded. Jason and Tania, a

pleasant meal behind them, were relaxing at a table by the window with coffee and liqueurs.

"I don't believe," Jason commented, "that you've heard a single word I said."

"Sorry, darling. There's a gorgeous man at the bar who hasn't taken his eyes off me since he came in. It's a little distracting."

"You should be used to it by now."

"It depends who's doing the looking; this is the sexiest guy I've seen in a long while."

"Thank you, sweetheart. You're always so good for my morale." Jason turned his head, met the eyes of the man at the bar – strange eyes, browny-green, with a disconcertingly penetrating gaze – and turned back to Tania. "I dislike extremely good-looking men on principle. They're usually narcissistic."

"I was – my God! What's in this drink?"

Heads were turning all over the lounge as Philip Selby joined his brother. "Anita said I'd find you here. Have you sighted the quarry?"

"Over by the window. I think you might say we've made contact."

"His wife's a corker, isn't she?"

"A bit too obvious for my taste. She's been giving me the come-on."

"Has his lordship deigned to look round?"

"Twice. Once for you and once for me. She must have said something."

Philip reached for his glass. "I hope he won't poke his nose where it's not wanted."

"If he does, he'll get more than he bargains for. I think we should keep tabs on him for a while – see where he goes and who he approaches. If he's genuinely

154

only up on holiday it'll soon become obvious and we can relax."

"It was a damn nuisance about that girl," Philip said broodingly. "It's drawn attention to the village just when we could least afford it."

Matthew did not reply. He had never mentioned the note he'd sent Jason Quinn, but privately he felt that it was the lure of a Macbeth prophecy rather than recent headlines which accounted for his presence among them.

Philip drained his glass and put it down on the counter. "If you've finished your drink, let's go. I promised Anita we'd call back to report, and enjoyable though it is being ogled by the delectable Mrs Quinn, I don't want to risk antagonizing her husband."

Tania watched with regret as the two men left the room, became aware of her husband's sardonic eyes on her, and smiled unrepentantly. "Relax, lover. It's good for my image to indulge in a little long-distance flirting!"

"If that comment masquerades as apology, don't bother. I've been quite content watching the boats on the lake. It must be extremely peaceful here out of season."

"Or dull!"

"Poor love, you miss the bright lights already don't you, and we've been here only a few hours! Never mind, you know the value of personal appearances. There's a man over there who's been trying for some time to pluck up the courage to ask for your autograph. Shall we give him another few minutes or are you ready for bed?"

As she bent to retrieve her handbag the man in

question finally made his move, confounding both of them by approaching Jason instead of Tania, who had difficulty in concealing her annoyance.

"For my wife, Mr Quinn," the stranger murmured. "She always enjoys your programmes."

"Long may she do so," Jason said smoothly, scrawling his signature on the back of the proffered business card.

"The fool doesn't even know who I am!" Tania said under her breath.

"Never mind, *liebling*. It'll dawn on him one day, and then he'll regret the one that got away!"

But the incident had soured her mood and she prepared for bed in sulky silence which Jason, tired by the day's travelling, made no attempt to break down.

He was at the window in his dressing-gown when the morning tea arrived, and took the tray from the girl with his best smile.

"Tell me about the local school, Sharon. What age group does it cater for?"

"Only up to eleven, sir, then they go to Barrowick."

"I see. That's very interesting. Thank you."

"What's very interesting?" Tania enquired, levering herself up in bed as the girl left the room.

"The fact that there's no child over eleven there. Since I can't believe an eleven-year-old would have written that note, we're left with the interesting probability that it came from a member of staff. Which gives it added importance. I wonder how many there are."

"Ask Sharon!" said Tania nastily.

After a leisurely breakfast they set off to walk up to the stone circle. The early morning sunshine had disappeared and a wind was whipping up the water of the lake. Tania pointedly turned up the collar of her jacket.

"Which way do we go?"

"Up the High Street initially."

"It's not far, is it?"

"Not more than a couple of miles."

"A couple of *miles*? Jason, I'm not walking that far!"

"We've little choice if we're to see the stones. Look at that staircase up the outside of the cottage – and there's a little cobbled square through the archway. It really is a most attractive village. It'd be interesting to learn something of its history. I wonder if there's a local guide."

He turned into a stationer's shop, meeting the owner in the doorway. "We're just about to close, sir. Only open till eleven on Sundays."

"I shan't keep you a moment. Have you any information about the village?"

"There's an illustrated guide, yes, sir, with a street plan."

Jason emerged triumphant. "We might as well know what we're passing," he commented, flicking through the pages. "It seems some of these buildings date from the fifteenth century, but the place is Norse in origin."

"So are these pavements, by the look of them. I nearly twisted my ankle just now."

"Are those what you consider walking shoes?"

"They're the flattest I have. I didn't know we were going hiking!"

The sound of an organ reached them from the squat stone church. "We'll have a look in there tomorrow, when it's empty. I didn't realize this was such a fascinating place – it's quite a bonus."

Tania paused to get her breath, looking apprehensively up the steeply rising path ahead of her. "How long is this street?"

"According to the plan it goes up to the top of the village and loops round, turning itself into Upper Fell Lane and then Fell Lane on the way down the other side."

"But how far up do we turn off for the stones?"

"At the top. We're here now, by the church. I should think we've come about half way."

"And when we get to the top, how far do we have to walk to reach the Circle?"

"A spot of exercise will do you good!"

Since she was patently not interested, he made no further comments on the bow-fronted shops, the pillars and stone steps, the colour-washed houses with their grey slate roofs. She was obviously going to be a liability when it came to exploring the village, as he found himself increasingly eager to do. Damn the girl: if she was going to complain all the time, he'd be better without her. Pity he hadn't let her go straight to France.

This exasperated thought took him by surprise, implying as it did that her departure would cause him no heart-searchings. Nor, he realized with gratified surprise, would the knowledge that she was in the company of Derek Paterson. If he was prepared to put up with her sulks and silences, he was welcome to her.

At the top of the High Street and a few yards short of the Ancient Monument sign, the smell of fresh coffee stole out to greet them and Tania stopped thankfully outside a small café.

"Praise heaven!" she said devoutly. "If you're set on going on to the Circle, lover, you'll travel alone. I'll wait for you here over a cup of coffee."

"Fair enough. Can't say how long I'll be, though."

"If I'm sitting down, I shan't care! Leave me that guide to look at."

A few spots of rain were falling as he turned into the steep alleyway leading up the hill. He glanced apprehensively at the sky, but it was clear over to the east and probably the rain wouldn't amount to anything. In any event, he had no intention of being diverted from his goal now that he was almost within sight of it.

A group of tourists was just ahead of him, anoraked against the uncertainties of the weather, and when he reached the Circle there were several other people moving round between the stones. Was it the monument that interested them, he wondered uncharitably, or the recent death?

Because of the tourists he did not immediately attach importance to the two boys squatting at the base of a stone. Only as he strolled towards them and they glanced up, did he register the two identical faces and with a jolt concluded that he had come upon Ted's twins. He stopped and they eyed him uncertainly, seemingly wondering whether to make a run for it.

"Good morning," he said pleasantly. They nodded acknowledgment.

"Is it going to rain, do you think?"

"Nobbut a little," vouchsafed one.

"You live in Crowthorpe?"

"Aye." Caution returned.

"If I were you, I shouldn't play around here, after what happened to Patsy Lennard."

There was a flicker in the dark eyes but neither boy answered. Suddenly, one of them raised his head, frowning slightly, as though he were listening to something. When his eyes returned to Jason, they were frankly suspicious. There was obviously nothing to be gained here. With what he hoped was a casual nod, Jason moved away.

"He was quizzing the boys," Philip said tightly.

"But only about the murder," Eve protested. "Nothing unusual in that – all the visitors are talking about it. Let's not get paranoid. There's no reason to think he's interested in us. If you ask me, he's genuinely here on holiday. In two weeks he'll go home, and that will be that."

But there she was wrong. As the days passed, Jason became progressively more interested in the village for its own sake. The good weather had returned, and each morning he left Tania sunbathing by the hotel pool and set off to wander in and out of the mews courtyards, down the twisting alleyways with their overhead arches, and into the dark recesses of the old churches. It was all so picturesque, so steeped in history. And how much easier it would be to settle down to write here, rather than in the hurlyburly of London, where friends and business contacts frequently interrupted him with their invitations and telephone calls.

By the middle of the second week he had made up

his mind. There remained the task of informing Tania, and her reaction was much as he'd expected.

"*Stay* here? All summer? You don't imagine I'm going to bury myself up here indefinitely?"

"I'm not asking you to. You came for two weeks, as we agreed, and I shan't persuade you to stay if you don't want to. In any case I'm hoping to write, and as you know, I'm not much company then."

"But at least in London there are things for me to do and people to see."

"Well, go home, then. Françoise will look after you."

"I'm not staying there by myself! You know how I hate being alone."

"You'll be in France for at least some of the time," he reminded her.

"Is that what this is all about? To punish me for going to France?" She sounded close to tears. "What's the attraction of this place, anyway? You must have examined every nook and cranny already, judging by the time I've spent by myself."

"That was your choice. I'd have been happy to have you with me."

Her eyes narrowed. "You knew I wouldn't stay, didn't you? You don't want me to."

"Let's not make an issue of it, Tania. It's not as though we're used to living in each other's pockets."

She spun the wheel of her lighter, ignoring the flame he held out for her. "If I'm lonely, I might find someone else to keep me company."

"That's up to you."

She flung down her cigarette. "Damn it, you could at least pretend to mind!"

"Oh, I did at first – quite a lot, in fact, but I realized that I'd brought it on myself, by pressing you to marry me in the first place."

"Which you now regret?"

He looked at her beautiful, flushed face and wide, angry eyes. "It hasn't been a resounding success, has it?"

"Damn you, Jason!" Her voice shook.

"Still, we don't need to go into all that now. For the moment I'm just staying up here to write. That's reasonable, surely, and an acceptable explanation for my absence, if that's what's worrying you. You can come for weekends whenever you like. I'll make sure I find somewhere with enough room to entertain you."

"You won't be staying on here?"

"Hell, no. In any case, the room will be booked to the end of the season."

"Where will you go?"

"I'll have to make some enquiries, but I wanted to discuss it with you first."

"Discuss!" She gave a bitter laugh.

"Somewhere quiet, that's the main requirement."

"So you're really only staying on to write? You're not going to bother any more about Ted's story or that letter you received?"

"On the contrary, indeed I am. They could well form the nucleus of the plot, but I'll have to move slowly and win people's confidence before they'll talk to me." He stood up. "Now we're agreed on that, I'll see if the receptionist here has any suggestions."

"What kind of accommodation are you looking for, sir?"

162

"Somewhere I can be alone, but have meals provided. My wife won't be staying and I don't want to fend for myself."

"I really don't know what to suggest. There are only three hotels here and I know they're all fully booked. So, I should think, are most of the boarding houses."

"A boarding house isn't quite what I'm after."

"Perhaps Barrowick might be easier? It's bigger, and—"

"No," he said firmly, "it must be in Crowthorpe."

"Well, Mrs Staveley lets out the bungalow at the bottom of her garden, but that's on a self-catering basis. I suppose you could try her."

Mrs Staveley, when he called on her that afternoon, was plainly overwhelmed by his enquiry.

"Oh Mr Quinn, if only I'd known! It's let, I'm afraid, for the next fortnight. There's a gap then, though, because I had two cancellations, one after the other. Right in the middle of the season – it was quite a let-down."

"Which might perhaps be to my advantage?"

"Well, yes, if you could wait that long. Would you like to see it? I'd have to ask—"

"It's not necessary. Just tell me what the accommodation is."

"There's two bedrooms, a nice living-cum-dining-room, kitchen and bathroom. All electric and very comfortable, though I say it myself. We had it built ten years ago when my parents were too old to live at any distance from us, but they've both passed away now. It's well equipped, with a nice modern cooker—"

"Ah, I was just coming to that, Mrs Staveley. Would it be possible for you to provide an evening meal? I

163

can just about manage breakfast, and if I'm writing I don't stop for lunch anyway, but one good meal a day is essential."

"Surely, sir, your wife—"

"My wife won't be with me." He gave her one of his most charming smiles.

"Well, sir, I don't know. The whole point of self-catering accommodation—"

"Yes, I do understand and obviously the terms would have to be adjusted accordingly, but if it's really out of the question, I'm afraid the cottage would be no use to me."

"Well sir, if you put it like that—"

He waited hopefully.

"If it was just one meal a day, a single serving – yes, I don't see why not. And if you're alone, you'd need laundry services too – sheets and towels and the like. You don't want to be troubling yourself with launderettes."

Jason drew a deep breath, aware of victory. "That's extremely kind of you," he said.

When Jason left her to call on Mrs Staveley, Tania was unable to concentrate on her paperback. Their conversation replayed itself in her head, with ominous overtones, and she realized that some time during the course of it, their relationship had subtly altered. '*It hasn't been a resounding success,*' he had said.

She stared broodingly into the glinting water of the pool, its brilliant blue dimmed to browny yellow by her sunglasses. Until now, though she'd suspected he knew of her affairs, Jason had maintained a discreet silence. It seemed that all at once he had stopped pretending.

She gnawed on her lip, reviewing the situation. They had been together for nearly six years, and in the early days at least his contacts had been useful. Now, admittedly, she could stand on her own, but since succumbing to Jason's pressure to marry him, she'd come to regard an eminent husband as something of a status symbol and, to her annoyance, found she was reluctant to give him up. Also, on a practical level, she was by no means certain that Derek had marriage in mind.

She stood up suddenly, dropped her book on the sun-lounger and looked about her. All at once she was tired of the pool and the comatose brown bodies surrounding it, and, in search of something more interesting, set off across the gardens towards the gateway on Lake Road.

In the market place opposite, a coach had parked and its complement of tourists in shorts and open-neck shirts was spilling across the road towards her, making for the iron-topped tables in front of the Pavilion café. Their offspring meanwhile crowded round an adjacent ice cream kiosk, eager hands reaching up to the counter.

Tania hesitated. She had no destination in mind, but not wishing to be caught up in the crowd she turned off the footpath and made her way diagonally across the grass bank down to the lake. Queues were forming at the public jetty and she stood for a moment or two watching in amusement as the inept mariners scrambled in and out of their unaccustomed craft. Behind her, a voice said quietly, "Good afternoon."

She turned quickly and to her surprise recognized one of the men who had been in the bar their first evening.

"Good afternoon."

"I hope you're enjoying your holiday?"

She met his eyes, green-brown and oddly probing, and felt a tremor of excitement. "Not particularly."

"I'm sorry to hear that. Though we can't compete with the south of France, we're rather fond of our little village."

She shrugged. "It's pretty enough, I suppose. As to the south of France, that's precisely where I shall be in a couple of weeks." He inclined his head with a smile and she had the absurd notion that that was why he'd mentioned it. Except, of course, that he couldn't possibly have known.

"Have you been out on the lake?"

"Not yet."

"Like to try it? It's very pleasant drifting over the water on a hot afternoon." As she hesitated, he added, "Perhaps I should introduce myself. Philip Selby at your service. Doctor of that ilk, and most respectable, I assure you."

She smiled back, warmed by the obvious admiration in his eyes. "I don't doubt it. Is your brother a doctor too?"

"No, one in the family is sufficient. Matthew's a schoolmaster."

"Really?" That might interest Jason.

"So what do you say, Mrs Quinn? May I take you sailing?"

"I'm not sure my husband would approve."

"If he leaves you unattended, he has only himself to blame. What could possibly drag him away from you on an afternoon like this?"

It was no business of this stranger's what Jason was

doing, but to her surprise she found herself answering, "He's trying to arrange accommodation for the rest of the summer."

The change in her companion was startling. His head snapped up and the lazy flirtatiousness faded from his eyes.

"But – what about the south of France?"

"I said I'm going. Jason prefers to stay here. He's gone to see a place called Rowan Cottage, and if—"

"Rowan – my God! Are you telling me Jason Quinn is thinking of taking Rowan Cottage?"

"What if he is?"

Philip Selby took a deep breath. "Sorry. It's just that my brother and I have a flat in Rowan House."

"Oh?" She waited but he appeared to think this was sufficient explanation for his reaction. The intent eyes were still on her face, though he was trying to speak lightly.

"He must have a very good reason for staying here instead of going abroad with you."

"He wants to write," she said briefly. Dr Selby appeared more interested in Jason than herself. As though reading her thoughts, he smiled placatingly.

"Then he'll have plenty of time to sail if he wants to, but you won't. Please come with me. I think you'd enjoy it."

But his lapse had disturbed her and she was no longer willing to spend an hour or so in his company. That he'd envisaged a pleasant afternoon's dalliance was obvious. How had Jason described handsome men – narcissistic?

She snapped shut the case of her sunglasses with a little click. "I don't think so, thank you. I'm going back to the hotel for tea."

"Can't I persuade you to have it with me at the Pavilion?"

She shook her head. "Jason will be expecting me. Goodbye, Dr Selby."

He gave her a rueful bow and she walked away, leaving him looking after her thoughtfully.

That little exchange had proved useful, even if it had not turned out as he'd hoped.

Jason was indeed waiting for Tania, ready to report the success of his negotiations.

"All fixed," he told her. "I'll go back to London with you for a couple of weeks, then Rowan Cottage is mine."

"How long for?"

"She didn't say definitely. Five or six weeks, I gather. Perhaps longer. She's getting well paid for the privilege of having me, but it's worth it from my point of view."

"As it happens, I've some news for you, too. I met an admirer down by the lake."

"Oh?"

"One of the Greek gods who was here the first evening. His name is Dr Philip Selby and he was considerably put out to hear you're staying on, especially when I mentioned Rowan Cottage. He and his brother have a flat in the house."

"Is that so? I wonder why my plans should concern him."

"Furthermore," she added deliberately, "the brother, Matthew, is a schoolmaster."

"Here? At Crowthorpe?"

"I didn't ask, but I should think so."

"Well done, my love! What else did the handsome doctor have to say?"

"He did his best to persuade me to go out in a boat with him. I'm pretty sure he had designs on me, for all he insisted he was respectable."

"And you didn't go?"

"I don't oblige every man who asks me, Jason!"

"But the sexiest you've seen in so long?"

"Yes, well I changed my mind. I didn't particularly care for him at close quarters."

"His loss is of course my gain," Jason said gravely.

She looked at him sharply, but his face was inscrutable. "Suppose you stop making clever remarks and order some tea," she said.

Eleven

"You're going back?" Ted repeated incredulously over the phone. "When?"

"At the end of the month, when the cottage is vacant."

"What does Tania think about that?"

"Tania isn't coming."

"Ah-ha!"

"No cryptic comments, if you please. I liked the place enormously and an idea for a play developed while we were there. I shall be able to lock myself away, and apart from food at regular intervals there'll be no-one to disturb me. Added to which, since the play will be based in a similar location, all the local colour will be to hand. The arrangement couldn't be bettered."

"And what will your pretty wife do while you're away?"

"She's planning a holiday, which will fill in most of the time."

Ted thought it wise to change the subject. "I presume you went to see the Circle?"

"Not only that, I found your twins *in situ*."

"My God! You were taking a chance, weren't you? I trust they didn't put the influence on you?"

"No, but they weren't particularly forthcoming. Incidentally, they're not the only twins we came across."

"Oh yes, those two at the pub. It's unnerving, isn't it? Can't be good for business – you automatically think you've had too many!"

"What pub? What are you talking about?"

"The Crow's Nest. Isn't that what you meant? The landlord and his blind brother?"

"No, it isn't. Don't tell me there are *three* pairs. I find that hard to believe."

"I don't know about that, but the two I saw gave me the willies, especially the blind one. Mind you, I was edgy by then anyway, after my experience on the hill. I didn't see a third pair, though. Who were they?"

"A doctor and a schoolmaster. According to Tania, they were perturbed to hear I was going back."

"I wonder why." His voice sharpened. "A school master, did you say?"

"Precisely. Could be the sender of the note. I certainly intend to find out."

"Jason, be careful. There's something not quite right about that place."

"I dare say, but with due respect I don't go along with all that mind-bending rigmarole. If they're up to something, and they could well be, it's very much of this world, believe me. A drug ring, perhaps. If poor Patsy what's-her-name stumbled across it, it would be sufficient motive for murder."

"But what about my amnesia? You can say what you like, those gypsy boys were behind it."

"Oh come on Ted, you imagined it. All right, so you had amnesia. People do, from time to time."

"*I* don't," Ted retorted. "And those kids *were*

responsible; I'd swear to it. Look, mate, you're a substantial part of my meal ticket. I don't want anything to happen to you."

"Such concern! As it happens, it's your meal ticket I'm thinking about, in the shape of my next play."

"Don't force us to produce it posthumously, that's all!"

"My God, you are a ray of sunshine! You've been telling me to take it easy and relax, and when I try to do just that, and write a bit at the same time, you're full of the croak of doom. I'm perfectly capable of looking after myself, I assure you."

Ted was sufficiently anxious on Jason's behalf to try to enlist Penelope's help.

"You know what an obstinate devil he is," he told her. "I wish you'd have a go at him."

"My dear Ted, he won't take any notice of me. He never has."

"But you must know how to get through to him! Hell, you were married to him for ten years!"

"Being married to Jason," Penelope returned dryly, "simply means sharing his bed and his dining table. He doesn't allow you to know him any better than his television audiences do."

"Then you won't try to dissuade him?"

"I can't, and to be perfectly frank, I don't know why you're making so much fuss anyway."

Ted sighed and reluctantly changed the subject. "Are you going to the Lamberts' party? I can give you a lift if you like."

Had Jason needed convincing that he should get away

from London for a while, the Lamberts' party provided the final proof. Marcia Lambert was known as a celebrity-hunter, and everyone who was still in London in late June was invited to join in her frenetic pursuit of enjoyment. It was therefore inevitable that Derek Paterson should be among the guests. He and Tania had received glowing notices in the play they'd just finished, and Marcia was not one to withhold such an invitation out of consideration to another of her guests. Jason knew, tiredly, that under the laughter and brittle chat, curious eyes were watching the three of them. Deliberately therefore he sought out Derek's company.

"Hello, Jason." The younger man looked slightly apprehensive, as well he might. "I hear you're off to the Lakes again."

"And you to France."

"I – yes, that's right." He cleared his throat. "The grapevine has it you've a new play in the pipeline."

The grapevine no doubt being Tania, Jason reflected ironically. "I hope so, yes. I'm going native to give it a chance to burgeon."

"And Tania's deserting you, isn't she darling?" Lydia Marsh slid a long bare arm round his neck. "Any openings for a willing slave girl to attend the maestro?"

"I'm grateful for the offer but I already have one. Plain, over fifty and guaranteed not to distract me!" He bent his head and brushed his lips over Lydia's eager mouth. "If you were there, my sweet, I'd never put pen to paper!" Two, he thought, could play at that game.

He disentangled himself from her clinging arms, nodded to the rest of them and walked over to replenish his drink. Then, seeing the open window and the dark garden beyond, he went outside and stood leaning on the parapet accustoming his eyes to the darkness.

"Jason?"

"Pen. Come and join me."

"That was an uncharacteristic performance. It's not like you to indulge in flirting."

"Is that what it was? It just seemed the right dialogue for that particular scene."

"Lydia's all a-twitter and your wife is not best pleased."

"Won't hurt her to be on the receiving end for a change." He drank from his glass. "God, Pen, is it always like this or is tonight particularly bad?"

"The social whirl? I'd say this is pretty standard."

"Can you tell me why we put up with it?"

"I, because beneath all the froth they are real people in there and I happen to like them. You—" she shrugged. "Perhaps because despite your high-flown contempt, you enjoy being lionized as much as the next man." She paused. "Is all this soul-searching a result of having had a breath of God's clean country air?"

"Could be."

"You're determined to go back?"

"I can hardly wait."

"Ted's worried about you for some reason. He was telling me a fantastic story about twins and stone circles."

"The ingredients for my new play."

"But based on fact?"

"Based on Ted's flights of fancy, actually."

"You found nothing up there to substantiate them?"

"Obviously there *is* a stone circle and there *are* twins. It's his interpretation of them I don't accept. However, there might be some connection with the girl's death. Ted's afraid I could get myself knocked off and there'd be no more commission coming his way."

"That's hardly fair."

"No," he agreed, "I'm sorry. You'd love Crowthorpe, Pen, though I'm afraid poor Tania was bored out of her mind."

"Is this a private party, or can anyone join?"

"We were just talking about you, Ted. Pen's been adding her words of warning to yours – possibly at your instigation. I can't imagine what you're both so bothered about."

"Then I'll tell you. I don't care for the fact that you were originally invited up there by some nut in connection with that weird Macbeth phenomenon. Secondly, there is something peculiar about those gypsy boys, whatever you might think. Give me credit for being able to distinguish between what actually happened and what didn't. Thirdly, you yourself discovered a connection between the dead girl and some gypsies, and fourthly since your phone call I've been wondering if this concentration of twins could be significant. How's that to be going on with?"

"Circumstantial, the lot of it. I shan't take unnecessary risks, I promise, but don't expect me to tote round a clove of garlic or whatever, for protection against evil!"

"I shall be thankful," said Ted with feeling, "when this play is safely written and you're back here where you belong."

Jason was remembering his words a week later as he drove in pouring rain along the shores of Lake

Crowswater. Was he doing the right thing? he wondered belatedly. It almost certainly heralded the end of his marriage. Last night, he and Tania had made love for the first time in weeks, but it had been, he knew, a farewell performance. He was tinged with sadness by the thought, aware of impending loneliness. For all his aloofness he did not care for being alone. Acknowledging the fact, he recalled one of Pen's more penetrating assessments towards the end of their marriage: "You need a few acolytes around to bolster your ego, but don't try to tell me you give a damn who they are."

Perhaps, he reflected bitterly, he should have accepted Lydia's offer after all. Pushing such thoughts from his mind, he turned into Ash Street and drew up outside Rowan House.

"Ah, Mr Quinn! You've made good time." Mrs Staveley came out on to the porch, putting up a large umbrella.

"I was wondering about the car."

"Yes, I should have said. We haven't one ourselves, so there's room for yours in the garage. Have you much luggage? I'm afraid you can't get any nearer the cottage to unload it, but if you'd like to wait till the rain stops my husband will give you a hand."

"There's no need to trouble him, thank you, I haven't much. I'll put the car away now and unload it when the rain eases off a little."

The garage at the back of the house was amply big enough for his car to go alongside the small Peugeot already there. He retrieved his raincoat and brief-case and, sharing Mrs Staveley's large umbrella, set off with her across the soaking grass to the bungalow. A gate in the picket fence gave access from the main garden, and they walked round the bungalow to the front door. Jason saw that a gravel path led from it down to a small gate in the wall, giving him his own access to, presumably, Fell Lane.

"Here you are then," Mrs Staveley announced, opening the front door and stepping aside for him to go ahead of her. "Your bed's aired and I've put towels in the bathroom. There's milk and butter in the fridge, and tea, coffee and so on in the cupboard. That'll see to your breakfast for the first few days. After that you might like to do your own little bits of shopping, but if not let me know what you need and it can go on the bill at the end of the week. Now, what time would you like your evening meal brought over?"

"Would seven-thirty be all right, or is that too late for you?"

"Seven-thirty it is. Don't worry about me, the house is like a cafeteria at tea-time anyway, with everyone coming in at different times. My niece, Madeleine Peachey, will bring it across for you."

Jason raised an eyebrow. "Peachey? Sounds like a girl out of James Bond!"

A sound at the open front door made them turn.

"Oh, you're there, Madeleine. I was—"

"Sorry to interrupt but there's a phone call, Aunt Alice. Mrs Braithwaite, about the Mothers' Union."

"Right love, I'm just coming. I was telling Mr Quinn you'd bring his supper over."

The sherry-coloured eyes met his coolly. She hadn't appreciated his attempt at humour and he thought he understood why. For if she sounded like a Bond girl, she certainly did not look like one. Glamour was the last word to be applied to Miss Peachey. She wore no

177

make-up and her skin had a polished, sunburnt sheen to it. Her hair, long and straight and the same colour as her eyes, was caught back in the nape of her neck by an elastic band, and she was wearing grass-stained jeans and an old anorak which she'd pulled round her shoulders to run across the garden.

For a moment longer she held his gaze. Then, without the vestige of a smile, pulled the door to on her aunt's fussy departure. Jason was left staring at the polished wood with an oddly deflated feeling. It was not the most auspicious introduction to someone he would presumably be seeing daily. He resolved to try to remedy it when she brought his tray later. In the meantime, he must explore his domain.

The tiny hallway where he stood boasted five doors apart from the entrance. He opened them one after another. The one on the left led to the sitting-cum-dining-room, which was some fourteen feet long and took up the whole side of the house. There was a gasfire in the grate, adequate chairs, sofa, coffee table and television set. At the far end was a rather scarred dining table and four chairs and beside it a door which presumably led to the kitchen. The long wall of the room was taken up with a large picture window which looked across the streaming garden to the towering grey shape of Rowan House.

The kitchen was small, compact, and interested him not at all. He intended to use it as little as possible. The larger bedroom at the front of the house had been prepared for him and the bed was decently covered with a candlewick spread. Its window looked down the neat front path to the gate. The second bedroom proved too small and too dark to make into a comfortable study, but since he wouldn't be entertaining there was no reason why he shouldn't litter the sitting-room with his papers.

He went back to the kitchen and began to read through the typewritten notes left on the table for his guidance: meters, nearest public telephone, doctor's number. The name given, he noticed, was Sampson, not Selby: the senior partner, presumably. The rain was still coming down heavily. He filled the electric kettle and made himself a cup of tea, drinking it standing at the sitting-room window staring at the house across the garden. It was three storeys high and the enlarged attic window at the top was presumably the Selbys' flat. He thought he caught a flicker of movement up there, but it might just have been a reflection on the glass. Remembering Philip Selby's reaction to the news of his staying on, he wondered again why it should have disturbed him. One of his first tasks would be to acquaint himself with all three pairs of twins. After that, he could either eliminate them from his list of queries or make a more detailed investigation.

As the rain was at last beginning to ease off, he decided to unload the car, and he had just put the last empty box away when Madeleine Peachey returned with his supper. He saw her coming across the grass and went to open the front door. She nodded an acknowledgment and went past him to the kitchen, where she set the tray down on the table.

"It had better go in the oven for a minute or two to warm through."

He found her voice with its slightly flattened vowels oddly attractive after the clipped southern speech he was used to. It made her sound sensible, homely, dependable – though it was no proof that she was any of those things.

She was already moving towards the door and he said quickly, "I'm just about to pour myself a drink. Can I persuade you to join me?"

"Sorry, I'm going out. They're waiting for me."

"Another time, perhaps."

She gave him a brief smile which committed her to nothing and pulled the door shut. For the second time he was left staring at it feeling vaguely disappointed. He didn't seem to have recovered any lost ground.

"Has his lordship settled in?" Matthew asked caustically as Madeleine slid into the car beside him.

"It looks like it. He invited me to have a drink with him."

"And you turned him down, the great Jason Quinn? That must have been a novel experience for him!"

"How did he strike you?" Philip enquired from the back seat.

"Only slightly larger than life. He wasn't as highly coloured as I'd expected."

Philip smiled. "Perhaps you should have your television set adjusted!"

"I'd give a lot to know what he's doing here," Matthew commented.

"Hoping to write a new play, isn't he?"

"But why here? And without his wife, to Philip's disappointment!"

"A lot of writers go into retreat, I've heard. He has Aunt Alice eating out of his hand, anyway."

Matthew was silent. He couldn't explain the reasons

for his uneasiness, but he was far from satisfied as to the real reason for Jason Quinn's return.

The following morning Jason decided to go to church. There was, admittedly, an ulterior motive for his decision, since he reckoned that the vicar would know more than most people about the local inhabitants. Accordingly, not unaware of turning heads, he took his place in one of the old, highly polished pews just before ten thirty. He'd explored the little church during his previous visit, and as before its grey stone walls exuded a peace which had no place in the tempo of his own life. He let it flow soothingly over him, while his dramatist's eye revelled in the ritual and pageantry of the service.

When it was over, he delayed his departure to allow the rest of the congregation to disperse, reading the memorial slabs which lined the aisles until the vicar stood alone at the door. "Mr Quinn, isn't it? Welcome to Crowthorpe."

"Thank you. As a matter of fact, I was hoping to enlist your help. There are one or two local points I'd like some information about."

"Certainly. Perhaps if you have a moment you'd care to come back to the vicarage for a glass of sherry? I'm sure my wife would be delighted to meet you. My name's Braithwaite, by the way."

He led the way among the ancient sloping tombstones to a gate which opened on to the vicarage garden. "What in particular were you wanting to know?"

"Firstly, I'm interested in the Gemelly Circle. It's a curious name, that. Has it any particular significance?"

181

The vicar hesitated. "It's derived from the Celtic, of course. A number of theories have been put forward but nothing definite established."

Jason glanced at him curiously. He had the impression that the man was not telling him as much as he could, and wondered why. Braithwaite opened the front door and ushered him in.

"Eve!" he called. "Mr Quinn's come back for a sherry. Can you spare a moment?"

Mrs Braithwaite was an attractive woman in her early forties, with curly red hair and wide-set eyes. She smiled pleasantly enough and held out her hand, but again Jason thought he detected a faint reserve, as though she were on her guard. He was becoming fanciful, he told himself derisively.

"Mr Quinn is wanting some information, dear," the vicar was saying as he handed her a sherry, and this time there was no mistaking the quick, warning look she flashed him.

"About the stone circle principally," Jason enlarged smoothly, "and the death up there."

"Yes indeed, that was a shocking affair. In a village this size, the whole community is shaken by something of that nature."

"They're no nearer finding who was responsible?"

"Not as far as we know. The police have interviewed hundreds of people but at this time of the year Crowthorpe has a floating population. In all probability it was some stranger who was well away before the crime was even discovered."

"Perhaps." Jason rested his head against the back of the chair and studied the ceiling. "Personally, though, I'd have been more inclined to that view if it had

182

been a run-of-the-mill killing. Since it bordered on the ritualistic, it seems more likely to be someone local. Which is why I was wondering about the Circle, whether there are any legends attaching to it that might account for the more lurid features of the case."

The grandfather clock ticked for some seconds into the silence. He lowered his head to find Eve Braithwaite staring at him. Meeting his eyes, she gave a strained smile.

"Come now, Mr Quinn, surely you of all people don't give credence to old superstitions?"

"Not personally, no, but someone else might have. What *are* the superstitions, Mrs Braithwaite?"

"Nothing to account for poor Patsy's death, I can assure you."

Since skirting delicately round the subject had produced no result, Jason said baldly, "Her eyes were pecked out, weren't they? That was the word used by one of the witnesses – 'pecked'. Which obviously suggests birds – crows, perhaps, in view of the name of the village." He smiled slightly, but his smile wasn't answered. "So I wondered if there are any myths concerning the stones which are connected with crows?"

Douglas Braithwaite cleared his throat. "As it happens there are, but they're very far-fetched. In Celtic times, one of the cults in the area was that of a Crow goddess, who was supposed to live at the bottom of the lake."

"Ah! And she ventured as far as the Circle?"

Before he could reply, there was the sound of a door opening and a voice called, "Eve? Are you there?"

Eve Braithwaite jumped out of her chair and ran to the door, but she was fractionally too late. As she reached it, it was pushed open and her twin sister came into the room.

Jason's hand tightened convulsively round his glass. Thank God he hadn't got on to his question about the twins. He rose slowly to his feet.

"My sister, Anita Barlow," Eve said woodenly.

"How do you do?"

The newcomer took his hand eagerly. Her face was flushed and there was a feverish glint in her eye. "This is a surprise. I knew you'd arrived, but I didn't expect to see you here."

"Mr and Mrs Braithwaite were telling me about your stone circle. Did the Crow goddess ever visit it?"

"Oh yes." Eve put out a warning hand, but Anita continued breathlessly, "She had a confrontation up there with a rival cult and turned them all to stone." Then she put a hand to her mouth and looked fearfully at the frozen faces of her sister and brother-in-law.

"She didn't by any chance peck their eyes out first?"

It was Eve Braithwaite who answered. "Not according to the legend." She paused and added tightly, "I'm sorry to disappoint you."

"Oh, but you haven't, Mrs Braithwaite. Far from it."

The vicar cleared his throat again. "Might I ask why you're interested in all this?"

"I'm thinking of writing a play around some standing stones, and I want to get the background right. Perhaps you can tell me—"

"Can I get you a drink, Anita," Eve broke in, "or are you in a hurry?"

Anita turned from Jason and her eyes met her sister's. "Oh – no, thank you, I mustn't stop. We're fully

184

booked for lunch today. I just wondered if you've finished with that book I lent you—"

Eve had taken her arm and was leading her out of the room. At the door Anita turned. "Goodbye, Mr Quinn, I hope we meet again."

Oh, we shall! Jason assured her silently as he smiled and bowed. "Mrs Barlow has a hotel?" he asked Douglas Braithwaite blandly.

"Yes, the Greystones, in Fell Lane."

"I must give it a try." He put his glass on the small table. "Talking of lunch, I hope I haven't delayed yours. Thank you so much for the sherry – and the information."

And for my own lunch, he thought, walking thoughtfully down the High Street, I'll try the Crow's Nest and see if I can run to earth Ted's second pair of twins. Perhaps, who knows, even more. There seemed to be no end to the duplication in Crowthorpe.

But had he not been told the landlord was a twin, there would have been no way of discovering the fact that day. The blind brother who had so disturbed Ted was not in evidence and the man behind the bar was too busy to pay any attention to his distinguished customer. Damn it, who could he ask about the twins? Not the vicar, evidently. Was his reluctance to speak of the legend anything to do with the fact that his wife was one?

Jason gave himself a mental shake. He was becoming infected by Ted's imaginings. There was nothing sinister in twins as such. But four identical pairs, all living in a village the size of Crowthorpe?

Eve said, "He came straight to the point. The girl's eyes

185

had been pecked out: could it have been a crow? I was terrified Douglas might say something. I flashed him a warning, but God, Anita, it was you I should have worried about! I thought you were going to blurt out the whole thing!"

Anita's hands twisted in her lap. "Of course I wasn't, and I didn't appreciate being bundled out like that. Anyway, Jason Quinn's charming. I know none of you like him, but I do – I always have. He's attractive and intelligent, and since he completely discounts anything supernatural, I don't see what you're all so worried about."

"He's obviously up to something," Matthew said slowly. "Don't forget he was quizzing the Smiths last time he was here."

"We didn't tell him nowt," Davy said sulkily. He turned to Philip. "He can't hurt us, can he? We only wanted to make Patsy forget, like that man. It was Granny and the crow that killed her, to teach us not to meddle, she said."

"But if you hadn't made her unconscious," Tom Hardacre answered sternly, "the bird wouldn't have attacked, Granny or no. You're partly to blame and don't you forget it."

Philip rubbed his hand across his eyes, trying to close his mind to the memory of the girl's body. All his medical experience could not dull the horror of that mutilation, knowing as he did that it had been caused by a viciously stabbing beak. And it had all been so pointless; just an old woman's revenge on the two grandsons she feared and hated.

"The cops came to see Uncle Buck again," Kim said, hoping to deflect attention from himself and his brother. "They'd heard Patsy 'ad caught him nicking lead off that roof. He were all right, though, because he'd taken Benjie fishing that evening and folks had seen him over at Scarthwaite."

Anita stood up agitatedly. "What are we waiting for?" she demanded. "That's what I don't understand! We have sufficient power, God knows! Why can't we go ahead and reclaim the stones?"

"Nay, lass," said blind Fred gently, "don't take on. We must bide our time till we get the word. It'll come, never fear."

"In any case," Matthew added, "we have to wait till Claire and Nicola come home at the end of the month and we're at full strength. After that, Jason Quinn can interfere as much as he likes, and much good may it do him!"

Twelve

That evening when Madeleine brought his tray, Jason said abruptly, "How many pairs of twins are there in Crowthorpe?"

The cutlery rattled slightly on the tin tray as she put it down. "Five," she answered, bending to put the plate in the oven.

"*Five?* Ye gods! Who have I missed?"

"Claire and Nicola Marshall, I should think. They're away at boarding school." She made a move towards the door but he leant against the frame, deliberately blocking her way.

"Doesn't it strike you as unusual, to say the least, that there should be so many in such a small area? Identical twins are not all that common, after all."

"There've always been twins at Crowthorpe."

Jason frowned. "How do you mean?"

"All through history. My aunt told me. She was born here and knows all the old stories about the Twin Bear gods and so on."

"*Twin* Bear gods?" The "rival cult" that Mrs Barlow had been so vague about?

"That's why it's called the Gemelly Circle, from the Celtic word for 'twins'. Now, if you'll let me pass—"

"Is that so?" And it was the vicar who had neglected

188

to mention that. "Do they have much contact with each other, all these twins of yours?"

She returned his gaze, her eyes hostile. "You ask a lot of questions, Mr Quinn."

"And you're damned if you're going to answer any more?" He smiled wryly. "You know, far from being 'Peachey', you're more like a prickly pear! You dislike me, don't you?"

Her head lifted. "Does it matter?"

"I'm interested to know why, since it was obvious even at our first meeting."

"That wasn't the first time I'd seen you."

"Prejudged by television? It seems a trifle harsh. And I don't improve on acquaintance?"

She smiled very slightly. "I'll let you know. Now if you'll excuse me, my supper's waiting."

Damn him! she thought as she hurried back across the garden. How dared he cross-examine her in that slow, beautiful voice of his? She shouldn't have allowed herself to be drawn into conversation at all, but it had been solely for the pleasure of hearing him speak. Accustomed to the flat northern dialect, a southern accent had always attracted her, even as a child when her friends had mocked what they considered the la-di-da voices of radio announcers. Jason Quinn might be a playwright but he had an actor's voice, capable she felt sure of doing full justice to any of the world's great love poems.

Love poems? She pulled herself up sharply as she reached her aunt's dining-room. What could that arrogant, self-centred man know of love?

"Why have you gone red?" Deidre enquired with interest, as she took her place at the supper table.

"Don't ask stupid questions!" Madeleine snapped, and ignored the expressively raised eyebrows of her uncle and aunt.

Strange how he'd immediately attached importance to the twins, though. As it happened, she had indeed noticed, over the last year or so, how often they sought each other out. It had made her vaguely uneasy, for what, other than their basic twinness, could the little gypsy boys, for instance, have in common with the old men at the Crow's Nest? She felt instinctively that there was something unhealthy in the relationship, but there'd been nobody to discuss it with, for the twins' influence was wide. Between them, they effectively blocked off confiding in the vicar, the doctor, the headmaster, the "squire"—

She frowned, realizing for the first time the stronghold they had established for themselves. If they'd been planning a takeover, they could not have been more strategically placed.

Swallowing her supper without knowing what she was eating, her thoughts turned reluctantly to the Selbys. They'd changed in the three years she'd known them. There were times, ridiculous though it seemed, when they actually frightened her – like the conversation she'd recently had with Matthew. They'd been discussing a child in her class who had resisted all attempts to teach her and was now, at the age of seven, still unable to read.

"Silly little fool!" he'd exclaimed. "I'd have forced her to learn!"

She had smiled at his vehemence. "Do you mind telling me how?"

"By willpower, of course. Since she isn't capable

of deciding what's good for her, the decision should be taken out of her hands. Believe me, that doesn't apply only to children. Life would run much more smoothly if people could be gently steered in the right direction."

"You sound like a mad professor!" she'd said with an uneasy laugh.

"Not at all, it's just a question of mind control. If you could regulate how people behaved, you'd have an ideal world!"

"Of robots!" She couldn't believe he was serious, but he'd frowned anxiously.

"It wouldn't be wrong, though, if it was for their own good."

"Of *course* it would be wrong, Matthew! Who's to decide what's good for another human being? If you blot out people's free will, what have they left? It's – manipulation, totally and completely unacceptable!"

He'd looked at her for a moment, all the enthusiasm draining out of his face. "You're right, of course. Don't they say all power corrupts? Perhaps they have a point."

Nor was their strangeness the only trouble she was having with the Selbys. Over the last months she'd become unhappily aware that Philip's feelings for her were deepening and she didn't know how to deal with the situation. She was fond of them both but it went no deeper than that and it never would. She'd tried to make that clear to Matthew years ago; now it seemed she would shortly have to convince Philip of the same fact.

She was washing up the supper dishes, still busy with her thoughts, when there was a tap at the back door.

Drying her hands on her apron she went to open it and was startled to find Jason with the tray.

"I was going out so I brought it back to save you having to collect it."

"Thank you." She reached for the tray but he didn't immediately release it.

"After all, it's a little hard having to wait on someone you so obviously disapprove of."

She felt the colour in her cheeks again. "I'm sorry if I was rude."

"Not rude, merely direct. It was a refreshing change."

She took the tray from him and put it on the table. "Thanks for bringing it over."

"And now go, and let you get on with your work?"

She looked up defiantly. "You're putting words into my mouth."

"They were already in your head."

"If you'll excuse me, then." She turned back to the sink, acutely conscious of him still standing in the doorway. Should she ask him in? It seemed pointless when he'd said he was on his way out.

"Might I be allowed one more question?"

She continued rubbing vigorously at the dirty plates. "About the twins?"

"No, the school this time."

Surprise made her turn. "The school?"

"Do you know anything about it?"

"I should, since I teach there."

She saw that she'd surprised him in his turn. "You teach at Crowthorpe School? That's a stroke of luck. You've saved me the trouble of seeking out Matthew Selby. He's there as well, I believe?"

So he hadn't dismissed the twins after all. "He is."
She waited, leaning against the sink and watching him
curiously.

"How many members of staff are there?"

"Five, including the headmaster."

Jason felt he could discount the headmaster at
this stage. He was unlikely to be the anonymous
correspondent. "Would you tell me who they are?"

"If you'll first tell me why you want to know."

He hesitated. "I suppose that's fair. I think one of
them wrote to me a few months ago."

"You think?"

"The note was unsigned." He looked at her with
sudden interest. "It wasn't you, by any chance?"

"It most certainly was not! I've better things to do
with my time!"

His mouth quirked. "I rather thought you might
have. But if you'd give me the names of your colleagues I should be most grateful and then I'll leave
you in peace."

"Matthew you know about. He teaches the top year.
Then there's Steve Ellis who takes Form Three, I take
the Seconds and Liz Davey the Firsts."

He had jotted down the names on the back of
a cigarette pack as she spoke. "Thanks. Who else
has access to the building, other than the children?
Presumably there are cleaners, a caretaker?"

She frowned. "This seems an awful lot of fuss
about a letter. Are you sure that's all you're interested in?"

"I want to find out who wrote to me. Surely you
can understand that?"

"What was it about, then?"

"It's better that I keep that to myself for the moment. One more favour, though; I'd be grateful if you didn't mention the letter to any of your colleagues."

"You don't want them put on their guard?"

"Quite so."

"But if they wrote to you and you came—" She broke off. "*Is* that why you came here? Because of an anonymous letter?"

"Only partly. It's a little involved."

"You're not writing a play at all? That was just a cover?"

"Most certainly I'm writing, or shall be, when the research is complete."

"Research on the twins and the school?"

"Among other things. Now, I've taken up enough of your time. Good night."

At last he was gone, but he'd left her with a lot to think about. When she finally turned back to the sink the water was quite cold.

Jason had decided to call at the Lakeside Hotel that evening. He would have liked to see the chambermaid Sharon again but wasn't sure how that could be achieved. He could hardly ask for her, nor, as a non-resident, would it be possible to prowl along the upper corridors where she was most likely to be found. As a preliminary measure he went first to the cocktail lounge where, last month, he and Tania had seen their first Crowthorpe twins.

He settled himself at a small window table and took out his note pad. It was time he started to be more methodical about his enquiries and he began to list the points which interested him in the order in which they had come to his attention.

Firstly, the mysterious letter. He copied out the names Madeleine had given him, putting a cross beside her own. He had no proof that she'd not lied to him but there was a directness about Madeleine Peachey which made it seem unlikely. Which left Selby, Ellis and Miss Davey.

However, the problem could be approached from another angle. Who had issued the Macbeth prophecy in the first place? The obvious assumption would be a fortune-teller and since the youngest set of twins were gypsies, there would be more of them about. Which conveniently led him to the second point of interest: Ted's alleged experience on the hill. Why, if indeed he hadn't dreamt it, should two seven-year-old boys cut the throat of a sheep and drain away its blood?

"Good evening."

He looked up, startled, to find a tall, grey-haired man standing at his table.

"Forgive me for intruding, but it is Mr Quinn isn't it?"

Not another damned autograph hunter! "It is."

"I'm Geoffrey Marshall." He glanced down at the note pad on the table. "Forgive my curiosity, but are you really here to write, or is it something else that interests you?"

Jason leant back in his chair. "Perhaps you'd better sit down, Mr Marshall." The name sounded familiar but he couldn't quite place it.

"Thank you." He smiled suddenly and Jason saw that he was younger than he'd first thought: probably only a couple of years older than himself. "I thought you'd tell me to mind my own damn business!"

"I have a reputation for old-world charm."

"But you see, Mr Quinn, unlikely as it may seem, it could very well *be* my business."

Jason signalled to the waiter, aware of a flicker of interest. "What are you drinking, Mr Marshall?"

These priorities sorted out and a couple of glasses in front of them, Geoffrey Marshall went on: "I have twin daughters, you see. Does that mean anything to you?"

Of course – the pair who were at boarding school. "It very well might."

"Look, I know it's a bloody cheek approaching you in this way, but we're desperate, my wife and I. You've made quite a name for yourself debunking the so-called supernatural and exposing it as fraud. I hope to God you can do it this time."

"You think something supernatural is going on?"

"There's certainly something unusual and it's a threat to my daughters. The worry's made my wife quite ill. We thought they'd be safe if we sent them away to school but unfortunately that hasn't been the case."

"If it's as serious as that I'm surprised you haven't moved right away."

Geoffrey Marshall met his eyes. "It wouldn't do any good. It's not – physical presence that's important."

Jason stared at him and the other man smiled. "Yes, I know, I sound like a crank myself. That's why I need a sounding board. I might as well confess that I came here specifically hoping to see you. The second half of my mission is to ask you to dine with us at the earliest opportunity. Would you do that? It's impossible to go into everything here."

"I should be pleased to."

"How about tomorrow, or have you other plans?"

"Tomorrow would do admirably. I shall look forward to it."

Jason was thoughtful as he walked back up Fell Lane. Geoffrey Marshall had struck him as a sound, clear-headed businessman, not given to looking over his shoulder or listening for bumps in the night. Yet something had frightened him badly and it was something he didn't understand. It would be interesting to learn what it was.

The top window of Rowan House was a rectangle of light as he turned up the path to the cottage and the outline of a man stood silhouetted against it. Was it chance, or were the Selbys keeping note of his movements? As he closed the front door behind him, Jason reflected that his first full day back in Crowthorpe could not be considered unfruitful.

Waking the next morning to lashing rain, Jason wondered how best to occupy the day. Madeleine and Matthew would shortly be leaving for school, Philip no doubt for the surgery. Might Mrs Staveley, with her knowledge of "the old stories" be of any help to him? He had an excuse for going over, since he must tell her he would be out for dinner; which also meant foregoing his daily sparring match with Madeleine. A pity; he quite enjoyed their confrontations.

He bathed and dressed leisurely and carried the newspaper to the kitchen where he partook of slightly burned toast and instant coffee. But London news might have been from another planet for all the interest it held for him. He turned to the arts page. *Clouded Crystal* was still playing to full houses. There was a boxed advertisement for it: "Third Phenomenal Year". He thought back to the week it opened when he had taken part in that TV programme with the American professor. But for that chance appearance his unknown correspondent would never have contacted him, nor in all probability would he himself have come to Crowthorpe.

He rinsed his coffee cup under the tap and left it on the sink to drain. It would be as well to go over to Rowan House straight away, before Mrs Staveley embarked on any preparations for his evening meal. He pulled on his raincoat, turned up the collar, and went over the perpetually wet grass to the house.

"Come in, Mr Quinn. I'm just making some coffee. Would you like a cup?"

The smell of the freshly ground beans expunged the memory of the tepid liquid he had just consumed. And how better to involve her in conversation? "I'd love one, Mrs Staveley."

He hung his dripping raincoat on the back of the door and sat down at the table. "I really came to tell you I shan't need feeding tonight. Mr and Mrs Marshall have invited me for dinner."

"At the Grange? That'll be nice." She poured the steaming coffee into a mug and put it in front of him.

"No milk or sugar, thanks. I believe their daughters are away at boarding school."

"That's right; have been for some time now, but they were never at the local school. Went to St Margaret's in Barrowick. Not that they're Catholics, mind. Their father's our church warden. Pretty girls. Must be about sixteen now, just a bit older than our Deidre."

"Your niece was telling me there's a long history of twins in Crowthorpe."

"Yes, we've had them since way back. They haven't always behaved themselves, either, not by a long chalk. Burnings at the stake, court cases, running off with other people's wives. There's usually some kind of trouble attached to them."

"And this time it might be murder?"

She looked startled. "Oh, now I wouldn't say that, Mr Quinn. That wasn't what I was getting at at all. Far more likely to be one of those gypsies if you ask me. There's a permanent camp on the hill, more's the pity. The women come round selling clothes pegs and wheedling money out of you to tell your fortune. I don't like it but I'm afraid something might happen if I refuse them."

Jason took a sip of coffee and burned his tongue. "They tell fortunes, do they?"

"Well, you'd expect it, wouldn't you? What I say, though, is they shouldn't come round the houses touting for business. I've no objection to the tent at the fair. It's up to you then whether you go in or not. Mind you, who would, in their right mind, beats me! That Janetta Lee'll tell you anything."

"You mean she's not a very good fortune-teller?"

"She's not a very good anything, if you ask me! Married to Jem, but it's common knowledge the three little girls were fathered by Luke Smith. Pretty, mind you. That I will say, with her bold black eyes and come-hither looks."

Out of this spate Jason selected the fact that most interested him.

"And who is Luke Smith?"

"Her brother-in-law, Nell's husband and father of the twins. They're in Madeleine's class at school, though she was saying this morning they haven't turned up for some time now and their brother and sister aren't saying anything."

"There must be quite a colony up there."

"Only three caravans but it's enough, what with Granny Lee and that ugly great bird."

"Bird?" Jason repeated, more sharply than he'd intended.

"Enormous great crow it is. Goes everywhere with her, humped up on her shoulder. I've even seen her take it out in a boat, though why she wants to go rowing up and down at her age, I couldn't say."

The Crow goddess lives at the bottom of the lake, said a voice in Jason's head, and he almost laughed aloud at the absurdity of it.

"Anyway, the police have told her to keep it chained up," Mrs Staveley was continuing. "They think it might have killed the Lennard girl, and if so it'll have to be destroyed." She shuddered. "I wouldn't like to be the one to tell Granny that."

She drained her mug of coffee and, pushing back her chair, started moving round the kitchen collecting her basket and shopping list. Jason realized the conversation had come to an end. He couldn't ignore the hint, but there was so much more he wanted to ask, and each question resulted in a wealth of additional information.

"Well, I mustn't hold you up," he said reluctantly. "Thanks very much for the coffee."

The rain showed no signs of stopping, and he spent the rest of the day typing such information about the village and its occupants as he had so far managed to glean. With luck, the evening should add considerably to that knowledge.

Crowthorpe Grange, a small manor house in Lakeland stone, was approached by a long drive leading off the High Street. Geoffrey Marshall greeted him at the door and his wife came forward to be introduced. From the hopeful look in her eyes, Jason had the uncomfortable feeling that they were looking to him for deliverance of some kind.

The drawing-room was large and attractively furnished, with white walls and some interesting modern paintings displayed on them. On top of a piano stood a framed photograph of two girls and Jason went over to study it.

"Claire and Nicola," said his host quietly.

Jason glanced from him to his wife's tense face. "What exactly is worrying you?" he asked.

Slowly, hesitantly, it all came out, starting with the inexplicable visit of the little girls to the vicarage where the other twins were gathered, and the gradual development of the telepathic bond between them all.

Jason said quietly, "I believe Crowthorpe is noted for its twins. Have you any idea why?"

Geoff smiled, motioning him to a chair. "Rationally, no, I haven't, none at all. Irrationally – well, there's the legend of the Circle."

"The Bear Twins being turned to stone?"

"You're well informed! But it goes on to claim that one day, when there are sufficient twins around, they'll unite to overthrow the Crow goddess."

Jason moved incredulously. "You're surely not suggesting—"

"I'm suggesting nothing, merely repeating the legend. Nevertheless, there are a lot of twins at the moment and I'm sure they're building up to something. You probably won't accept this – I hope you don't – but they contact each other by means of the television."

After a moment Jason said, "When it's switched off, you mean?"

Geoff nodded and drained his glass. "If you can convince me it's all imagination, I'll be more than grateful!"

Jason looked at him consideringly. "I had a letter from Crowthorpe a few months ago."

Geoff looked blank. "A letter?"

"Inviting me to come here and see – something working itself out."

"Well, I'm damned. Who was it from?"

"It wasn't signed."

"You think it was referring to the legend?"

Jason said slowly, "That hadn't occurred to me, but it might have been."

"Well, all I can say is that if that letter brought you here, I'm grateful to whoever wrote it."

Felicity appeared at the door. "Dinner's ready, if you'd like to come through."

Conversation was determinedly light and inconsequential throughout the meal, but when the coffee had been served, Jason reverted to the subject uppermost in their minds. "Hasn't the old gypsy woman a pet crow?"

"She has. The locals swear she takes it out on the lake and they slip over the side of the boat and disappear under the water." He gave a brief laugh at Jason's expression. "It constantly amazes me, the hold that superstitions and old beliefs still have in out-of-the-way communities."

Jason smiled. "And I used to think the country was dull!" He turned to Felicity. "Was there any one thing in particular that made you decide to send the girls away?"

"It was really a combination of things," she answered slowly, "but we'd been having a very bad time with Nicola. A boy had been pestering her on the school bus and when he suddenly had a stroke of some kind, she seemed to imagine she was to blame. For months we couldn't do anything with her at all and I thought she was heading for a complete breakdown. When at last she began to pull round, it seemed wisest to get her right away."

"But you say it hasn't made much difference?"

The Marshalls exchanged glances. "No." It was Geoff who answered. "Jason, what I'm going to say now, I must ask you to swear not to repeat to anyone."

Jason raised an eyebrow. "If you say so."

"A few weeks ago we had a phone call from the girls. They were extremely upset and at first we couldn't understand what they were saying. Finally we established that they were clamouring to know who had died up by the Circle. We were totally bewildered, because at that stage we hadn't heard anything about it." He paused and added heavily, "Nor had anyone else. The body wasn't found till the next morning."

After a moment's silence, Jason said quietly, "What are you saying, Geoff? That it was an example of premonition?"

"Or their infernal telepathy."

"In which case some of the other twins must have been involved, or at least known about it. Did you tell the police?"

"Of course not. What kind of evidence would that have been?"

"Mrs Staveley is of the opinion that the gypsies had a hand in the death."

"If so, Davy and Kim would have known, and possibly our two registered some echo of their reactions."

"You believe it works as directly as that?"

"I'm convinced of it, God help me. Are you beginning to have some inkling of what we're up against?"

As he drove home, Jason was reviewing the extraordinary disclosures which had come to light during the evening, and it wasn't until he got out of the car that he noticed the Selbys' Peugeot parked in the shadows and the entwined figures inside it. He hesitated, but since it was too late to retrace his steps, continued towards the garage. As he put his key in the lock, a car door slammed behind him and footsteps went running round the side of the house.

All thoughts of the Marshalls suddenly erased from his mind, Jason carefully drove his car into the garage and, without glancing at the solitary figure in the other vehicle, set off across the garden towards the cottage.

Thirteen

Madeleine spent a sleepness night as the scene with Philip endlessly played itself over in her mind. Although she had been fearing such a development for some time, its actual occurrence took her by surprise, as did the force of his kisses. It seemed she had overestimated her ability to maintain a platonic friendship with the Selbys and her only option now was to spend considerably less time in their company. Having reached that decision, she was conscious of relief. Emotional tensions apart, she was no longer comfortable in their presence. She could not forget Matthew's wild talk of mind control, and an unacknowledged corner of her brain related this to the fact that the children in his class, whatever their previous school record, seemed to blossom almost miraculously into near-geniuses.

It was almost dawn before she allowed herself to wonder which in fact had upset her more; Philip's kisses or the fact that Jason Quinn had witnessed them.

The discovery that yet again the Smith twins were absent that day did little to improve her temper. "But where are they, Cora?" she demanded impatiently. "Do your parents realize they haven't been to school for two weeks now?"

"Don't know, miss." Apparently the answer served

for both halves of her question. Madeleine sighed and tried to anchor her thoughts to the water-table in the Thames valley.

She had not been looking forward to seeing Jason that evening, but contrarily, when he made no attempt at conversation, she prompted, "No catechism today?"

"No."

"You think you have all the answers?" There was more sarcasm in her tone than she'd intended and she saw his eyes narrow.

"Not at all," he answered evenly, "but I realize I might not be getting unbiased information."

Her face flamed. "If that's a reference to last night, you got completely the wrong impression."

"Indeed? It seemed pretty unequivocal to me."

"Which only shows how blinkered you can be!"

The door slammed behind her and Jason pursed his lips thoughtfully. As it happened, he had been considerably disturbed by the evidence of Madeleine's involvement with the Selbys. From his conversation at the Grange, all the Crowthorpe twins seemed suspect to some degree and though he still closed his mind to anything supernatural, the death on the hill was real enough and the Marshall girls had known about it.

While he ate his supper he pondered his next move. There was no immediate excuse for visiting the Selbys, and whichever of them had been with Madeleine the previous night no doubt resented his intrusion as strongly as she did. It seemed wise to allow some time to elapse before approaching them, and dismissing them from his thoughts, he reviewed the remaining twins. At their brief meeting, Anita

Barlow had struck him as the most likely to respond to tactful questioning, and he decided to visit the Greystones Hotel in the hope of being granted that opportunity.

She was behind the reception desk when he arrived, and again he was conscious of the feverish excitement in her. "Mr Quinn! Have you come for dinner? I can offer you—"

"No thank you, I've already eaten. I was hoping for the chance of a word with you, if you could spare the time."

"I should be delighted. If you'd like to go through that door on your right, I'll join you as soon as I can find someone to take over here."

The Barlows' private sitting-room was empty. Jason wondered where her husband was and if he'd approve of his wife being interrogated. It was possible that he knew nothing of her activities with the other twins.

"Since you've had dinner I've brought coffee and liqueurs."

"That's very kind. Thank you."

She set a silver tray on the coffee table and motioned him to take a seat opposite her. "Now, Mr Quinn, how can I help you?"

He took the cup and saucer she held out. "I think perhaps you know that I hold somewhat rigid views about – paranormal phenomena?"

"Yes indeed." Her eyes, a deep, luminous grey, were fixed on his expectantly.

"Since coming to Crowthorpe I've been bombarded on all sides by highly improbable stories of gods and goddesses, telepathy, presentiment and so on, which I conclude must be specifically designed as a blind for something else. I should be very interested to know what it is."

She smiled. "You dismiss it all that easily? Mr Quinn, it would be a privilege to broaden your mind for you!"

"In the sense you mean, I doubt if that's possible." He could feel her mounting excitement.

"Suppose I were to give a demonstration? Would that convince you?"

His interest quickened. "What kind of demonstration?"

"Telepathy, perhaps. One of the things you consider 'highly improbable'."

"You propose to read my mind?" Scepticism permeated his voice.

"Your subconscious, actually, since you'd raise mental barriers to any straightforward mind-reading." Her eyes, deep and mesmeric, were intent on his and despite himself he felt a flicker of unease. Such total conviction in her own ability was unnerving even if he didn't share it.

"You're not a happy man, Mr Quinn," she began. "Despite all your success, you're restless and unfulfilled. You pity yourself because both your marriages failed, but you didn't love either of your wives."

He moved protestingly at the past tense but she continued inexorably, "Your grandparents, who brought you up after your parents were killed, died within months of each other soon after you came down from Cambridge, and you married the first time because you were unsettled after their deaths and wanted to establish some roots."

She could have read most of that in a newspaper

profile, Jason told himself, though no journalist would have disposed of his marriages so summarily.

"She was a girl you'd known at university, who'd already made a name for herself in the literary field and therefore provided not only stability but a challenge. You had no intention of taking a back seat while she received all the plaudits, and you set out to prove you could do better."

Jason frowned, resenting this in-depth resumé. Though the facts she'd outlined were correct, their interpretation disturbed him. Was it true he'd married Pen to give himself roots? Though they'd been attracted to each other, he accepted he'd not been deeply in love. But that he'd used her as a spur for his own success, that accusation stung. Because, to his shame, there might well be a grain of truth in it, unacknowledged till now.

"But it was too easy, wasn't it? You achieved success with your first play, which was unfortunate for your marriage, because without the stimulus of competition you quickly became bored, and even the birth of your children didn't rouse you to much interest."

Jason moved uncomfortably. "I thought this was an exercise in telepathy, not psychoanalysis."

"Then," she continued as though he hadn't spoken, "Tania Partridge appeared on the scene, which sounded the death knell for your marriage. She was young, beautiful, talented. Everyone was talking about her, and she chose you, a man fourteen years her senior, as her lover. Heady stuff, Mr Quinn, but again, hardly a basis for marriage."

He said tightly, "Apart from the amateur psychology, you could have read most of that in the press."

She smiled. "If it's any comfort, your next marriage will be a very happy one."

"Now you *have* succumbed to fortune-telling." There was an edge to his voice that he didn't attempt to disguise. "As you're well aware, my wife and I are still together, so talk of a third marriage is to say the least uncalled for."

"You're annoyed with me and I'm sorry, but do you at least admit that I proved my point?"

He shrugged. "I wouldn't rule out inspired guess-work. What does interest me, though, is why you're so anxious to develop this faculty. What do you propose to do with it?"

She stared at him, pleasure at her success fading as for the first time she doubted the wisdom of it. "I was only showing you it's possible."

"But you've all taken trouble to augment it, haven't you? The gypsy boys, and the Marshalls—"

She stood up abruptly, smoothing down her skirt with hands that were shaking. "I don't know what you're talking about."

He rose to his feet. "It was only a thought. Thank you for the coffee and brandy, and also the demonstration. It was quite an eye-opener." And with a pleasant smile he left her trying to define his last remark.

Outside the hotel gateway he paused, wondering what to do. It was only nine o'clock and the empty cottage held no appeal for him. The character analysis had left him introspective and depressed. "Restless and unfulfilled," she had said – and she was right, though he hadn't fully realized it till now. He thought of Penelope with unaccustomed tenderness. His attitude having been what it was, their marriage was probably doomed from the start. Feeling the need to speak to her, he set off briskly down the hill in search of a public telephone.

"Penelope Quinn speaking."

He dropped his coins into the box. "Hello, Pen. It's good to hear you."

"Jason! Where are you?"

"Still in the wilds of Cumbria."

"Why are you phoning? There's nothing wrong, is there?"

"No, except that I'm at a loose end and rather lonely."

"Poor lamb! And there's there no-one nearer than London that you can talk to?"

Fleetingly he thought of Madeleine. "No," he said.

"How's the investigation going?"

"Slowly."

"If you're not getting anywhere, I should give up and come home."

"A few things are beginning to emerge but it's pretty complicated." He hesitated. "I suppose you wouldn't consider coming up to join me for a few days?"

He heard the amusement in her voice. "You're not by any chance propositioning me?"

"Only if you want to be propositioned! Bring the children as chaperones!" It had rankled, being told he'd no interest in his son and daughter.

"We couldn't come before the end of term – three weeks away."

"You can't manage a weekend?"

"Not really. Alexander's in the cricket XI as I told you, and he has matches most Saturdays."

"Forget it, then. It was just a thought. Pen, you are happy, aren't you?"

"My goodness, what is this? Pangs of conscience?"

"Perhaps."

"Then rest assured. I'm happy and so are the children. How about you?"

"Not particularly."

Her voice softened. "You're thinking about Tania?"

"No," he said truthfully, "I'm thinking about myself, as usual."

"Well, cheer up! Give me your number and I'll ring back in a day or two. I'm sure you'll be feeling better by then."

"Unfortunately I'm not on the phone, and I doubt if Mrs Staveley would appreciate trailing over to look for me." Nor, most assuredly, would Madeleine. "Forget it, Pen," he added. "I'm just feeling sorry for myself. It'll pass." With which assurance, for himself as much as for her, he put down the phone.

"Nell, I'm right bothered about owd Granny." Nan pushed a pile of dirty clothes off the rickety chair and sat down. "She's not been after them twins again, has she?"

Nell hooked a wisp of mousey hair behind her ear. "Not as I know of. They'd not tell me if she had."

"She keeps on about 'em all t'time, them and t'other lot in t'village. Talking to herself, like, whether anyone's there or not."

"Aye, well she has the sight and at times it worrits her."

"She's never been this bad. I could hear her when I woke in t'night, sitting on the steps of her van

212

chuntering away. Fair made me flesh creep. Yon dog's eating babby's rusk," she added, with no change in tone.

Nell glanced at the floor where her youngest child crawled, shadowed by the tail-wagging mongrel. She aimed one of her tattered slippers at the animal but hit the baby, which howled briefly.

"Jem says as she's started brewing her potions again," Nan continued when the noise had subsided. "Won't say what they are, neither, but they're not her usual mix, so tell t'lads not to drink owt she gives 'em."

"Nay, she durstn't harm 'em. Rants away at 'em, allus has done, but she kens Dr Selby has his eye on her."

"Happen you're right, but she's up to summat and no good will come of it, mark my words."

A clatter of feet on the steps heralded the return of Cora and Bobbie.

"Twins weren't at school again," Cora remarked, helping herself to a hunk of bread. "Teacher was cross."

"And what can I do about it? Takes me all me time feeding and clothing the five of you, wi'out worriting what you're up to every minute of the day."

"Janetta's feared for t'babbies," Nan said, returning to her original theme. "Yon pesky bird flew at little Rose yesterday and between 'em they set up a terrible racket." She stood up and stretched. "Eh well, I've worries enough of me own wi' Benjie." She glanced out of the dirty window, then back at Nell. "Luke's coming," she said briefly.

"Oh drat! If he's been drinking, I know what he'll be after."

"I'm going, anyroad. Mind you watch out for t'owd woman." She nodded to Luke, whose towering strength seemed to fill the caravan.

He stared after her. "What were that about t'owd woman?"

"She's at her muttering again."

"Nowt new i' that. Out!" he added to Cora and Bobbie. "Your mam and me have things to do."

"Oh Luke!" Nell whined, "I'm just getting tea!"

He jerked his head again and the children sullenly slouched down the steps, leaving the baby playing unconcernedly in the middle of the floor.

"What's me Mam and Dad doing in there?" Cora asked curiously as she and Bobbie squatted on the grass outside.

"Making more babies," he replied, whittling at a stick.

"But what do they want more babbies for? Mam cried when Sarah came."

He didn't answer and after a moment Cora said tentatively, "Where do twins go every day?"

"Dunno."

"I'm right glad I've got you, our Bobbie. Davy and Kim aren't like brothers at all."

Bobbie lifted his head suddenly, like an animal scenting the breeze. "Someone's coming," he announced. "Happen it'll be Miss Peachey."

Cora turned in time to see Madeleine emerge from the trees and they both sat watching with coal-black eyes as she came towards them.

"Hello, children. Are your Mum and Dad here?"

"Aye, but you can't go in," Cora piped. "They're—"

Bobbie dug her with his bony elbow. "If it's about

214

twins, Miss," he volunteered, "Mam don't know any more than us. They go off when we leave for school and come back after us."

"But they *must* come to school, Bobbie. It's not only I who say so, it's the education authorities. Your parents will get into trouble."

He shrugged. "Twins is different," he said, adding slyly, "Ask Mr Selby!"

Madeleine bit her lip. "I'll wait a little while and speak to your parents. They'll have to be warned about the position."

The caravan door swung open and Luke Smith came down the steps buckling his belt. Madeleine regarded him with interest. She'd never seen him at close quarters but there were plenty of tales about him. "Better be good or Luke Smith'll get you!" Crowthorpe mothers told their children, and once she'd heard her precocious cousin retort under her breath, "Happen I'd not mind, at that!" He was dirty, uncouth, no doubt illiterate, but beneath it all she could sense a basic animal attraction. His eyes moved over her and she lifted her head to withstand the scrutiny.

"Is yon school miss, Cora?" Then, directly to her, "What do you want wi' us?"

"Davy and Kim haven't been to school for two weeks, Mr Smith. Cora says they're not ill so I wondered if there was some other reason for their absence."

He scowled. "Never fear, Miss, I'll give them a hiding when they get back and they'll be there tomorrow."

She said quickly, "I don't think there's any need—"

"I'll be judge of that."

She hesitated but his steady gaze disconcerted her.

"Yes, of course. Thank you. Good afternoon, then."
She started to walk away from them and had covered
several yards before she realized she was heading for
the screen of trees rather than the more direct route
back to the village. However, Luke Smith was still
staring after her and she had no intention of retracing
her steps.

Once out of his sight, her footsteps slackened. This
route would take her past the stone circle and she
hadn't been up there since the murder. As far as she
could see there was no-one about, and despite herself
her heartbeat quickened. As if the murderer would still
be hanging round there! she chided herself; but as she
came level with the stones she couldn't prevent a quick
glance in their direction, and her eyes widened in sudden horror, for between two of them sprawled the body
of a man. She came to a halt, the blood hammering in
her ears. Oh God, not again! Panic beat at her. Should
she run for help or see first if he was still alive? The
attacker might be concealed behind the stones.

With dry mouth and racing heart she started moving towards them and as the figure came more fully
into view, horror suddenly became more personalized.
Jason? It was Jason!

Caution forgotten, she sped over the grass and dropped to her knees by the motionless form. He was lying
on his back, his head turned to one side, and a sluggish
stream of blood, dark and ugly, had caked on the bright
hair. She slid her hand under his sweater, feeling for his
heart. It was beating fairly strongly and the intensity of
her relief left her trembling.

"Jason?" she said softly. "Jason – are you all right?"
Ridiculous question in the circumstances. She laid a

hand on his brow and after a moment his eyelids flickered.

"Madeleine? What the hell—?" He tried to raise himself and winced, one hand going to his head. It came away sticky with blood and he stared at it uncomprehendingly.

"Can you sit up if I help you?"

Between them they managed to achieve a sitting position.

"How do you feel?"

"Decidedly groggy. What happened?"

"I don't know, I just found you lying here."

"My head hurts like hell."

"We'd better get you to a doctor. It's quite a way to the village, though."

"I'll manage, but I wish I could remember what happened."

Infinitely slowly and laboriously they made their way down the hillside.

"We'll go straight to the surgery," Madeleine said encouragingly. "It won't have started yet, but Dr Sampson'll be there."

"Not Philip Selby?" Jason asked through clenched teeth. The wound had opened up again and they had to keep stopping to staunch the blood with his handkerchief.

"Wednesday's his free day," she said briefly.

"Just as well. He might have finished me off."

She looked at him quickly. "I don't know what you mean by that. Philip's a wonderful doctor, everyone says so."

"Joke," said Jason succinctly as they turned into Caldbeck Rise.

*   *   *

217

"Looks as though you must have fallen against a sharp piece of stone," the doctor commented some minutes later. "There are minute chippings and dust in your hair."

"I'd hardly have slipped with sufficient force to knock myself out."

"It's possible to fall surprisingly heavily. Fortunately your hair was thick enough to prevent any serious damage. Take things easily for a day or so and you'll be as right as rain."

Madeleine was sitting anxiously in the waiting-room. "All right?"

"Marvellous!"

"Would you like me to ring for a taxi?"

"Having managed to get this far I think I should make it home."

At the front door of the cottage Madeleine hesitated. "Will you be all right now?"

"Could you make a cup of tea before you go? I'd prefer a stiff drink but since I've enough of a headache as it is, it probably wouldn't be wise. You'll join me, won't you?"

"It will have to be a quick one, I mustn't be long. I've quite a few compositions to read through."

"Not going out with the Selbys tonight?"

"If you're going to cross-examine me, you can make your own tea!"

He smiled and lowered himself gingerly into a chair. Madeleine put the kettle on and came back to stand in the doorway. "Have you remembered what happened?"

"I'm beginning to think I must have blacked out, though I never have before." The words brought unwelcome memories of Ted's experience and he hastily dismissed the connection. Yet vague sensations were beginning to come back and they were not reassuring. When he'd reached the Circle, he'd been aware of what could only be described as a feeling of animosity – which was patently absurd.

Obviously he must have been ill even then, without realizing it. All kinds of thoughts had started chasing through his head, needling, prodding, harassing – a veritable psychic bombardment. He had put out a hand to steady himself against one of the stones, and – yes, that was it! As he rested his palm on the rough surface he was suddenly hurled backwards with incredible force, for all the world as though he'd received a high-voltage shock. The next thing he remembered was Madeleine bending over him. It looked as though the doctor had been right after all.

She was watching his face. "Something's coming back, isn't it?"

"I think I must still be suffering from concussion."

She turned away as the kettle came to the boil, but as she brought through the tray she said, "Tell me."

"Have you ever heard any suggestion that there might be some kind of current in the stones?"

She looked at him quickly. "Yes, a lot of megalithic monuments have it. It's stronger at certain times of the year, I believe."

"Well it was certainly strong today."

"The *stones* knocked you out?"

"It seems so. I touched one and was flung violently backwards, presumably knocking my head on the corner of another."

"Matthew said once that it's possible to store power in the stones. I don't know what he meant." She frowned, connecting the idea for the first time with his later remarks.

"How close are you to the Selbys, Madeleine? No, don't fly off the handle again. I'm not being offensive, or at least I'm trying not to be, but I'm becoming increasingly interested in this twin syndrome and the more I see of it the less I like it." He met her eyes. "You told me yesterday to discount the – circumstantial evidence."

Her eyes fell. "Yes."

"So? How close are you?"

She said quietly, "Matthew's been in love with me for the last three years."

"And you?"

She shook her head.

"So it was Matthew the other evening?"

"No. That was part of the trouble."

He let that pass. "Have you ever noticed anything out of the ordinary about them?"

She spread her hands helplessly. "I feel so disloyal, discussing them like this."

"It's not just idle curiosity, I promise. Have they ever done anything to alarm you?"

"Not really. I was frightened one time, but there was a simple explanation. It was just a phobia."

"What happened?"

"Matthew and I were having a picnic and a crow came down to eat some ham we threw out. He was – terrified."

Jason stopped with his cup half way to his mouth. "What did he do?"

"Put his arms over his head and screamed."

"It must have been distressing for you, but phobias about birds are quite common."

"That's what was so strange, though. He's fine with most birds, it's only crows that petrify him. He said Philip's the same."

"Is he really?" Jason's voice was so soft she could hardly hear him.

She stood up. "I must go or I'll never get my work done. I'll bring your supper later."

He looked up at her and smiled. "I haven't thanked you yet for coming to the rescue. It must have been quite a temptation to leave me lying there!"

"Not really." She went quickly from the room.

There was a queer little ache inside her that she didn't want to analyze, but she knew his smile had caused it. It was the first genuine one he had given her, completely different from his usual sardonic mockery, and the effect it had had was as unexpected as it was unwelcome.

Fourteen

To his annoyance, the after-effects of Jason's accident lasted several days and he had to postpone his plans for seeking out in turn each individual set of twins. However his incapacity did serve its purpose, for on the Friday morning Douglas Braithwaite called to see him.

"I was so sorry to hear of your mishap. You tripped and fell, I believe?"

"No," Jason returned deliberately, "I was pushed!" And at the other man's startled surprise, he added flatly, "By one of the stones."

"Mr Quinn, you're the last person from whom I'd expect to hear a statement like that!"

"I'm not suggesting the megalith upped and hit me, Vicar, but there's a scientific basis, surely, for accepting that a force exists in some of these stones."

"And it was the shock that flung you backwards?"

"Precisely."

"Mr Quinn, you asked me before for help and I wasn't completely honest with you."

"Because of your wife?"

Douglas Braithwaite let his breath out in a sigh. "Exactly. I've been bending over backwards to protect her and closing my mind to a great deal I should have looked into long before this. Now I'm convinced the only way to help her is to come out into the open. What do you want to know?"

"Why there are so many twins in Crowthorpe and whether their presence can possibly have some connection with the Gemelly Circle." He stressed its name slightly, and the vicar smiled.

"Another point I concealed. I'm sorry. At the beginning of the century, you know, shepherds round here still used Celtic numerals to count their sheep. Think of it! Virtually unchanged for thousands of years! Now, alas, the Gemelly Circle is our last link with the Celtic language. But to answer your question, yes, I'm sure there's a connection between the twins and the stones, but it's of their own making, and that's what worries me. They're letting the legend prey on their minds to such an extent that they actually believe it will be fulfilled."

"And what would that involve?"

"Presumably releasing the spirits of the Bear Twins from the stones. Insane, isn't it? And quite frankly, this has been my greatest fear – that some basic instability in the twins might lead to madness. It happened with the Carters."

"With whom?"

"There's another set you mightn't have heard of, making six in all. Women in their sixties, in a mental home near Carnforth. I know for a fact that the Selbys visit them but I can't imagine why. There must be a strong reason for them to go to so much trouble." He glanced at Jason. "Do you remember a programme you once did in which Macbeth prophecies were discussed?"

"I do indeed."

"I have a feeling we might be dealing with one here. Eve told me once that the gypsy girl foretold limitless power for the Selbys, 'over life and death, body and soul'. You can imagine how I, as a minister, felt about that."

"Then it must have been Matthew!" Jason said with satisfaction, and told him about the letter. "I wonder why he wrote, though. An act of bravado or a cry for help? In any event he must have regretted it; he's made no move to approach me since I arrived." He looked at his visitor. "So now I know who wrote to me and what the prophecy was. The final, sixty-four thousand dollar question is, did it come true?"

Douglas Braithwaite sat forward, hands clasped between his knees.

"To a certain extent, yes. Matthew undoubtedly achieves the most phenomenal results with his pupils, to the point where there have been complaints from neighbouring villages about unfair competition."

"And Philip?"

"Philip really believes he has power over life and death, and the human brain being what it is, his patients believe it too. There was an instance only the other day. Old John Armitage was terminally ill and the hospital sent him home to die, warning his wife he could linger for months in increasing pain. She said to me quite openly, 'Well, Vicar, I couldn't let that happen, could I?' So she sent for Philip. He simply went into the old man's room, sat down by the bed and took his hand. John had been delirious for days, but after a minute or two he opened his eyes, looked straight at Philip and said clearly, 'Thanks, Doctor.' Then he died."

"Telepathic euthanasia. You think that's wrong?"

Douglas shrugged. "I can only be thankful for John's sake. Mind you, there've been occasions when Philip's powers haven't been used so sympathetically."

"But you'd say these powers are based on telepathy?"

"Mind control, brainwashing – call it what you will."

Jason hesitated. "We are still speaking of the Selbys?"

The other man ran a hand over his face. "No," he said in a low voice, "I think they all have it to some extent. They can communicate with each other whenever they want."

"You must forgive my ignorance on the subject. I still have the greatest difficulty believing it exists at all. Are you saying that one of them transmits a message and the others receive it?"

"Even that isn't necessary. They share the same psychic field and are automatically aware of the signals."

"My God!"

The vicar smiled tiredly. "It's hard to accept, but I went into it very fully when all this started. Telepathy's an established fact, though it usually works between only two people at a time. I did try to stop it, but with such total lack of success that I gave up the attempt. I hold myself very much to blame for that weakness."

"Yet even accepting all that – which I confess I can't – what's the purpose behind it? The Selbys might be gratifying their lust for power, but what do the others get out of it?"

"Whatever it is, it's taking its toll. Anita is becoming progressively more unstable and the Marshalls had a bad time with their girls a few years ago. If some kind of climax is imminent, it could have a devastating effect on all of them." He stood up. "I imagine I've given you some food for thought. I hope you can make something of it."

"Even if I can, what do you suggest I do about it?"

The vicar met his eyes. "That, of course, is entirely up to you."

When he had gone, Jason sat for a long time thinking over what he had said. A week ago he would have dismissed the whole thing as fantasy, but a week ago he was still safely in London, where folklore was buried more deeply beneath the surface than in this Lakeland village. And a week ago he had not been subjected to the barrage of sensations which had resulted in a visit to the doctor's surgery. There was a certain kind of justice in that he, who had always derided the supernatural, should have been brought so uncompromisingly face to face with it.

"How are you this morning, Mr Quinn?" It was Saturday, and Mrs Staveley had arrived to give the cottage its weekly turn-out.

"Much better, thank you."

"It was a nasty bang you had, Madeleine said." She hesitated. "I wonder if I could ask you a favour."

"Ask away, Mrs Staveley."

"We're having a social next Saturday at the church hall – the Mothers' Union, that is. I was wondering if you would mind presenting the prizes for us?"

"Well, I—"

"Everyone would be so thrilled. The judging will be done during the afternoon, and in the evening we're holding a wine and cheese party when the prizes will be awarded. It would be such an honour if you'd do it."

"Very well, Mrs Staveley, I'll present your prizes for you." And, cutting short her expressions of thanks, he made his escape.

"Madeleine – wait!" Matthew increased his pace, catching up with her on the corner of Broad Walk. "I was beginning to think you're avoiding me! You haven't waited for me after school all week."

"Sorry. There's been quite a lot going on."

"So I gather. I hear you found our eminent friend unconscious among the buttercups?"

"In a manner of speaking."

"What happened?"

"He apparently received some kind of shock from the stones. Matthew—" She glanced at him and surprised a gleam of intense excitement in his eyes. "You told me once that they store up power. What's it for?"

"Not Jason Quinn, as he discovered."

Something in his voice sent a chill through her. "But perhaps," she said very softly, "for you?"

He gave a breathless laugh. "Clever little Maddy!"

"If it's liable to knock you out, I can't think—"

"It wouldn't do that to me. I helped to build it up."

She stopped and stared at him, coldness spreading inside her. "You're trying to tell me it could distinguish between you? It would attack Jason and not you?"

"Exactly. The shock is only a deterrent, an anti-burglary device."

"But he wasn't trying to steal anything! He didn't even know it was there!"

"No, being Jason Quinn he wouldn't. Well, he does

now. Perhaps it showed him there are one or two things he doesn't know about after all."

The expression on her face belatedly penetrated his elation and he took her arm and drew her forward again. "But why are we wasting time talking about Quinn? You don't like him any better than I do! Let's go to the Crow's Nest for a pub lunch and you can ask Fred about the stones. He's the expert."

They found the saloon bar crammed with people. Matthew steered Madeleine to one end of the counter where Mabel was taking orders.

"Any chance of a bit of lunch?"

"They're queuing for the dining-room, love."

"We only want a snack. Ploughman's, or something like that."

"I'll see what I can do. Go out into the garden – there's more room there – and Sadie'll bring it. What do you want to drink?"

"A pint of bitter and half of lager. Thanks, Mabel. Where's Fred, by the way?"

"I think he went outside, too."

The pub garden was gay with coloured umbrellas and beneath one of them, deep in conversation, Fred was sitting with Jason Quinn.

"Damn!" Matthew said softly.

Jason had seen them and made some comment to the old man, who raised his hand. "Matthew? Come and join us, lad."

They had no choice but to go across. Jason rose and pulled out a chair for Madeleine. She didn't meet his eyes. No doubt he was wondering whether her rebuttal of closeness with the Selbys was as reliable as he'd hoped. Be that as it may, having settled himself again, it was at Matthew that he directed his attention.

"So we meet at last, Mr Selby. I've been wanting to thank you for your letter."

The two men's eyes locked for a long minute before Matthew said, "I'm afraid I don't understand."

Jason smiled; one of his mocking variety, Madeleine noted. "Just as you like. Can I get you both a drink?"

"We've ordered, thanks."

Fred said deliberately, "Mr Quinn here was asking about them stones."

"That's quite a coincidence. So was Madeleine."

The old man turned towards her. "What did you want to know, lass?"

"We were talking of Mr Quinn's accident," she said hesitantly. "It looks as though he received a shock from them, and Matthew seems to think it was deliberate; a personal attack." She paused, aware that she held the attention of all three men. "Surely, Mr Hardacre, that's impossible? How could an inanimate lump of rock distinguish one person from another?"

Fred said slowly, "Well, love, stones are made up of the same groups of atoms and molecules as the rest of us. Only a hundred years ago country folk believed they were alive, since every time they cleared their gardens of pebbles, another lot 'grew'. As for standing stones, they've had strange powers over the years and there's a lot about them we don't understand. If he'll forgive me saying so, Mr Quinn probably knows less than most, being as he's kept his mind closed to that kind of thing. Happen they wanted to teach him a lesson."

Matthew had suggested the same thing.

Jason leant forward. "Enlighten me, then. What powers have the stones had over the years?"

"Eh well, now you're asking! They've been used for healing, for cursing, and for fertility. Kings have been crowned on them, treaties sworn over them and bishops ordered to destroy them. Even today we're somehow drawn to them. Show me the boy or girl who hasn't at some time collected a handful of pebbles on the beach – though ask them why and they likely couldn't tell you." The old man sat placidly staring ahead with his sightless eyes.

After a moment Jason prompted; "And what about the energy they're supposed to store?"

"Well, sir, it could come from the earth, or even from the stars if the circles were built to read them. Or it might just be a build-up of human energy, from all those years of ritual dancing among the stones."

"And what is it to be used for? Can you tell me that?"

Fred turned his head slowly and Madeleine felt a superstitious shiver down her back.

"Aye, I can sir. It's to free the imprisoned and restore that which was stolen."

Sadie Perkins, plump, fair and cheerful, banged down the tray containing the ploughman's lunches and drinks Matthew had ordered. To the people sitting round the table her normality was an intrusion which violated the atmosphere they had unwittingly built around themselves. Since it was irretrievably dispelled, Jason stood up.

"I'll leave you to enjoy your lunch. Thank you, Mr Hardacre, that was fascinating. I'll treat stones with more respect in future."

"Supercilious bastard!" Matthew said softly, staring after him.

"Did I answer your questions too, lass?"

"Some of them."

"What else do you want to know?"

"When this – restoration is going to take place."

"That'd be telling, now, wouldn't it? It'll not be long, though, I promise you that. Not more than a month or so, possibly less."

"Really, Fred? As soon as that?" Matthew's voice was taut.

"Aye, I reckon we've waited long enough."

"*You've* waited?"

"Only a manner of speaking, miss. The whole village, like."

Madeleine's heart was thumping, her appetite gone. She wished Jason had stayed to hear that last piece of information. She needed his quizzical disbelief to counter the apprehension which was growing inside her. Matthew, on the other hand, merely added to it.

"By the way, Fred, Madeleine's been complaining about the Smith boys missing school."

"Oh aye? That were partly my fault, I'm afraid. There were things to be done and Tom's been right busy with all the holiday trade. So I borrowed them two to help out."

"Without their parents' knowledge?"

"Well, now, I've never known Luke and Nell bother about the lads one way or t'other."

"But they should have been at school, Mr Hardacre."

"Aye, well let's say I was educating them myself. They're young enough to come to no harm through a few missed lessons."

"What were you teaching them?" she asked curiously.

"Habits of birds, among other things. Crows in particular."

"Crows?"

"Aye, like yon black monster of their Granny's."

Matthew said tightly, "If it's all the same to you, Fred—"

"Sorry, lad, but she did ask. Anyroad, I've finished their training now."

And with that, sensing Matthew's discomfort, she had to be content.

During the days that followed, Jason worked steadily at the outline of the new play. Some of Fred Hardacre's remarks had given him a lead and his imaginary stone circle became impregnated with superstition and folklore which, characteristically, he intended systematically to demolish. The fact that Matthew Selby had denied writing to him did not surprise him, but Madeleine's appearance with him after their previous conversation had. She'd seemed ill at ease, though whether that was due to his own presence rather than Matthew's he could not be sure. Certainly the precarious friendship founded after his accident seemed to have dissolved and he found himself regretting this.

One evening, purely by chance, he ran into the little chambermaid, Sharon, down on Lake Road. She was more than willing to accompany him to the Pavilion for a coffee, while he plied her with further questions about Patsy Lennard.

To little avail. She appeared to have told him all she knew, and repeated what Mrs Staveley had said: that the police seemed to be coming round to the belief that the crow was the culprit and there was no murderer after all.

Jason received this view with scepticism. He was convinced there'd been human connivance behind the bird's attack, but he'd no grounds on which to base any accusation.

Finally he gave Sharon five pounds and she went happily on her way. Outside the café window, the grassy bank led down to the calm blue waters of the lake. He sat staring at it, his mind sifting through what he had learned and worrying at what he had not. Then, with a sigh of frustration, he pushed back his chair and went out into the darkening evening.

Saturday morning came round again, and with it a letter from Tania asking for a divorce. Jason read it through twice and tossed it into the waste basket. So, Mrs Barlow, your prediction was only a few days previous. His second marriage was about to follow his first down the road to failure. He was still brooding over the matter when Mrs Stavely arrived for her cleaning session, and only then did he remember his promise of the previous week to preside at the prize-giving that evening.

"The social starts at eight, but the prizes won't be presented till nine-thirty," she told him in reply to his questions. "If you'd like to come along with us—"

"It's kind of you, but I have some work to finish first. Will it be all right if I arrive just before nine-thirty?"

She looked disappointed. Obviously, regarding him as her own particular prize, she had hoped to show him off during the evening. "Well, if that's what you prefer—"

"I'll be there on time, I promise," he assured her, and wondered how soon he would be able to escape again.

A babble of voices met him as he pushed open the door of the hall that evening. The building had been the village school until the new one was built and the scuffed skirting boards and flaking paint told their own story. He walked down the corridor towards the double doors from behind which the sounds of revelry emanated. Mrs Staveley bore down on him with a cry of delight and her husband also came forward to shake his hand. Jason was relieved to find he was not, as he'd feared, the only male present. Among the sea of faces he recognized the vicar and his wife and the Marshalls and in the far corner caught a brief glimpse of Madeleine. No doubt she'd been coerced into attendance by her aunt.

He allowed himself to be led up to the platform and embarked on the speech they seemed to expect from him. One by one the worthy ladies came to receive their book tokens, boxes of chocolates and bathsalts from his hand. Then it was over and Geoff Marshall was waiting with a glass of wine to revive him. Jason stood chatting to him for several minutes before moving over to where he had last seen Madeleine. She had disappeared, but a curtain moving in the breeze gave a clue to her whereabouts and lifting it aside, he found an open door leading to the old school playground. It was almost dark with the moon hidden behind banks of cloud, but the cool breeze was welcome after the stifling heat inside the hall. As his eyes grew accustomed to the darkness, he could make out a figure on a wooden bench at the far end of the playground. He walked over to join her.

"Had enough?"

"I'm afraid so. I've a vicious headache and the heat and noise in there didn't help at all."

"Matthew not in attendance?"

"Can you imagine him at the Mothers' Union?" She paused and added heavily, "I know you don't believe me, but I really am trying to phase out seeing him. After three years, it isn't easy." She glanced sideways at him. "I gather you've decided it was he who wrote that letter?"

"It has to be."

"And you still won't tell me what it said?"

"'Come to Crowthorpe and watch a Macbeth prophecy coming to pass.' Words to that effect."

She looked at him in surprise. "A Macbeth prophecy? You discussed that once on TV, didn't you, but I can't remember what it was."

"One that fulfills itself."

"And Matthew thinks we have one here?"

"It would seem so."

She shook her head in bewilderment, then winced and pressed her fingers to her temples.

"Head still bad?"

"It'll be all right. You'd better go back to your admirers."

"Among whom you obviously don't number yourself! Am I being dismissed?"

"Excused would be a better word."

"Actually I prefer it out here, even though this bench is somewhat lacking in comfort. Try closing your eyes and leaning against me – it might help."

"No, really—" But he had already put an arm round her and it seemed wiser not to make an issue of it. Certainly it was a relief to close her eyes. After a moment she said, "Incidentally, when Matthew and I were talking about your accident, he claimed he'd helped to build up that power in the stones."

Jason's hand moved fractionally against her shoulder. "Having been knocked senseless, I can hardly deny there's some sort of energy there, but if Matthew Selby considers himself responsible for it, I'd say he's more dangerous than the stones. I'm only sorry I can't seem to convince you of the fact."

"After you'd gone the other day, Mr Hardacre was saying everything would come to a head within a month or so."

"He's quite a character, that old man. I can't imagine how he's managed to amass so much knowledge on such an erudite subject."

Madeleine said slowly, "I don't think he 'amassed' it. I'd say it's something he just knows instinctively."

Jason snorted. "You're starting to talk like they do! The trouble is that under all this airy-fairy nonsense there's a more concrete danger. Matthew can talk till he's blue in the face about personalized attacks by inanimate objects, but the fact remains that a girl died up there, and it wasn't the stones that killed her."

She raised her head quickly. "It wasn't Matthew, either!"

"Maybe not, but I'm damn sure he knows who did."

She stared at him wide-eyed, trying to read his expression through the uncertain light, and he felt a shaft of fear for her. She was so appallingly vulnerable.

He said urgently, "Madeleine, you must stop seeing

them – all of them. Don't you realize the danger you're in? If you found out too much, or if they only thought you had—"

"Too much about what?" she whispered.

"Hell, I don't know! Whatever it is they've got going at that infernal Circle. You could get drawn into it before you knew what was happening, and you don't want to be the next one found with her eyes pecked out."

She gave a little gasp and he said more gently, "I'm sorry, I'm not trying to frighten you. Or rather, I am but for your own good. Don't you see how easily it could happen? Promise me that you'll keep right away from them."

She said tremulously, "But how can I? They're my friends."

He caught hold of her shoulders. "Haven't you heard a word I've been saying? They're lethal, the lot of them! Even if they've no power at all, they *think* they have, which is as bad! Why can't you just accept what I say?"

"Because I—" A second before he moved she divined his intention and tried to stand up but it was too late. As his hands tightened on her shoulders she said breathlessly, "No, Jason!"

"I think, yes."

The kiss which, if he'd thought about it at all, had merely been intended to put an end to her arguing, immediately got out of control. He was totally unprepared for the effect of her closeness and his own overwhelming response to it, and it was some minutes before the frantic beating of her hands against his chest restored some measure of sanity. As he released her she stumbled to her feet and ran unsteadily back across the playground to the lighted hall.

Jason sat immobile, waiting for his breathing to quieten and the tumultuous beating of his heart to subside. The fierce protectiveness, above all the tenderness which had tempered the flare-up of desire, were sensations completely new to him and he did not welcome them. His hands were shaking as he lit a cigarette and inhaled deeply. God, what must she be thinking? She didn't even like him.

A burst of applause from the hall made him turn. He'd have to go back inside; there was no way he could avoid it. He took another deep pull on the cigarette and sent it spinning away, a red arc in the darkness. Then with grim determination he started back to the hall.

Fifteen

A sleepless night and a restless day did nothing to settle him, and as Sunday evening approached Jason knew he did not want to see Madeleine with the tray. Obviously he'd have to apologize, but not yet.

He went swiftly down the path and across the road to the Greystones Hotel. From the call box in the hall he phoned Rowan House to report he would not be in for a meal. Fortunately it was the child Deidre who answered and no explanations were necessary. He went through to the bar and ordered himself a large whisky.

Deidre, relaying the message to the kitchen of Rowan House, did not notice her cousin's relief. For Madeleine the intervening hours had been equally uncomfortable as her memory circled relentlessly round those moments in the dark playground. That they had meant anything to Jason, she did not for a moment consider. He was no doubt missing his wife and, given his sophisticated background, presumably saw no harm in a few stolen kisses with a little country schoolmistress.

To be fair, he could have no idea of the havoc they had caused, for it was ironic indeed that they should have triggered in her the response she had longed for and not found in Matthew's kisses, and which by now she had resigned herself to never experiencing. Furthermore, far from the delight she'd anticipated from such response, it had left her with a yearning restlessness which she had no hope of gratifying.

"Will you be dining this evening, sir?"

Jason turned to find a waiter hovering with the menu.

"I shall." He ran a practised eye down the card. Very impressive, he had to admit. It would make a change from Mrs Staveley's appetising but homely fare. He ordered avocado to be followed by lobster, and a bottle of Meursault. He would enjoy this meal, he told himself grimly, if it choked him.

The dining-room was well appointed and a pianist played discreetly in one corner. He could almost imagine himself in some exclusive Mayfair club, and he wished to heaven that he were.

"Everything all right, sir? Would you care for a sweet to follow?"

"Just coffee, thank you."

"Good evening, Mr Quinn." Anita Barlow stood on the far side of the candle. He rose to his feet.

"Good evening. Will you join me for coffee?"

"I should be delighted."

She was wearing a lace blouse in navy-blue, high-necked and long-sleeved, which emphasized the creamy pallor of her skin. An attractive woman, Anita, even if her eyes were a little mad. Altogether more his type than that prickly, wide-eyed little—

He forced his mind back to his companion.

"I hear you paid a visit to our Circle," she was saying.

"I'm not expecting any sympathy," Jason said drily. "In fact, the news must have given you some satisfaction – sceptic gets his come-uppance, and so on. Or should I say fall-downance."

"Perhaps you were lucky to escape with concussion."

"Perhaps."

The waiter brought an extra cup and saucer and, at Jason's request, two brandies.

"You've heard from your wife?" Anita's eyes innocently met his over the rim of her cup.

"Damn it," he said resignedly, "you know I have."

She smiled and he bit his lip. If he were not careful, he'd find himself accepting more than he was prepared to.

"And how are your enquiries going? Have they produced anything of interest?"

"Very little that I can accept."

"But you're at least beginning to wonder?"

"That much I'll admit."

Her eyes moved over his face. "I believe your education is extending in other directions too, and that you're not finding all the lessons palatable. Do you regret coming to Crowthorpe?"

Jason tipped back his head to drain the brandy. "Not at all. My new play is taking shape satisfactorily."

"Of course. I was forgetting the reason for your visit." Her eyes mocked him. "What's the play about?"

"A stone circle and the evil influence it seems to exert over local people. In reality, of course, the evil is in their own minds."

For a moment she looked startled, then she smiled. "*Touché*, Mr Quinn. Your round, I think."

He met her eyes blandly. "That was a superb meal – my congratulations. Now, if I might have the bill—"

As he came out of the hotel driveway and crossed Fell Lane, Jason's mind was on the exchange with Anita and he did not see the dark figure in the shadow of the wall until he was within a few feet of it. Momentarily its distorted shape brought tales of griffins leaping across the years before resolving itself into the marginally more acceptable outline of an old woman with a bird on her shoulder. The gypsy and her crow. He felt the hair rise on the back of his neck and lashed himself with ridicule. Damn Anita's hints and superstitions: she was infecting him with her own credulity.

"Good evening," he said formally. The old woman nodded and the great bird fluttered its wings. Steeling himself not to look round, Jason walked along the pavement to his own gate.

But however enjoyable the meal had been, he could not seek refuge at the Greystones every evening, and the next day braced himself to face Madeleine. Her hands trembled as she laid down the tray, which caused him to speak more harshly than he'd intended.

"Don't look so apprehensive, I shan't attack you again." She made no comment and he added stiffly, "I owe you an apology for the other evening. I hope you'll accept it."

"Of course."

"I'm still concerned about you, Madeleine. You

know my opinion of the Selbys. Will you at least tell me if anything worries you?"

She said quietly, "They're my friends. They won't hurt me."

He turned abruptly and stared out of the window. "For God's sake be careful, that's all."

Her eyes moved over him, the thick shining hair, the square shoulders, the hands driven deep into his pockets, and she remembered the rough caress of that jacket beneath her cheek. Not trusting herself to reply, she left the room.

Jason stood motionless watching her hurry back across the garden. Well, he'd apologized and the status quo between them was more or less restored. Sourly, he supposed he could be thankful for that.

During that week, the Marshall twins returned for the summer holidays. Jason met them in the High Street with their mother. On the face of it they were perfectly normal schoolgirls, yet their eyes held that awareness common to all the Crowthorpe twins, not least blind Fred Hardacre, and he felt a tightening of the muscles in his stomach.

Felicity was watching his reactions nervously. "Geoff and I were wondering how your – play was coming along. We didn't have much chance to speak at the social."

"It's going quite well, thank you, though I still have a lot of research to do." He was aware that the undercurrents of their conversation were transparently obvious to the girls quietly listening.

"You must come for dinner again. Nicola's interested in writing – I'm sure she'd be grateful for any advice you could give her."

He had no way of knowing which was Nicola, but both girls smiled politely and made no comment. With a further exchange of pleasantries, they went their separate ways.

The meeting was reported at the next conclave of twins.

"Mother thought she was being so subtle, bless her, but it's obvious she's confided in him."

"He's been asking a lot of questions," Philip said shortly. "Matthew, Fred, Eve and Anita, the Smiths. He's gradually working his way round all of us. Much good it'll do him!"

"All the same," Eve said with a frown, "if Geoff and Felicity are on their guard, the girls might find it hard to slip away when the need arises."

"Aye," Tom Hardacre agreed, "folks are getting suspicious all round. Mrs Braithwaite's just said as the vicar's watching her more closely and even old Mabel played up when we came out tonight. If there's to be that much bother getting away, I reckon we'd do better taking 'em with us. Anyroad, it would be a back-up of energy, like."

The others stared at him in consternation. "But what reason could we give?"

"They'd never come!"

"Not voluntarily, no."

"Mass hypnotism!" Philip said softly. "It shouldn't be any problem. How many would be involved, would you say?"

"Only those closest to us – Mabel, in our case, and the vicar and Mr Barlow, Mr and Mrs Marshall, and maybe Miss Peachey. No call to bother with Luke and

Nell, they pay no heed to the boys anyroad. So it'd only be six between the ten of us."

"Twelve of us," Fred corrected quietly. "Mustn't forget the Carters."

Eve nodded. "We're keeping in touch with them. Philip has suggested they be allowed a weekend pass to visit their old home. I don't think the authorities would object if he accepts responsibility."

"That ties us to a weekend, then?"

"Or a Friday," Matthew replied, "and August the first happens to be the feast day of the Crow goddess. Quite a coincidence, wouldn't you say?"

"Next week?" Claire's voice shook.

"But suppose something went wrong?" Anita broke in jerkily. "Suppose at the last minute we couldn't put someone under? The whole project would be jeopardized!"

"She's right," Philip said. "This is all too important to be left to chance. We must have a dress rehearsal. The Carters won't be here but we should still manage. How about later tonight? There aren't any extensive preparations to make."

"Eleven-thirty, then. Agreed?" Matthew's voice rang with exultation. "By that time not many people will be about. We'll start exerting pressure at eleven-fifteen – wake those who might be asleep and give them time to dress. The trance must be total, so they remember nothing; and I think it would be better if we made our way there separately, so as to attract as little attention as possible." He looked round at their excited, apprehensive faces. "After all these years, my friends, the time is almost here. If we all keep faith, nothing can go wrong."

*   *   *

245

It was very close that evening. Even with all the windows open, Jason was uncomfortable and found it hard to concentrate on his work. As his attention wandered he found himself staring across the garden towards Rowan House. The Selbys appeared to be entertaining: he could see figures moving behind the wide expanse of picture window, and wondered if Madeleine were there. He seemed to spend most of his time these days thinking about Madeleine, which, as he repeatedly reminded himself, was a singularly useless exercise.

He went through to the kitchen and took a can of beer from the fridge, the coldness of it numbing his fingers. He drank it slowly, cursing the restlessness which had hold of him. It was after eleven but he was still too unsettled to contemplate either going to bed or returning to his typewriter. On an impulse he decided on a walk. There might be a breath of air towards the top of the lane and perhaps the exercise would clear his head.

The light at the Selbys' window had gone out. The sky was fairly bright, the moon three-quarters full. As he closed the gate behind him, he was startled to see three figures emerge from the corner of Ash Street some hundred yards ahead of him, and with a jolt recognized them as Madeleine and the Selbys. Apparently he wasn't the only one unable to settle tonight. He started to walk after them, resentful of the possessive way the men had hold of her arms. So much for his words of warning; he should have saved his breath.

The familiar road was alien in the moonlit darkness, trees and cottages well known by daylight taking on a sinister *alter ego* as though he walked some cosmic landscape. His rubber soles compounded the illusion since he made no sound while the footsteps of the three in front echoed in the stillness. As, suddenly, did others from behind. He had rounded a slight bend in the road and his quick turn revealed nothing. Acting purely on instinct, he moved back into the shadows of a tree to let whoever was behind him pass. He had no wish to appear to be following Madeleine.

Two figures rounded the bend and passed within six feet of him, identifying themselves as Anita Barlow and her husband. Jason stood staring after them, wondering whether they knew the other three were ahead or if this general ambulation was pure chance. He stood listening for a moment, but no further sounds came from lower down the hill. More cautiously this time, keeping well in against the cottage walls, he continued up the road and reached the final curve in time to see the three figures in the lead turn up the alleyway. They were going to the Gemelly Circle!

A shaft of primitive fear ran through him and he dismissed it instantly. It seemed he'd absorbed more than he realized of the myths and legends he'd been indoctrinated with since his arrival; but much more worrying was the fact that Madeleine, despite her alleged reservations about the Selbys, should accompany them up there after dark. Mr and Mrs Barlow had also turned into the alley and he was about to start after them when, from the direction of the High Street, yet another little procession appeared. The Marshall family. In the shadow of the wall, Jason stood stock-still. One group, possibly two, but three?

Did all the inhabitants of Crowthorpe take to the hills after dark? And Geoff had been so adamant about his mistrust of the twins.

Suddenly, the sweat still on his body, Jason went very cold. For this must surely be a meeting of the twins. Every group that had passed him had contained at least one of them. A social gathering, with their next of kin?

He quickened his pace, passing the entrance to the passageway and continuing to the top of the High Street where the descent began. Ahead of him the long street lay bathed in moonlight. No-one else appeared to be coming. Almost running now, he retraced his steps to the alley and started up it. In here between the walls it was darker and a primeval animal awareness took over. He could almost feel nostrils flaring and ears pricking as he made his way stealthily up the cobbled path. Out on the hillside he recovered some of his twentieth-century equilibrium and paused for a moment to take stock. There was no cover up here, and once he started to move he would have to crouch as low to the ground as possible. Though he had no intention of going too near the Circle, he was determined to find out how many people were up there and what they were doing.

Cautiously he began to make his way forward until he could see the figures fairly clearly. They seemed to be forming themselves into a ring round one of the groups of stones. Crouched in the bracken, Jason was conscious of a feeling of unreality, as though the scene he was watching had been enacted through countless centuries against the same backcloth of moon-bright sky. Only the fact that Madeleine was among the participants anchored him to the present and filled him with sick foreboding.

A soft, united cry reached him over the still air and he tensed as the distant figures raised joined hands high above their heads. The ceremony appeared to be ending, and if they were about to return to the village he would be directly in their path.

Keeping close to the ground he retraced his steps, wondering where he could conceal himself to watch them pass. At the foot of the alley a solution presented itself. A tall wooden gate had been let into the high garden wall of the cottage fronting on to the main street. It was old and fitted badly, leaving a six-inch gap down one side. Jason swung round the corner of the alley into Upper Fell Lane and pushed open the cottage gate. His luck held; there was no fence dividing front and back garden, and a moment later he had positioned himself behind the wooden gate with his eye to the gap.

He was only just in time, because footsteps were already echoing between the alley walls. The moon had moved round in the sky, so that it now shone directly into the passage, illuminating the faces of those who were coming down it.

In the lead were the Hardacre brothers arm-in-arm with a woman – the pub landlady, at a guess. Then Eve and Douglas Braithwaite. (The vicar, taking part in such pagan ceremonies?) Madeleine passed next, still with Philip and Matthew closely at her side, followed by the Marshalls, and, bringing up the rear, Anita and George Barlow. No doubt the gypsy boys had also been present, but their route home lay over the hillside.

For long minutes Jason stood in the dark garden. Had it all been an elaborate hoax, then, Douglas and Geoff seeming so anxious for his help? Were they hoping to throw him off the scent with their fake anxiety? And Madeleine. Had she reported back his worries on her behalf? Even, perhaps, his reaction to them in the old playground?

The coldness inside him no longer owed anything to the supernatural. They had all made a fool of him, and no doubt enjoyed much amusement at his expense. Hurt turned to anger. To hell with the lot of them! At least they'd given him his play, and perhaps its eventual success would compensate for this moment of bitter humiliation.

He let himself soundlessly out of the garden and started back down the long, empty street to Rowan Cottage.

Matthew said furiously, "You didn't have to paw at her like that!"

Philip spun round in the act of unbuttoning his shirt. "She's not your property, you know! She's made it pretty clear she doesn't want you!"

"That's not true. She needs time, that's all."

"Another three years? Look, Matthew, it's time you came out of cloud cuckoo land! She'll never marry you, and the sooner you face up to the fact and settle for Liz Davey, the better."

"You want her yourself, don't you? I've known that for years, but it turned my stomach the way you took advantage of her when she was in a trance and couldn't push you away."

Philip's eyes were flint-hard. "It might interest you

to know, dear brother, that she doesn't push me away when she's not in a trance, either. Or at least, not quickly enough to be convincing!"

The colour left Matthew's face. For the first time Philip, with a sense of shock, saw naked hatred in his brother's eyes. "I'm waiting for an explanation of that remark."

Philip's tongue moved nervously over his lips. "I'm only trying to make you see—"

"*Have you been with Madeleine?*"

"In a manner of speaking."

Matthew moved swiftly, grabbing his twin by the collar. "In *what* manner of speaking?"

"God, Matthew, calm down! I haven't slept with her, if that's what you are worrying about. It was only a kiss!"

Matthew's fist swung, and as Philip reeled against the wall he heard the door slam. Swearing, he straightened, feeling his already-swelling jaw. Matthew had struck him! After all those carefree years of girl-sharing, it was inconceivable that a woman could come between them. Still, Matthew had had ample time to win her round and he'd failed. Now Philip had every intention of making a bid for her himself. Moving painfully, he made his way to the bathroom.

The world was still a bleak place the next morning, and it was raining again. Jason lay on his bed listening to it drumming on the roof. Pity it hadn't started last night, and soaked the lot of them! What were they *doing*, raising their hands in that age-old gesture of acclamation? Recharging the stones to fend off any further intrusion? No doubt it was conscience that had obliged Madeleine to help him when she found him lying there.

He swung his feet to the floor and on his way through to the kitchen pulled the morning paper out of the letter-box, glancing at the dateline. Friday 25th July. Nearly the weekend again. At least this Saturday he shouldn't be obliged to attend any social.

Memory flooded him, mercilessly detailed: the cool flesh of her upper arm, the sweep of lashes as she rested with closed eyes, the softness of her mouth. He leaned heavily on the table, head lowered, waiting for the spasm to pass. He was behaving like a sixteen-year-old, he told himself disgustedly. How it would gratify the Selbys to see him now, and all those others over the years who had resented his command of himself. In retrospect, it was the loss of control which disturbed him most. Even in the early days with Tania he had remained mentally detached from physical involvement. It was the combination of emotional and physical longing he'd experienced with Madeleine which had proved so lethal.

He straightened, sluiced his face under the cold tap, and mechanically set about preparing his breakfast. He had never felt more alone in his life.

Somehow the day passed. He typed several pages, tore them up and typed more. Dialogue was clogged and unnatural, his characters refused to come alive. At five-thirty he consigned them all to hell and went to pour himself a drink. And it was then that the frantic knocking sounded on his door. As he opened it, Madeleine pushed past him into the hallway, slamming the door shut behind her and bolting it top and bottom before running to the sitting-room, where she pulled the window shut, secured it and drew the curtains. Jason stood in the doorway, watching her with growing amazement. If this was an act, it was a damn good one.

"Are we about to be attacked?" he asked mildly.

She turned, started to speak, shook her head helplessly and put her hands to her face. Slowly he went to her and put his arms round her. Though she made no sound, he knew from the shuddering of her body that she was weeping and steeled himself to withhold all but the most basic response to her distress. After a moment or two she moved away, drying her tears with her hands like a child.

"Sorry."

Silently he held out a clean handkerchief and she blew her nose. He was still standing in the middle of the room and she looked up apprehensively.

"You did tell me to come, if—" She bit her lip, still far from composed. He did not trust himself to go to her again. He said evenly, "You'd better sit down and tell me what's happened."

"It's Matthew," she said. "Oh God, Jason, I think he's mad!"

He stared at her for a moment, then sat next to her on the sofa under the long, prematurely curtained window.

She swivelled round to face him. "Apart from school, I haven't seen him for nearly two weeks." She didn't notice his movement of protest. "When I came in this afternoon there was a parcel for him, from home. Deidre was at her dancing class and Aunt Alice doesn't like those stairs. Her balance isn't too good, which is why I have to bring your supper."

He said drily, "And I thought it was my irresistible charm!"

She gave an automatic, absent-minded little smile. "I hadn't been up to the flat for weeks. Philip wasn't there but Matthew'd just got in, as I had. He insisted I stayed for a cup of tea. I didn't want to, but I couldn't think of an excuse. I was drinking it as quickly as I could, when—" She caught her lip between her teeth.

"Go on."

"The television crackled suddenly – atmospherics, I suppose. The effect on Matthew was incredible. He rose slowly to his feet and stood looking at the thing as though it was about to explode. He didn't seem to hear me when I asked what was wrong. Then he – he – oh God!" She reached out blindly for his hand.

"Jason, he said I mustn't be frightened by anything I'd seen or heard, because it wouldn't hurt me, and he'd help me to forget the message because it was better that I shouldn't—"

"Message?" Jason cut in sharply.

"Yes. He seemed to think there'd been some announcement on the television. He wouldn't believe me when I said I hadn't heard anything. He took my hands and held them tightly and said everything would be all right because – because he was immortal—" She choked to a halt.

Jason sat unmoving and after a moment she shuddered back to control.

"He said he and Philip were the twin bear gods Matunus and Artio, and they were going to reclaim their kingdom! *Jason, he really believed it!*"

Without warning she flung herself across his knees,

sobbing uncontrollably. Half of his mind incredulously recorded her words; the other, more urgent half had other problems. Gently he began to stroke her hair and as her sobs lessened he said carefully, "I could make a better job of this without that damned elastic band. Why do you wear it? My wife says they tear the hair."

She said in a muffled voice, "Do you have to talk about your wife?"

"I'm sorry, it was hardly appropriate, especially since she won't be my wife for much longer."

She made no movement as his fingers clumsily freed her hair from the tight elastic. Released, it was like a live thing, rippling and shining in his hands.

"Madeleine—" His voice shook slightly and he started again. "I have to know the truth. You said you hadn't seen Matthew for nearly two weeks."

"That's right, since we were all at the Crow's Nest."

He said very quietly, "What about last night?"

She sat up, shaking her hair back. "Last night?"

God help him, he couldn't doubt her when she looked at him like that. He forced himself to say, "At the Circle?"

Fear flashed across her face and he knew that momentarily she was doubting his own sanity. He took her hands.

"I saw you up there, with Philip and Matthew."

She was gazing at him, completely uncomprehending.

"And the Marshalls and the Hardacres and all the rest of those God-damned twins and their friends and relations."

She said in a whisper, "I don't know what you're talking about."

He believed her. Relief flooded through him, mixed with more concentrated alarm than before. "You don't remember?"

"Jason, I didn't go. Really. I went to bed early."

"Darling, I *saw* you. You might not have known you were there, but believe me you were. You must have been – conditioned in some way, and the others with you – Geoff and Felicity and Braithwaite. God in heaven, if they have sufficient power for that we'll have to move fast."

She said on a high note, "I'm frightened. Please hold me."

His arms came tightly around her. She could hear his heart thundering under her cheek but her fears were too strident to allow her to dwell on his closeness. "What happened?" she asked fearfully. "Up at the Circle?"

"I couldn't see very clearly. You all formed a ring round two or three of the stones and raised your hands in some kind of salute."

"I can't *believe* it – that I was there without knowing. It's terrifying!"

"I know."

"Could anything like that have happened before?"

"I've no idea."

Her mind switched back to her original fear. "Matthew must be mad, mustn't he; paranoid, in some way? It would explain all his talk about the stones. You see, the stones are actually supposed to be the Bear Twins – and the girl they both loved."

She looked up at him quickly as the full measure of her danger struck them both at the same time.

"God, Madeleine, we must get you away – immediately."

"But I can't. I've promised to stay with Deidre while my uncle and aunt go on holiday. They haven't been away by themselves since she was born."

"Damn the Staveleys' holiday, your life might be in danger. If the Selbys really believe they're the Bear Twins and they're both in love with you, your presence must be central to whatever they're planning. The first priority is to get you away, and once you're safe I'll have to set about trying to convince someone in authority of the danger. God knows how. Even now, with all the evidence piling up, I have difficulty believing it myself. Perhaps if I had a word with Douglas Braithwaite—"

"But could you rely on him? He might hold back because of his wife."

"It's too late for that now. The whole village is in danger. If, as now seems likely, the twins can overrule people's wills any time they want, they're considerably more powerful than I realized. So no more arguing, please. You'll have to go into hiding till it's all over. We can't risk anything happening to you."

She met his eyes and something in her expression started his blood pounding again. "Can't we?" she said softly.

"After my exhibition the other evening, you're surely not in much doubt about my feelings."

"I thought you were just amusing yourself while your wife is abroad."

"That was why you ran away?"

257

She nodded. Her eyes were still locked in his and her breathing had quickened. He said barely audibly, "And now?"

"I shouldn't run away again."

He reached for her with an eagerness that was almost pain and this time she was waiting for him, body straining, hands caressing, and his total commitment was no longer a cause for disquiet but of wild, exploding joy.

When finally the tumult was over and the inevitable cigarette in his hand, he said teasingly, "It's just as well you drew the curtains!"

She smiled and nestled against him, but he felt a tremor go through her and cursed his thoughtlessness. Once more the menace of the Crowthorpe twins hung heavily between them.

He stroked her hair gently. "I think it would be as well if no-one knew about this for the moment. There's enough trouble brewing without stepping up any vendetta between myself and the Selbys. Do you think Matthews realizes you came here?"

She shivered and pressed against him. "I don't know."

He brushed her hair with his lips. "Trust me, darling. I'll work something out."

But as he drew back the curtains to watch her walk across the grass, his eyes were drawn inexorably to the blind staring window of the Selbys' flat and a feeling of helplessness clamped over him.

Sixteen

"Girls, which of you borrowed my new shoes?" Felicity appeared in the doorway, her face flushed with annoyance, and her daughters calmly returned her accusing gaze.

"Not me."

"Nor did I."

"One of you must have, because there's mud caked on the side. It really is too bad of you. I've never even worn them myself."

Geoff's voice called from upstairs and she turned away. "The least you can do is clean them for me," she added over her shoulder.

The twins exchanged glances. There was no way they could tell their mother she had worn the shoes herself on her visit to the Circle – and been unfortunate enough, on that hot dry night, to step into the little pool of blood which Kim, in an excess of zeal, had poured at the foot of the Bride Stone.

Nicola said softly, "It's weird, somehow, knowing she can't remember."

"What's worrying me," Claire remarked, "is what'll happen next time. I'm not looking forward to seeing the Miss Carters again. Do you remember when we were little, how they used to shuffle round the village making those peculiar noises? I was terrified of them."

"Yet Mrs Braithwaite said they were the ones who recognized the Selbys." Nicola looked across at her sister. "It's only symbolic though, isn't it? I mean, Philip and Matthew aren't going to appear with bear-skins round their shoulders and expect us to worship them?"

Claire shuddered. "I have a creepy kind of feeling they just might."

After a lifetime of surface emotions, Jason had that day been experiencing uncomfortable extremes of happiness and anxiety as he tried to work out the most convincing means of alerting someone to the danger of the twins. He had still not solved the problem when, at four o'clock, he saw Madeleine come running across the garden and a wave of premonition swept over him. He pushed back his chair and hurried to meet her.

"There's a phone call for you, from London. She said, 'Tell him it's Penelope.' She sounded upset, Jason."

He started to run towards the house, Madeleine at his heels, and caught up the phone lying on the hall table.

"Pen? What's wrong?"

"Oh Jason! Thank God you mentioned that woman's name when you phoned! It's Alex – he's been hurt."

Jason's hand tightened on the receiver. "How?"

"At a cricket match this afternoon. The ball caught him on the back of the head. He's unconscious. I'm at the hospital now. Jason—" Her voice rocked. "Will you come?"

"Of course. How serious is it?"

"I don't know. The X-rays aren't very conclusive but until he regains consciousness—" Across the miles he could hear the unspoken dread in her voice. He glanced at his watch.

"I'll be there about ten. Will you be at the hospital?"

"Yes, I'll stay here. Please hurry."

As he put down the phone Madeleine appeared fearfully in the kitchen doorway. His eyes went to the room behind her and he raised his eyebrows interrogatively.

She shook her head. "Everyone's out."

He moved forward and pulled her against him. "My son's been hurt. I'll have to go, but I can't leave you here. Come with me."

"You know I can't. You must be with your family."

"But—"

"Don't worry about me, Jason, nothing's likely to happen yet. Mr Hardacre said 'a month or so'; it could be another two weeks, and you'll be back long before that."

He said worriedly, "I hope you're right, because there's no time to make contingency plans – I'll have to leave right away. Oh God, darling, promise me you'll take care. I'll phone every evening and you can get me at this number if you need me." He jotted it down on the flap of his cigarette pack. "Now, are you sure—?"

"Go on with you!" She forced a smile and gave him a little push towards the door, but moments later, as he backed the car out of the gate, a wave of desolation swamped her and it took all her courage to keep the smile in place until he was out of sight.

Reassured that Madeleine was safe for the moment, fear for his son blotted everything else from Jason's mind as he fought his way down the motorway, solid with returning holidaymakers. Jam after jam, hold-up after hold-up. The hands of his watch crept steadily round and round the dial, and he cursed the fact that, thinking he'd not need it on holiday, he'd left his mobile phone at the London flat.

When at last he reached the M1, he stopped at a service station to fill up with petrol and phone the hospital. There was no change in Alexander's condition. "Tell Mrs Quinn I'll be there in a couple of hours," he said.

Penelope was waiting for him and went straight into his arms. "Oh Jason, I'm so frightened!"

Alexander lay in a screened-off bed at one end of a ward. A nurse was sitting beside him but she stood up as they pulled back the curtain.

"We'll take over for a while," Penelope said with a strained smile.

"Of course, Mrs Quinn. I'll bring another chair."

They sat close together, Penelope gripping Jason's hand. "He looks so little!" she said with a break in her voice.

"Hasn't he come round at all since it happened?"

She shook her head. "They were playing at Lynton Park. The first thing I knew was when the games master phoned from the hospital."

"Where's Emily?"

"With a school-friend. She'd gone there for tea so I rang the mother and asked if she could stay."

"He'll be all right, Pen. Children are tougher than they look; they're always knocking themselves out."

"Yes. Yes, of course." She drew a deep breath. "We should keep talking, I think, because our voices might get through to him. So tell me what you've been doing since you phoned. As you didn't ring back I presume you found someone else to talk to?"

He smiled. "Yes. Actually things are hotting up at the moment."

"Did you find out who killed her?"

"What?"

"The chambermaid – I thought you were trying to discover who killed her?"

Jason realized with surprise that he hadn't spared a thought for Patsy Lennard for some time. "Among other things, yes, but there's not much progress there. It's the twins I've been concentrating on."

"Oh yes, the twins. A classical connection! Didn't Jason take Castor and Pollux with him on the Argo?"

"If he did, I hope they gave him less trouble than I'm having."

"With the little boys Ted saw?"

"Among others. There are no fewer than five pairs of identical twins in Crowthorpe."

"Good grief! That's unusual, surely?"

"Very unusual. And not a little sinister."

They were interrupted by one of the doctors who came to check Alexander's condition. When he'd finished he said kindly, "I think it would be as well if you both went home and had some sleep. This could be a long job and I'm quite sure there'll be no developments during the night. If there were, we should contact you immediately."

Penelope hesitated. "I'd rather stay."

"As you like, of course, but there's nothing you can do at the moment. Later, we might well be glad of your help and you'll want to be fresh for that."

"The doctor's right, dear," Jason said gently. "Let me take you home."

As they drew up outside the house in Blackheath, Penelope said, "You'll stay here, won't you, since Tania's still in France?"

"If I may. I want to be on hand."

"You can have Alexander's room."

It was after midnight but the night was still warm. He followed her into the dark, quiet house.

"Would you like a drink?"

"An excellent idea. It'll help us to sleep."

They sat in the sitting-room, its uncurtained windows giving on to the darkness of the garden and reflecting back their images.

"Tania's asked for a divorce," Jason said suddenly.

"Oh no!"

"It's been on the cards for some time."

"I'm so sorry."

He shrugged and put his glass down while he lit a cigarette. "It's more of a relief than anything."

"Is that what you said about me?"

"Pen, I'm sorry. I'm a callous devil. Of course it wasn't."

"I'm sorry too. Put it down to exhaustion."

"We should go to bed."

When she had left him he went to the little room which belonged to his son, his eyes moving over the model aeroplanes on a table and framed photographs of the school First XI with Alex himself proudly in the centre. On a chair was the rumpled T-shirt he had presumably discarded when he changed into cricket whites that afternoon. Jason picked it up and clenched it tightly in his hand. So many dangers seemed to be hovering over those he loved, and his new vulnerability left him no armour to withstand their menace. God keep them safe, he thought, and wearily began to prepare for bed.

Up in Crowthorpe the days crawled by. The airlessness persisted, clothes stuck to hot bodies and tempers frayed. Mr and Mrs Staveley, unaware of their niece's misgivings, duly left for their holiday in Cornwall.

Madeleine watched them go with a feeling of dread, yet there was nothing concrete she could put forward to delay their longed-for break. Keep away from the Selbys, Jason had told her, but now school had broken up she and Matthew would have long days to put in at Rowan House, and if she continually refused to see him, he might begin to guess at her reasons.

All of this she tried to hide from Jason during his nightly telephone calls. It seemed that far more than three hundred miles separated them. He was tense and preoccupied, deeply concerned about his son's continuing coma, and she reflected that his ex-wife and child had far more claim on him than she had. Perhaps, back in London, he would realize that their brief happiness together had no real substance.

"You're sure you're all right?" he would say brusquely, and repeatedly she assured him that she was. Possibly Penelope was in the room when he phoned. Certainly there was nothing she could not have overheard in their stilted conversations.

But on the Wednesday, for the first time Jason sounded guardedly optimistic. "The doctors think he's coming out of it. We should know in a day or two."

"Thank God! How – how's your ex-wife?"

"She's been wonderful. What about you? Any developments up there?"

"No, things are just the same. We had a card from Cornwall today."

"Hell, I'd forgotten the Staveleys were away." His voice sharpened. "And school must have broken up, too. Has Matthew been round?"

"He suggested a picnic but I managed to put it off. I'm taking Deidre out tomorrow, so that'll be a help."

For the first time he was aware of the anxiety behind her determined cheerfulness. With his attention exclusively focused on Alex, he hadn't appreciated the extent to which, for his sake, she'd been playing down her fears. Out of that awareness and a resurgence of love and fear, he said urgently, "I miss you, Madeleine."

"Me too."

"Just another couple of days, darling. I should be back by the weekend."

Penelope came into the room as he put down the phone. "I do wish you wouldn't leave money there every night, like a lodger!"

"I am a lodger!"

"Who is it you keep phoning, anyway?"

"Madeleine Peachey, Mrs Staveley's niece. I need to keep in touch."

"You said before things were hotting up. Tell me about it."

So he told her the whole story as it had unfolded for him and she listened carefully, her eyes on his face.

"No wonder you're worried," she commented when he finished. "Are they all insane?"

"I wish I knew. They're certainly dangerous."

"And this girl Madeleine; do you think they'll harm her?"

"Not intentionally, but she could get hurt. I'm damn sure she figures in their plans."

"You're in love with her, aren't you?"

He met her eyes. "Does it show that much?"

"I noticed at once that you seemed different, but I was too upset to wonder why. Does she love you?"

"Yes, thank God!"

"So how are you going to protect her?"

"Try to persuade her to go into hiding while I sort things out."

"She can come to us if you like."

"You wouldn't mind?"

"Why should I? I'll be fascinated to meet a girl who can wreak such a change in you! But I'm sorry I dragged you away at such a critical time. Thanks for staying, Jason. I couldn't have got through this week without you."

He bent and kissed her cheek. "What are ex-husbands for?" he said.

"Meddling again?"

The Smith boys spun round to see Granny Lee in the caravan doorway, the huge bird balanced on her shoulder, wings outspread.

"We picked you some herbs, Granny," Kim said quickly, holding out the bunch he'd brought for just such a contingency.

She brushed the excuse aside and advanced on them, black and menacing.

"Spies! Traitors, betrayin' yer own! Yer *Crows*, ye hear me? Never been twins in our family, nor wouldn't be now wi'out Artio's meddlin'! Ye were promised to *me* – it were in the cards – Nell's third child wi' special powers, like in the oud times." Her voice rose in a shrill paroxysm of fury. "But he split ye in the womb, one fine babby into two scrawny mites, and stole ye for his own!"

Her eyes were glittering and the boys, backed into a corner, instinctively raised their arms to ward her off.

"It'll come to nowt, all this plotting and planning! I'm more'n a match for the ten of ye! The power will be divided again, and the Bears lost for ever!"

She flung out her arm and the great crow, unseated, fluttered forward. Ducking, the two boys raced for the door and clattered down the steps to safety.

"Mummy? My head hurts!"

Penelope bent and slid her arms under the little body. "I'm not surprised, my darling! Oh Alex – thank God!"

Alexander's eyes went to the tall figure of his father. "Daddy, I made fifteen, not out!"

"Very creditable," Jason said, "but you were certainly 'out', my lad! "Alex, I have to go back to Crowthorpe now. But I'll be home in a couple of weeks, and you and Emily and Mummy and I are going to get to know each other a lot better. Right?"

Penelope reached up a hand. Jason took it and bent to kiss her. "All right with you too?"

"Wonderful. Give my love to Madeleine. I'm looking forward to meeting her."

At last he was free to go, and with the anxiety for Alex removed, Crowthorpe and all its dangers came surging to the forefront of his mind. Friday afternoon, and London full of shoppers and tourists. The traffic lights were all against him and as he fumed helplessly he became aware of growing unease. Impatiently he pushed it aside. He might have changed, as Penelope informed him, but not, please God, to the extent where he accepted presentiments of doom! He put his foot down and shot through the next set of lights on amber. Once on the M1 he should be able to make good time.

Eve said, "I hope they'll be calmer than they were last time."

"Don't count on it," Philip warned her. "They know as well as we do that this is D-day."

"You told the staff what time to expect us?"

"Yes, about four. They'll have time for a rest when we get back."

"Douglas isn't at all happy about their staying with us. He hasn't said much, bless him, because he doesn't want to sound unchristian, but I can tell he's apprehensive."

"If the worst comes to the worst we can sedate them, but we need all their faculties for tonight."

"I can't believe it, can you?" Eve's voice trembled. "Tonight! After all these years, the time has finally come!"

"All these years," Philip repeated softly. "Several thousand of them!"

"You think she knows, the Crow?"

"Almost certainly. The boys said she was rambling on about it yesterday."

"What will she do?"

"There's nothing she can do. The power we've amassed will far outweigh hers."

Eve looked across the still, grey waters of Lake Windermere as they drove alongside. "What's happened to the blue sky we've been seeing all week? It's even closer today." She ran a finger round the neckline of her dress.

"We could do with a good storm to clear the air. I shouldn't be surprised if it's on its way. At least it would keep people indoors and we could start that much earlier. We want it all over by midnight, while it's still the first of August."

She looked at him curiously. "Have you any idea what's likely to happen?"

"Not really." His voice shook with suppressed excitement. "We can begin as we did the other evening and see how it goes. The Crow is certain to be there for her feast day. She might set things in motion herself."

The first drops of rain were falling as Jason came out of the motorway café where, having had no lunch, he had stopped for coffee and sandwiches. By now his disquiet had grown to an extent where it overshadowed everything and, conscious of an urgent need to speak to Madeleine, he turned into one of the telephone alcoves. Her voice in his ear brought profound relief. "Nothing's happened, has it?"

"Not really. Philip and Mrs Braithwaite went out just after lunch in his car. I was in the garden when they left and they seemed on edge. I haven't seen them since."

"At least that's two fewer twins for the moment! Darling, I'm at Keele. I should be back in about two and a half hours, all being well. Is it raining up there?"

"It's just starting. It's been getting darker all afternoon."

"How's my friend Deidre?"

"Fine. She's staying the night in Barrowick with a couple of school friends."

"So you're alone with Matthew?"

"Hardly! He's at the top of the house and I'm at the bottom."

"Keep it that way, for heaven's sake. I don't know why, but I have a persistent feeling you're in danger."

"You, Jason? A 'persistent feeling'?"

"All right, it's illogical but please indulge it. Lock the doors and keep out of sight, and with luck he'll think you've gone to Barrowick too."

His advice came just too late. As she put down the phone there was a tap on the front door, which immediately opened to admit Matthew.

"All alone? I thought I heard voices."

"I was on the phone, but I'm – just going out."

"Where?"

Desperately she searched for somewhere plausible but he was continuing, "Unless it's urgent I shouldn't bother. The rain's getting heavy now and there's thunder in the distance. We're overdue for a storm."

He walked past her into the living-room and stood at the window.

"Where's Philip?" she asked uneasily. His patent restlessness, combined with Jason's uncharacteristic anxiety, brought the first positive wash of alarm.

"He's gone to collect the Carters. They should be back any minute."

She stared at him uncomprehendingly. "Those two old ladies you used to visit? Why on earth?"

"They have a forty-eight hour pass. It sounds like the army, doesn't it?"

"But why, Matthew?"

He turned from the window, and with his back to the light she couldn't see his face clearly.

"They want to see Crowthorpe again. They haven't been here for about nine years." He came towards her, put his arm round her and held her tightly, his face in her hair. She could feel the excitement moving in him, a tingling current of anticipation, and sought frantically for some means of escape.

"Oh Maddy," he said softly, "it seems an age since we were together. Have you been avoiding me, or am I just imagining it?"

"You must be." It seemed imperative not to upset him and she stood without moving as his lips moved across her face to find hers. Oh God, if only Jason were here, just across the garden in the cottage! She started to tremble and as Matthew's arms tightened round her, gently pushed him away. "Something's going to happen, isn't it?"

"Yes, my darling, it is."

"Tonight?" Hurry, Jason!

"Tonight. It's the feast of the Crow goddess."

"But you hate crows!"

"And you know why? Because, thousands of years ago, they took away my kingdom, mine and Artio's."

She moistened her lips. "You think all these ancient forces are still here?"

"Of course, locked in the stones."

"And the Crow goddess?"

He let out his breath in a long sigh. "Granny Lee."

Oh God, he really was mad and she hadn't the slightest idea how to deal with him. Keep him talking – wasn't that one of the basic rules? She said vibrantly, "And you're going to use the power you've stored in the stones to overthrow her?"

"Good girl! Exactly that! I knew you'd understand but the others said I shouldn't tell you. You'll come with us tonight, won't you? If you agree it won't be necessary to hypnotize you." He smiled into her face. "We had a dress rehearsal last week and you were all there. Does that surprise you? Douglas and George, the Marshalls, Mabel—"

Her mouth was dry again. "Why did you need us with you?"

"The extra energy was useful. We could harness it, even without your knowing." The clock on the mantelpiece struck six. "Come upstairs with me, Maddy. Philip'll be here soon and we can spend the evening together till it's time to go. It'll be like old times."

"I've some letters to write," she began hopelessly, but he caught her hand and pulled her with him to the door. With a last despairing look over her shoulder, she

273

followed him into the slanting rain and up the outside staircase to the flat.

The rain was sluicing down the windscreen and there was thunder in the air. The car radio crackled, reminding him of the Selbys' television when the psychic messages flashed. How much of that welter of suggestion and myth had any basis in fact?

He frowned, putting his foot hard on the accelerator, aware of the suddenly sluggish response. If the thing should break down now – And as the thought formed in his mind the engine stuttered and he felt the power drain away as the needle of the speedometer swung down to 60 – 50 – 40.

Swearing, he steered the car up on to the hard shoulder and came to a halt. Holding the choke out he tried again and again to restart the engine, with no result whatever. Resignedly he reached for his mackintosh on the back seat and, shrugging it on, stepped out into the driving rain.

Five minutes later he straightened, staring down into the body of the car with a feeling of helplessness. There were no plug leads missing, nor were the leads from the distributor loose. Yet the bloody thing still wouldn't start. Despairingly he looked up and down the road. Only one car had passed since he'd stopped and there was no sign of any others. His only choice was to set off in search of an emergency telephone and pray the nearest wasn't too far away.

"Right, sir," said a voice reassuringly in his ear. "We'll be with you in about half an hour."

"Can't you make it any quicker?"

"We have to come from Preston, sir, but we'll be there as soon as we can."

Swearing under his breath, Jason went back along the verge. It was years since he'd had any trouble with his car and this could hardly have come at a worse time. He slid inside and lit a cigarette, churningly aware of the passing of time. It seemed an age before the breakdown van pulled up just ahead of him, but the upsurge of hope did not last long.

"I'm afraid this won't be a quick job, sir. I've checked the plugs but there doesn't seem to be any electrical fault. The next thing will be to remove the carburettor. If a jet's blocked that could be the cause of the trouble."

"How long will it take?"

"Depends what's wrong. Could be under an hour, could be longer."

"God, I can't wait that long! Have you any cars for hire?"

"Yes, we can arrange that for you."

"Then for God's sake let's tow this thing back to the garage and I'll hire one. I have to get to Crowthorpe urgently."

"That's a good hour and a half's drive you've got."

"I know, and I should have been there some time ago."

Even with the decision reached, everything seemed to happen at a snail's pace: the fixing of the tow rope, the crawling journey back to the garage, the signing of papers. By the time he regained the motorway it was almost two hours since the breakdown and during the enforced delay his fears for Madeleine had escalated. Particularly since there had been no reply when he'd tried to phone from the garage. Please God she'd gone out as he'd suggested, and was out of harm's way. He put his foot down and shot forward. The rain showed no sign of lessening and the thunder was now much closer. Jason gritted his teeth and concentrated on his driving.

It was as he approached Penrith that his fiercely submerged disquiet momentarily surfaced and he was convinced he heard Madeleine's voice. Just once, above the roar of the car's passage and the onslaught of rain – taut with fright and calling his name.

He swerved dangerously, fighting the wheel to straighten the car. Imagination! he told himself through clenched teeth, yet it had sounded as clear as if she'd been in the car beside him. Oh God, don't let those maniacs harm her!

The Keswick road stretched ahead of him, and in the hills to his right the lightning stretched and died. If this was indeed the night the twins had chosen, he thought grimly, he couldn't fault their stage-management.

Philip said, "All right, Madeleine?"

She forced her eyes to meet his. *Where was Jason?* He should have been back hours ago. Could something have happened to him? Driving conditions must be appalling. "Yes. I'm all right," she answered.

"Then I think we'd better be going."

Panic clutched at her. Not yet! Give him just a few more minutes! "Aren't you going to wait till the rain stops?"

"We have to stick to schedule. We said ten forty-five and the others will be setting out now." He put an arm round her and across the room she saw Matthew

276

stiffen. "Don't look so apprehensive, love! It'll be an experience you'll never forget, but nothing can go wrong."

Matthew said curtly, "You can't go up the hill in those sandals. I'll come down with you to get your boots. We'll meet you at the gate, Philip."

Oh, why hadn't she thought to lock the front door earlier? Yet even if she had, even if she'd gone, safely as she thought, to bed, they'd have roused her as they had before and she would still have been compelled to make this fantastic journey up the hill. Since there could be no escape, it was better that she should at least know what was happening. Oh Jason! Again the twist of fear. Even allowing for the weather, he couldn't be as late as this unless something had gone wrong. Perhaps in his anxiety for her he had driven too fast on the wet roads.

The heavy knot of misery dulled her more personal fear as they turned into Upper Fell Lane. Could she perhaps, fully conscious as she was, break away, run and hide somewhere? But Philip and Matthew had hold of her and there was nothing she could do. In her confused state she no longer knew which of them was on her right and which on her left. They both held tightly to her hands and in this alien landscape on this fateful night she was glad even of their human contact.

As they rounded the top of the lane they came face to face with a small group of people, but her brief spurt of hope was stillborn. It was only the Hardacre brothers with Mabel. Meeting her alert gaze under the street lamp, Tom exclaimed and turned to Matthew.

"You've not put her under?"

"There was no need. We can blot it out later if need be."

Tom nodded and turned into the darkness between the cottage walls. As they set off after him a sudden soft babbling reached them from the foot of the alley, chilling and inhuman. Madeleine stiffened and would have turned but the Selbys kept her moving forward.

"The Carters," Philip said briefly, "with the group from the vicarage."

White lightning momentarily spotlighted the strange procession and a crash of thunder echoed painfully down the narrow chasm they climbed. Stumblingly, linked together, they came out on to the exposed hill and, with heads bent against the rain, turned in the direction of the Circle.

It was not until she felt a simultaneous tightening on both her arms that Madeleine realized their arrival had been forestalled. Gathered round the Wedding Group of stones, motionless in the driving rain, stood the gypsies: Luke and Nell, Jem and Janetta, Buck and Nan and poor gangling Benjie, and, just in front of them, the bird as always on her shoulder, the slight bent figure of Granny Lee.

Still holding on to Madeleine, taking her with them, Philip and Matthew went forward to meet her, the others clustering behind them. The opposing camps had met at last and battle was about to be joined.

When shall we three meet again
In thunder, lightning or in rain?

The words rang in Madeleine's ears with superstitious dread. In a last effort to free herself she turned her head and as another flash knifed through the darkness, encountered the blank gaze of Douglas Braithwaite

278

immediately behind her. Hope died. There would be no help forthcoming; he was as powerless as the rest of them.

Philip's voice rang out exultantly, making her jump. "It is over, Macha! Your long tyranny is ended. We have come to claim our own!"

"Nay, Artio o' the Dark Hills. You'll never be free." She turned and scrabbled with surprising agility on to one of the lower stones so that she stood some three feet above them.

As Madeleine fearfully raised her head, she saw to her horror that the beady black eyes were fixed unblinkingly on herself.

"Which one of you claims the Bride?"

Philip raised Madeleine's hand, clasped in his. "I do! My brother had his chance and lost it. I claim her!"

Matthew turned swiftly. "Damn you, Philip, let her go!"

They faced each other across her, protagonists in some ancient play outside of time yet part of it, helpless to extricate themselves from the fate already decreed.

Matthew dropped her hand, swinging round to challenge his brother, and in the same moment a voice rang out: "Take care! Divided we fall!" One of the Carter twins, lucid for the only time in her life, but the warning came too late. Above their head the gypsy shrieked a command – in Celtic? Romany? – and the huge bird came swooping down on the tableau.

Matthew twisted round as its great wings beat into his face and his scream filled the whole storm-ridden night. His body arched in a paroxysm of terror, went slack and slumped to the wet grass.

Philip hurled himself forward and began to claw dementedly at the gypsy's long black skirt, and to Madeleine's fear-crazed eyes it seemed in that moment that the shabby material and his own drenched coat blurred into the fur and feathers of a far more ancient conflict. The illusions was transient and even as she blinked, nature or a force almost as old played the final hand. A tongue of lightning snaked to earth, splitting the stone in half and sending both the old woman and the man who clutched her crashing to the ground.

With a high keening note the Smith twins flung themselves across Philip's body and somewhere on the edge of the crowd Eve screamed, "Break the trance for God's sake! Douglas – Douglas wake up!"

Blinded, numb with horror, Madeleine was aware of people running forward, bending over the three motionless bodies; aware, too, that they had no need of such ministrations. The drama was played out, and any power the Circle might have contained was draining harmlessly away into the waiting earth. And she knew instinctively that from this day forward, twins in Crowthorpe would be no different from any others. They had had their chance and lost it, for all time.

Incapable of movement, she continued to stand there, her mind fretting at the edges of concepts too vast for comprehension, and it was Jason's ringing call, clear above the confused babble within the Circle, that finally broke through her paralysis. Sobbing with terror and relief, she threaded her way through the milling crowd and ran stumbling to meet him.

Epilogue

St Botolph's Vicarage,
Crowthorpe.
30th August.

Dear Jason,

I'm sending you under registered cover an incredible document which has come into my possession. It was deposited in a bank safe by Matthew Selby about a year ago, with instructions that in the event of his death it should be sent to me to deal with as I think fit. No doubt it would be of interest to psychiatrists but I'm reluctant to let it "out of the family", since it deals with a part of all our lives. I'm inclined to think that the best course would be to give it, like its author, a decent burial.

I think you'll agree that the Selbys emerge from it as the closest and also the most susceptible of all the twins, and we're left with the unanswerable question of whether or not events would have taken the course they did, had they not been subjected to Janetta's fatal "Macbeth prophecy".

Regarding their mental state, Eve is convinced that after the Carters' proclamation of divinity – how incredible it feels to write that! – they actually identified themselves as the bear gods. The one fact

281

that emerges from the whole sorry business is the danger inherent in these old superstitions and the power they can still exert.

Things here are teetering back to normal. The post mortem confirmed that Matthew's death was due to heart failure, brought on no doubt by extreme fear. The Hardacres, I'm glad to say, have left Crowthorpe, and the Smith boys have been taken into care. We can only pray that no irreparable harm has been done to them.

I hope that Madeleine has now recovered from her ordeal. Please give her our regards, and we hope to see you both again one day, in much happier circumstances.

With best wishes from Eve and myself,

DOUGLAS BRAITHWAITE.